TROUBLE

IN

LOVE VALLEY

Published by Lorimer Press
Davidson, North Carolina

Printed in China

Book Design - Leslie Rindoks
Cover - based on photos by Cotton Ketchie
Author Photo - Vickie Ketchie

Library of Congress Control Number: 2011930682

ISBN 978-0-9826171-8-2

TROUBLE

IN

LOVE VALLEY

a novel by

"COTTON" KETCHIE

LORIMER PRESS

Davidson, NC

2011

ALSO BY "COTTON" KETCHIE

Memories of a Country Boy

A Country Boy's Education

Little Did They Know

For Vickie: You are the wind beneath my wings.

CHAPTER 1

"WHO'S OUT THERE?"

"It's me. Open up. I gotta talk to you!"

Eighty-two year old Bud Beckett unlatched the chain and opened the door of his mobile home to a bearded man with breath that reeked of beer. "What do you want? It's late and I'm gettin' ready to go to bed."

"I need some money," the man said, slurring his words. "That's all. Just loan me a little for beer and I'll be on my way."

"I ain't loanin' you nothin'," the old man barked at the half-drunken, late-night visitor.

"Why not?"

"Because you're lazy, and you won't work long enough to get your own paycheck, that's why. You're drunk now, so go on and git outta here."

"I ain't goin' nowhere 'til I get some money!"

Beckett turned the man around and shoved him toward the

open door. The inebriated trespasser stumbled down the front steps and eventually ended in a heap on the ground. He lay there briefly, trying to organize his thoughts before attempting to stand. He looked up at the closed door of the trailer and managed to reach the step's handrail and pulled himself to an upright position. The angry intruder yelled in a loud voice to be sure the old man heard him, "Damn you, old man. You can't treat me like this!"

On wobbly legs, the man turned and staggered to his truck, extracted a tire iron from behind the seat and then stumbled back to the trailer and banged on the door. "Open up or I'll break the damn door in!"

Knowing he would not get any sleep until the matter was settled, Beckett opened the door slightly. "Now what do you want? I already told you I ain't loanin' you no money. Now, git off my property, 'fore I call the sheriff."

Not to be denied, the intruder shoved Beckett backwards so hard, the old man stumbled and fell against the kitchen table and onto the floor.

"Now give me some money or I'll beat it out of you!"

Surprised by the brutality of the man, Beckett looked up at him from where he lay and stammered, "Alright… I'll… give you some money, just don't hurt me."

"You done made me mad now," the intruder said. "But, I might not hurt you if you give me all the money you got." The thief brought the tire iron from behind his back and waved it menacingly in front of Beckett.

"Please. There ain't no need for that," Beckett pleaded. "I'll give you all I got."

"You're damn right you will," the man said, clutching the tire iron in his right hand and striking it into the palm of his left hand for emphasis. The symbolism was effective.

While keeping his eye on the tire iron, the elderly man

grabbed a chair for support. With much effort, he pulled himself up and leaned against the table.

"Well, hand it over!" the thug demanded.

Beckett now feared for his life. He would do anything to get this man out of his trailer. With shaking hands, he reached into his overall pocket, withdrew his wallet, and handed it to the ruffian.

Rifling through the wallet, the unsympathetic hooligan spat, "Is that all you got old man?"

"Yeah, that's it. I wouldn't hold out on you," he said trembling.

The thief stuffed the wallet into his jacket pocket and demanded, "You're bound to have some more money around here somewhere. You'd better tell me where it is or I'll tear this damn trailer apart."

Beckett stammered, "I...I have a little savin's in the bedroom."

"Alright, let's go get it and no funny stuff!"

"Okay, just don't hurt me," Beckett said and led the man to his bedroom and opened the door. "It's in here. I got it hid under my pillow."

"Well get it out!

The old man was shaking, but reached under the pillow and withdrew the .45 caliber Colt revolver he kept hidden there and turned and fired at the astonished intruder. A tongue of flame exploded from the barrel when he pulled the trigger. The noise was deafening in the cramped trailer. The bullet barely missed its target and struck the bedroom wall behind the thief, splintering the paneling.

"Why, you old son of a bitch!" the big man screamed in rage. He swung the tire iron in an overhand arc, and in one smashing blow, crushed the skull of Bud Beckett.

The old man crumpled from the force of the blow. The gun

fell from his grasp as he spun and landed face up on the bed; his eyes wide-open, staring into nothingness.

With his ears still ringing from the gunshot, the thug searched and found the money that was hidden under the pillow and quickly stuffed it into the pocket of his jacket. He took one last look at the old man lying on the bed staring up at him and then picked up the pistol from the floor. He quickly retrieved the blood-stained tire iron and left the bedroom.

He stood briefly at the opened front door and scanned the driveway to see if anyone was coming. After seeing no one, he raced down the steps and fled to his truck.

The thief sat in his truck thinking, *did I touch anything in there?* Trying to satisfy himself that he did not, he thought through the whole event once again just to be sure. *The old man opened the trailer's front door and the bedroom door. I got the codger's wallet in my pocket and I got his gun and the tire iron.* He wiped beads of sweat from his brow with the sleeve of his jacket, started the truck, and drove away into the night.

CHAPTER 2

WATERCOLORIST, JAKE MCLEOD, was painting more at home since his wife Marci and he had been blessed with the birth of their daughter. His gallery was still open six days a week on Main Street in downtown Mooresville, but Jake liked being at home as much as possible, especially in the mornings. His painting table took up a corner in their not-too-spacious kitchen.

Marci, dressed in her navy blazer and tan slacks, had just washed her hands and was drying them with a paper towel. "What did you say, honey, I had the water running and didn't hear you?"

After a quick glance at their daughter who was sitting at the table eating Cheerios, Jake repeated, "It's hard to believe Meredith's four years old." He then turned back to his work and continued applying a wash of cerulean blue onto a sheet of Arches 300 lb. hot-pressed watercolor paper.

"It surely is," Marci agreed as she looked over at their precocious child who was innocently slurping the cereal from her spoon. Marci was still amazed that just watching her daughter eat breakfast could give her so much joy.

Out of the corner of his eye, Jake noticed how Marci relished her role as a mother. "What're you thinking about?" he asked.

She poured herself a cup of coffee, leaned against the kitchen sink, and took a sip before answering. "Oh, I was just admiring my family," she said. "Just think how much our lives have changed since the first day we met."

"I know," Jake said. "If James Caldwell hadn't called me that day, we would have never met."

"I'm glad he did," Marci said, smiling. "I had no clue being the first female detective of the Iredell County Sheriff's Department would help me find a husband, especially when I wasn't even looking for one."

She had never tired of looking at Jake since that first day she saw him. Jake McLeod was a man with rugged good looks. A scar over his right eyebrow, earned during a childhood mishap, was more prominent when he smiled and added a little mystery to his weathered face. His teeth were white and fairly straight except for one wayward canine. Even though his brown hair was giving way to gray, he still struck a handsome pose for a man in his early fifties.

Jake smiled at Marci and dipped his brush into the jar of water on his table and turned back to his painting. He found himself thinking back on those four days in October five years earlier when Gail Caldwell, the wife of his friend James and three other women had gone missing and the newly promoted detective, Marci Meredith, had led the search in finding them.

"You know, I still remember the very first moment I laid eyes on you," Jake said. "I was sitting in the temporary sheriff's office on Brawley School Road with James and here you came bouncing through the door carrying a box of Krispy Kreme doughnuts. You said they were for Sid Bellman, but you ate half of them."

"Listen here, fella, I didn't bounce," Marci said jokingly. "And furthermore, I only ate four of those doughnuts."

"Yeah, yeah," Jake said, playing along with her banter. "It was only by sheer luck that I got to ride along with you in that Crown Victoria while we were searching for Gail and the other missing women. I'll never forget the days we spent riding together to Wilkes County."

Marci smiled, "I remember that first kiss you planted on me, too, and me, a poor innocent, young woman."

"Me, planted a kiss on you," Jake said incredulously. "Think back a little bit. You were the one driving the car. You were the one who pulled the cruiser over and made me get out and walk down the dark road. You're the one who put a kiss on me that I never got over."

"Well, you didn't seem to mind it too much, if I recall," the red haired, green-eyed, Marci said in a sultry voice.

Jake laughed, "You're something else, Marci McLeod; did you know that?"

"You've told me that at least once a day since I met you."

"Well, I mean it," Jake said, "I really do. You are truly the most remarkable woman I've ever met. I feel most fortunate to have been the one who won your young heart."

"Young heart my rear end," Marci chided. "I wasn't even that young back then, but now I'm over forty."

"And a 'hottie' if I ever saw one," Jake said.

"What do you know about 'hotties'?"

"Just because I'm old, doesn't mean I've lost my eyesight. Don't forget, I'm an artist and artists find and appreciate beauty in everything they see."

"Yeah, I guess you do," Marci conceded.

With fondness, Jake looked over at their daughter busily eating her breakfast, "Do you think Meredith will take after her old man and become an artist?" he asked.

"I was kind of hoping she'd become the first female sheriff of Iredell County someday," Marci replied, tongue in cheek.

Jake laughed and turned back to his painting. His mood became more somber as he peered down at the blue wash in his sky and dabbed the still-damp paper in a few places with a tissue to make puffy clouds appear as if the wind had just blown them in on a March day.

"Pray for me," Jake said seriously looking up at Marci. "I still get scared when I start a new painting." Even after painting thirty years, Jake still got butterflies in his stomach each time he began a new painting.

Marci rinsed her coffee cup in the sink, leaned over his shoulder and studied the work in progress. "Well, the drawing looks good, so you better not mess it up."

"And you wonder why I'm afraid to start a painting. I work my butt off drawing the doggoned thing and I'm scared to death I'm going to ruin it when I start applying paint and then you tell me not to mess it up."

"Oh, Jake, hush up!" Marci said as she massaged his shoulders. "Look at the hundreds of paintings you've done and the following you have. People love your work. Just get it done and quit complaining."

"That's easy for you to say. All you have to do is catch a few crooks once in a while."

"Speaking of which," Marci said, "I gotta run. There's been a rash of break-ins at the northern end of the county and a gunshot was heard last night near the Alexander County border, too. A deputy went out there then to check on things, but didn't find anything unusual. Just in case, the sheriff wants me and a couple of deputies to run up there, ask some questions, and poke around a little bit. Sometimes things take on a different slant in the daylight."

"Do you have to go now?" Jake asked.

"Yes, I have to go now. I'm meeting a couple of deputies up there in forty-five minutes, so shut up and kiss me."

Jake was always ready to oblige Marci with a kiss. She was a demanding woman when it came to lovemaking. That was another reason he loved her so much. She was either going to keep him young or kill him.

"What about me, Mama?" Meredith asked dolefully looking up from her Cheerios.

"What about you, young lady? You're the apple of my eye. Come here and give me a big hug."

Meredith climbed down from her chair and ran over with open arms to accept her hug and kiss.

"Now, you be a good little girl for Daddy and help him run the gallery today."

"Okay."

"I gotta run. Love you both." And with that, Detective Marci McLeod was out the door and on her way to the beginning of an investigation that would change her life.

CHAPTER 3

"CAN WE TAKE a ride, too, Daddy?" Meredith asked. "Mama's goin' for a ride."

"She has to, that's part of her job," Jake explained.

He never painted very long at a time—his back muscles would stiffen and ache as a result of a fall he'd experienced years before. He looked briefly at the detailed drawing in front of him with only a blue sky and a few clouds. *Maybe it is time for a break,* he thought.

"Why not? Let me call Joanie to come and watch the gallery and you and I will have a daddy/daughter day in the wonderful sunshine."

Meredith waited anxiously until Jake hung up the phone. "Oh boy! Can we leave now?"

"No, sweetheart, we have to go to the gallery and wait for Joanie."

Jake packed up the watercolor he was working on, buckled

Meredith in her car seat, and headed to Jacob McLeod Fine Arts.

Jake had remained loyal to historic Mooresville and had rejected the idea of moving his gallery to the new shopping centers west of town near I-77. The entire downtown business district had been revitalized. New sidewalks with interspaced brick pavers lined each side of busy Main Street. Colorful flowers and attractive awnings adorned the shops giving one the feeling they were in a small village. Trendy restaurants had helped breathe new life into the heart of town. Jake was a hometown boy. Nothing was going to change that. Many of the gallery's visitors would ask him, "Have you lived here all your life?" Jake would smile and reply, "Not yet."

After Jake unlocked the door and turned off the alarm system, Meredith raced to the back of the gallery where she jumped onto the sofa in front of a widescreen TV.

"Will you turn on the TV, Daddy?"

"Sure, honey," Jake said, as he turned on the television and tuned it to the Cartoon Network.

"I'm going to sweep now, honey," he said.

"Okay," Meredith said as if she was giving him her blessing and dismissing him.

Jake smiled at his daughter, gathered the broom and headed outside. As was his morning ritual, Jake turned the sign around on the front door from Closed to Open, thus announcing to the small North Carolina town that he was officially open for business and began to sweep the sidewalk.

He was almost finished sweeping when he heard a familiar voice, "Hiya, handsome." He looked up and saw the vivacious Joanie Mitchell.

"You're looking well, Joanie," Jake said, and gave her a big hug.

"You always know the right thing to say to a gal," Joanie said with a hearty laugh and kissed him on the cheek.

Jake held her at arm's length and said, "Be careful, Joanie, we don't want people talking."

"Talkin' smalkin'," she smirked. "Who gives a shit in this town, anyway? Everybody knows that you love that Marci more than anything in the whole wide world and I sure as hell ain't leavin' the best thing that ever happened to me."

"Joanie, you're one of a kind," Jake said laughing.

"Hell fire, Jake. That was just a friendly little peck. You'd know it if I ever planted a real kiss on you."

Just about everyone in town knew about Joanie's harrowing experience five years earlier when she, Gail Caldwell, and Debbie Wells were kidnapped. After their rescue, Joanie remarried Ed Mitchell, sold her flower shop and retired. Now she just shop-sits for Jake when he wants a day off.

Joanie was the epitome of a southern, country girl. Her colorful vernacular and crazy antics made her fun to be around. One never knew what she was going to say or do next. Everybody loved Joanie Mitchell.

"What you got going on this morning?" she said, still laughing at Jake standing on the sidewalk with a red face.

"Come on in and I'll tell you about it," Jake said as he held the door for her to enter the gallery.

"Hey, Joanie," Meredith said with enthusiasm as she looked up from watching television. "We goin' ridin' in the country."

Joanie smiled, "Where you takin' this little princess?"

"I thought we might head up toward Love Valley" Jake said.

"Love Valley! I've heard of that place. That's the cowboy town, ain't it?" she asked.

"Yes it is. I used to go there years ago and had almost forgotten about it. I saw an article in the *Mooresville Tribune* last week about Love Valley's mayor, Andy Barker, and his town and I promised myself I would take Meredith up there one day—so I decided this morning that today is the day."

"Sounds like y'all are gonna have fun. Now y'all don't get into any trouble, you hear?"

Jake couldn't help but grin, "We hear," he said. "We should be back late in the afternoon."

"Don't you worry about a thing here. Y'all just go and enjoy yourselves."

CHAPTER 4

DRIVING DOWN the tree-lined driveway from Beckett's trailer, the thief heard a sorrowful whine rise from the nearby woods. He'd never been afraid of anything since his childhood. *Maybe my nerves are gettin' to me,* he thought. But the incessant whine had grown into an incessant howl and it brought a chill to the murderer's black heart.

What the hell was that? Was that one of them one-eyed wampus cats? He'd heard tales about those legendary animals when he was a just a little boy sitting around a campfire in the woods with boys from his neighborhood. He had actually believed the stories for a long time and was teased unmercifully by the older ones in the group. He was not embarrassed now, just frightened. *There it was again. What in the hell is making that awful sound?* The sound resembled some kind of wild animal in pain. It was a mournful, pathetic sound that rose from deep within whatever kind of beast was out there.

I gotta get outta here. Damn animals. His thoughts raced as he drove. *Why'd the old bastard have to go and pull a gun on me anyway?*

Still shaking, he drove without turning his headlights on until he had driven far up the lonely dirt road that headed back into the deep woods and across Fox Mountain. The ramshackle cabin he had discovered a few days earlier awaited him among the budding trees of the Brushy Mountains. He felt that the old man had held out on him and that there was more money still to be found in that trailer. He knew how the man was—just like his mother—she always stashed money away for a rainy day.

I wonder how much money I got from the old man. Damn him to hell for tryin' to hold out on me and damn him again for tryin' to shoot me. By God, I showed him though, didn't I?

CHAPTER 5

WITH MEREDITH BUCKLED securely in her car seat, Jake set out on Highway 115 toward Statesville, Iredell's county seat. He always pointed out landmarks to Meredith and tried to give her an appreciation for beauty and a love of history. Even at four years old, Meredith showed promise and could already recognize certain places. Driving through Troutman, she pointed toward a large, two-story, gray house on the left side of the street and exclaimed "Talley House, Daddy!"

"That's right, sweetie," Jake said, proud of his daughter's acumen for landmark recognition. Of course the McLeods ate there as often as possible, which may have helped in her recognition ability. The Talley House was known for its country cooking and Meredith loved their fried chicken legs…but then so did Jake.

As they passed through Statesville, Jake pointed out the old courthouse on Center Street before they crossed over the square.

"There's Hardee's," Meredith said with delight when she pointed to the restaurant on the left. "They got good biscuits."

Jake laughed. *Damn, if she doesn't take after me always thinking about food.*

Before long, he drove his aging Jeep Cherokee under busy I-40 and soon they were out of the city limits and surrounded by bucolic scenery.

"Look, Meredith! See the cows?"

"Lots of cows," she said with delight. "Where're the horses? I wanna see horses."

"You will, I promise. Just sit tight."

After another ten miles, Jake drove past Central School and turned left at a large sign that signified the Town of Love Valley was just a few miles farther down Mountain View Road. "We'll see some horses anytime now," Jake assured Meredith.

The excited little girl was looking intently out the window when Jake said, "There're some horses now." He pointed toward a pasture surrounded with wooden fencing where several horses were grazing in the lush, spring grass.

"I see them. They're pretty," Meredith said. "I like that one with the spots."

"Those horses are called paints," Jake explained.

"Paints?"

"You know, like the horse had been painted with lots of different colors."

"Oh," she said. "Like you paint with colors?"

"That's right," Jake agreed and glanced at her in his rearview mirror. He smiled with pleasure as he watched her scan the countryside for more horses.

After driving another mile, Jake said, "Let's turn here," and made a right turn onto a paved road at a sign that pointed to Love Valley.

The road led them beside an empty pasture that was covered with tall, green grass that waved in the gentle March breeze. Jake steered the Cherokee up and down a few hills and around a few curves before the pavement ended.

Meredith pointed to her left and then to her right and squealed, "There're some more horses!"

Jake saw them and bragged on her for finding them. The rolling hills were dotted with mobile homes and green pastures where horses were grazing peacefully. Some of the trailers had seen their better days, some were new. A rustic campground on the right was half-filled with small camping trailers and a few motorhomes.

He continued up the dusty road for several hundred yards and saw Andy's Hardware Store. As usual, a few battered trucks were parked in front. Jake smiled when he thought of Andy Barker, the town's affable mayor. *Andy must be in his eighties now.* He pictured the mayor in his mind, dressed in his blue jeans, western shirt, and cowboy hat leaning back in his chair spinning a humorous story. It was rare not to find him sitting before the huge woodstove laughing and talking with his visitors.

Jake decided to bring Meredith to meet the mayor another time and drove on up to the top of the hill past the hardware store. Nothing was behind him, so he stopped and gazed down the shady slope. Fond memories brought a quick smile to his rugged face. *That little dusty parking lot is still beside the blacksmith shop just as I remember.* He slowly edged the Jeep down the hill and pulled into the lot that was virtually empty this time of day. The sun was out and warm, so Jake pulled all the way up to the trees on the far side of the lot to take advantage of the shade.

Jake turned off the motor and quickly climbed out of the Jeep. By the time he had opened the rear door, Meredith was standing there ready to get out.

"We're here!" Jake said.

"Where?" Meredith asked with a serious frown on her small

face.

"Love Valley, isn't this a great place?"

At the sight of the rustic, wooden buildings lining the dusty street, Meredith said with some doubt, "I guess."

CHAPTER 6

IT WAS A BEAUTIFUL SPRING morning and Marci was glad to be out of the office. Driving through the pastoral hills of northern Iredell County gave her great pleasure. Her cell phone chirped and she answered the caller with a question. "What's up, Floyd?" Marci listened for a moment without saying a word and then asked her deputy incredulously, "a what? Where are you?" She paused again so the deputy could give her directions. "I'll be right there. I'm on Mountain View Road now."

Deputy Floyd Alexander met her at the beginning of the victim's driveway. "The body's down this drive in a trailer," Alexander said. "I walked out here to get some fresh air and show you the way in. I'll ride down there with you if that's alright?"

"Sure, hop in," Marci said, "and you can fill me in on the way."

An aging, blue and white trailer underpinned with cinder blocks was at the end of the drive. Another deputy, Leroy Ingle, was stringing yellow crime scene tape around the perimeter when they drove up and stopped.

Marci got out of the Dodge Charger first, but she waited on Alexander to lead the way. "It ain't pretty, Marci" he told her. "His head's bashed in. What bothers me so bad is that his eyes are still open…just staring up at you."

"Death's never pretty, Floyd," Marci said, and then added, "for the life of me I'll never understand it either."

"Understand what?"

"What makes a person take the life of someone else? I just don't get it. I guess I never will. Take me to him," Marci said.

Alexander led the way to the back bedroom where the victim lay, just like the deputy had described.

Marci stretched on a pair of latex gloves and leaned over the body. After examining the wound, she straightened up and said, "Looks like he was killed last night. What's your take on it, Floyd?"

"That's kinda what I was thinking, too," Alexander agreed. "We'll know more about it soon. The crime scene techs should be here shortly."

"Do we know who the victim is?"

"Not a clue," Alexander said. "We checked the neighboring houses and didn't find anyone home. Most of the property owners come up on the weekends. Only a few live around here year-round."

"Well, tell Ingle to stay here to protect the scene until the techs arrive," Marci said, "and let's go into town and see if we can find anybody who can identify the deceased."

They climbed back into the Charger and drove up to the town of Love Valley.

CHAPTER 7

J AKE LOOKED at his daughter whose eyes had grown large with excitement. "Can we go up there?" she asked motioning toward the town.

"Sure we can," he said, "c'mon." Jake took hold of her hand and they walked across the dusty parking lot and on to Henry Martin Trail. He called her attention to the large sign that was suspended between two weathered poles and spanned across the unpaved main street. In large white letters were the words: *Love Valley*. The bold letters stood out against the Carolina blue of the March sky.

"What's that say, Daddy?" Meredith asked.

"It says, Love Valley. It's a real cowboy town."

"Love Valley?" Meredith said wrinkling her nose.

Jake explained to her that no cars or trucks were allowed on the main street. "Only horses, dogs, and pedestrians are permitted."

They stood there for a moment gazing down the dirt street that was about as long as a football field. Weather-boarded buildings with six-foot wide, plank sidewalks lined both sides of the street. There was a combination restaurant and saloon, a general store, and tack shop. A gift shop and a bar rounded out the downtown amenities.

"Look at the horses," Jake said and pointed out several that were tied to hitching rails along the main street. A few buckskins, a couple of sorrels, a dapple gray, and a pinto were switching their tails in the warm sunshine.

"I like this place," Meredith said, grinning from ear to ear.

The door to The General Store opened and several cowboys dressed in western garb emerged, mounted up, and rode down the street toward Jake and Meredith. Seeing them, one of the cowboys pulled away from the others, reined in his horse, and stopped a few feet from where they were standing.

"Howdy," said the lanky rider sitting astride his beautiful dapple gray. "Have y'all been here before?"

"I have," Jake answered. "It's been years, but everything looks just about the same."

"Nothin' changes around here very much."

"I can see that," Jake said and extended his hand to the cowboy. "My name's Jake McLeod and this is my daughter, Meredith."

The weathered looking rider, sporting a handlebar mustache, leaned down and grasped Jake's hand with a calloused grip and said, "Rodney Phillips, but people around here just call me Wish."

"Wish?" Jake asked, not sure he had heard correctly.

"Yeah, Wish. It's short for Wishbone. My mama loved to watch *Rawhide* on TV years ago. He was the cook, you know?"

"I remember that," Jake said. "And Clint Eastwood played Rowdy Yates, right?"

"Yep, that's the one."

"Well, Wish, how long have you been in Love Valley?"

"Long as I can remember, I was born here in 1962." He paused briefly and then asked, "Are you that artist feller?"

"I sure am," Jake said. "Do I know you?"

"Probly' not, I don't get out much, but I've sure heard of you. Are you goin' to paint a picture of our town?"

"I hadn't planned on it. I just brought my little girl up to see the sights. She really just wants to see some horses."

"You ever rode on a horse?" Wish asked Meredith.

"Noooo."

"You wanna try it?" Before she could answer, Wish reached down and swiftly hoisted Meredith up onto the saddle in front of him.

Frightened by the sudden action of the cowboy, Meredith called out to Jake, "Daddy, I wanna get down."

Jake, too, was a little uncertain when this stranger suddenly grabbed his daughter, but remained calm and reassured her with a tentative smile. "You'll be fine, honey. Just let your new friend ride you up to the end of the street and back."

Meredith turned and looked up into the eyes of the cowboy and saw nothing but kindness and then peered down at Jake, "Okay, Daddy." She relaxed a little, but held on to the saddle horn with all of her might.

Wish turned the horse around and walked it back up the main street, slowly but surely, letting Meredith get used to the idea of being on a horse. Jake watched with pleasure as his daughter rode up the street of Love Valley on the back of the big dapple gray with the friendly cowboy. He wished Marci was here to see Meredith take her first ride.

Wish wore a weather-beaten, sweat-stained Stetson and sat his horse as if it was as natural as breathing. Wrinkles, from years of being outdoors, framed his eyes when he smiled.

Turning her head to look at Wish, Meredith asked, "What's your horse's name?"

"His name's Applejack."

Meredith laughed, "What kind of name is that?"

"I just thought it sounded good, so that's what I named him. I never heard him complain about it one time."

The little girl was warming up to the cowboy and said, "Aw, Wish, horses can't talk."

"Well you never know, he might start any minute."

"You're funny," Meredith said laughing.

"And you're pretty," Wish countered.

"My mama said I'm 'posed to say thank you when somebody tells me I'm pretty."

"Your mama's right. You listen to her."

"I always do...well sometimes."

They both laughed.

"Do you paint like your daddy?" Wish asked.

"Nobody paints like my daddy."

"I've seen some of his paintings and they're really good. I wish I could paint like that. Maybe some day, I'll give it a try. Your daddy is a smart man," Wish said.

"I know," Meredith agreed.

The cowboy smiled as he guided the horse up the street. *This is one smart little girl,* Wish thought.

"Will Applejack go any faster?"

"You betcha, but let's take it easy for a while yet."

"Okay."

"Let's ride back to your daddy and see if he wants to ride, too."

The friendly cowboy turned Applejack around and headed back toward a relieved Jake McLeod.

"Your turn, Daddy," Meredith squealed. "This is fun."

"I don't have a horse, darling, maybe another time."

"Wish'll let you ride Applejack, won't you, Wish?"

"Sure thing," he said as he handed Meredith down to Jake.

"Are you sure about this?" Jake asked.

"I wouldn't let just anybody ride Applejack, but since you're the daddy of my friend, Meredith here, I think it'll be alright."

Wish dismounted and handed the reins to Jake and said, "Enjoy."

Jake took the reins, put his left foot in the stirrup and swung up onto the saddle. "It's been a long time since I've been on a horse. Wish me luck."

Jake turned the animal and loped off up the street. *Well, damn. I haven't forgotten how. This ain't so bad.* He turned Applejack around near the broken windmill and galloped back to where the cowboy and Meredith were waiting.

"You done good, Mr. McLeod," Wish said with approval.

"You know, I didn't think I could do that after all these years. Actually it was kind of fun to get back in the saddle again," Jake said.

"I could tell you've been on a horse before," Wish said.

"When I was growing up, our neighbor had horses and I used to ride all the time. But, you know how things go. He sold his farm and moved out West and along with him went my opportunity to ride." Jake dismounted and handed the reins to the cowboy. "Thanks, Wish, you just made our day."

"No problem. You sure you don't want to paint our town, Mr. McLeod?"

"I'll definitely think about it," Jake said. "After all Love Valley is a piece of history and I've dedicated my career to preserving North Carolina's heritage." He really liked the cowboy and suggested to him, "Please just call me Jake."

"I'd like that very much. It's Jake from now on."

CHAPTER 8

"**I**S THAT A SIREN?" Jake asked, turning his head to the distant sound.

"I think it is," Wish agreed.

"Wonder what's going on?"

"I don't know, but there's been a lot of break-ins lately. It might have something to do with that," Wish said. "I thought I heard a gunshot last night, too, and that's something you rarely hear at night up here."

"My wife was telling me about the break-ins this morning. She's a detective for the Iredell County Sheriff's Department."

"You kiddin' me? Your wife's a detective?"

"I'm serious," Jake said. "Her name is Marci McLeod."

"Marci," Phillips said, rolling the name over his tongue. "You don't hear that name every day. There used to be a deputy named Marci Meredith that came up this way once in a while. She was a nice lady."

"Well, that deputy's now my wife."

"Well, I'll be doggoned," Wish said.

"Her husband, Mark Meredith, was tragically killed in an auto accident seven or eight years ago," Jake said.

"I'm sure sorry. You know, it seems like I remember something about that. He was a deputy, too, wasn't he?"

"Yes he was. Did you know him?" Jake asked.

"I didn't know him. But I'll never forget her! Several years ago, I watched her arrest a guy I know."

"Why did she arrest him?"

"Well, he was drunk and then he borrowed somebody's horse without askin' and just rode off. The poor feller that owned the horse had to get somebody to take him home. He thought it was stole. Everybody got all excited and one thing led to another."

"What happened?"

"Well the old boy came ridin' the horse back into town the next morning and that was when he got into trouble. Your wife was here then tryin' to sort stuff out. Everything was going pretty good 'til he started sassin' her. That's when she spun him around and slapped them cuffs on him before he knew what happened. That woman didn't take no junk off'n nobody."

Jake grinned, "She still doesn't."

Wish laughed.

Meredith had waited patiently for several minutes as they carried on their conversation, but she finally pulled on Jake's sleeve and said, "I'm hungry, Daddy!"

Jake looked down at his daughter and then back to the cowboy, "Let me buy you some lunch, Wish."

"Okay," he agreed, "but there ain't many places to eat around here right now, 'ceptin' the Silver Spur."

"Do they have anything on their menu a hungry little girl might eat?"

"They got great hot dogs," Wish said. "I betcha she likes hot dogs."

"I know I do," Jake said with enthusiasm. "Lead the way. We like hot dogs, don't we Meredith?"

"We sure do, with lots of ketchup!"

CHAPTER 9

BUD BECKETT'S KILLER spent a fitful night tossing and turning on the lumpy mattress. Now that morning had come, he was cold and hungry. He raked his fingers through his straggly beard and hair and struggled to his feet. A shaft of light slanted through the window and lit up dust motes as they floated in the morning sun. He surveyed his surroundings. *I like it here in Love Valley. It's so laid back and quiet up here in this old cabin. I shoulda come here sooner. Uncle said they didn't have much law around here, either. If I'm gonna stay here for a while and see how the pickin's are, I'd better lay in a supply of food.*

The sound of a siren far away caught his attention.

What in the hell is that? It must be an ambulance. Hellfire, they couldn't have found the old coot that quick.

He listened intently as the sound grew closer. A bead of sweat suddenly appeared on his forehead and ran down his brow. He wiped it off with his sleeve, opened the door to the cabin, and stepped outside. The sound had stopped. *I wonder if that really was an ambulance. I'd better check in town and see what's goin' on.*

Back inside the cabin, he pulled on the same dirty jeans he had worn the day before and tucked his shirt into the waistband...the same shirt in which he had slept. He found his hat where he had thrown it when he'd stumbled in during the night. His boots were caked with mud, but he pulled them on over the socks he had forgotten to take off before he collapsed on his mattress last night.

Fully dressed, but worse for wear, he stepped out into the day and climbed into his old truck and headed down the mountain.

CHAPTER 10

THE SILVER SPUR SALOON and Restaurant was housed in a cinder block building, unlike most of the wood buildings that lined the town's main street. A covered porch stretched over the plank sidewalk that ran the length of the town. In front of the Silver Spur was a large, log hitching rail where two horses stood, patiently waiting for their riders to come and free them from their tether.

Jake, Meredith, and Wish strolled up the dusty street toward the Silver Spur all the while looking at the variety of horseflesh hitched along the rails in front of the businesses.

Two rowdy cowboys emerged from the restaurant, laughing and talking with each other. When they saw Wish walking toward them with Jake and Meredith they grew quiet.

In a low voice, Wish said, "It's probably best if you just keep your distance from those two."

The larger of the two's mood quickly turned dour. He glared at Wish as he swung up onto his saddle. Both men then turned their horses and rode down the main street without even a nod.

"Not very friendly, are they?" Jake pointed out.

"No, they're not. They don't like me at all and I don't like them too much, either," Wish admitted.

"Oh," Jake said, waiting to hear more.

"Well," Wish began, "I don't know if I should tell you this or not."

"Go on," Jake encouraged.

The cowboy took in a deep breath and began again. "Well, I started to say that the big one with the beard…well, that's Dewayne Allison, he's the guy your wife arrested several years ago. He's always in some kind of trouble and drinks most of the time. He's a mean one when he's been drinkin'."

"Oh," Jake said, "I can see why she was quick to put him in his place."

Wish thought a little bit and continued. "I can still remember him cussin' her and sayin', 'I'm not gonna forget you deputy. I'll get even with you someday. You just wait!'"

When Jake heard the veiled threat, a sudden chill ran down his spine and the hair on the back of his neck bristled.

"I don't guess I shoulda told you all that," Wish confessed.

"That's alright," Jake said. "It's better to know." He knew that Marci's job was sometimes dangerous, but he was also confident that she could handle it.

His thoughts were interrupted by another tug on his sleeve. "Are we gonna get some hot dogs, Daddy?" Meredith asked.

"Sure," Jake said and he reached down and clutched Meredith's hand a little harder than usual and followed Wish up onto the plank sidewalk in front of the Silver Spur.

At the door, he turned around to see where the cowboys had gone, but they were already out of sight. Jake tried not to show it, but a bad feeling was worming its way into his psyche.

CHAPTER 11

"DID YOU SEE WISH kissin' up to that fancy dude and his little girl?" Allison asked.

"Yeah, I did. Who was them people?" his friend, Shorty Parsons asked.

"How the hell should I know? He looked like he coulda been a lawyer or something, maybe even a real estate salesman… Lord knows we need more of them."

His sidekick laughed and then grew more serious, "Wonder what they was doin' up here?"

"Just tourists, I guess. Wantin' to see how us country folks live. I doubt they'll be back, I didn't see no mama with them and that tells you somethin' right there."

"It does?"

"It sure does. That means there ain't no mama in the picture. He's probably divorced and it's his time to be with his daughter, don't you know nothin'?"

The little man said, "You always figure things out. I wish I was as smart as you."

"Never happen," Allison said. "Never happen."

"I know I ain't too bright, but you don't have to rub it in all the time."

"Aw, hell, let's go get a beer and I'll make it up to you. How's that sound, Pard?"

"Hey, that sounds good to me!"

As they neared Andy's Hardware, a dog ran out of a nearby barn and began barking at the heels of Allison's horse. His sorrel jumped sideways and almost threw him to the ground. "Settle down you damn knothead," he yelled at his frightened horse and finally reined him back under control. "Damn dogs everywhere up here," he said and then turned and guided the animal down the road as if nothing happened.

Parsons admired his friend's horsemanship. "Boy, I thought he was gonna throw you for a minute there."

"Not this bag of bones," Allison bragged. "Now that I got this damn horse straightened out, let's go get them beers. We'll get in my truck and drive down to the gas station and get us a twelve-pack."

"I'm with you," his little shadow said.

CHAPTER 12

"Y'ALL ARE GONNA like this place," Wish said as he led the way into the Silver Spur. Half of the huge room was dimly lit with a few overhead lights that strained to brighten the space where a few diners were eating their noon meal. The other half of the room consisted of an empty dance floor, a large stage, and more tables that sat forlornly waiting for the nighttime crowd.

Wish waved to a couple of his friends sitting at a table near a large woodstove. The man dressed in western clothes motioned for Wish to come over to their table.

The couple rose to meet them and Wish introduced Jake and Meredith to Beth and Charlie Nance. Everyone shook hands, even little Meredith.

"Why don't y'all sit with us?" the gregarious cowboy asked. Jake noticed the laugh lines around the man's eyes and liked him immediately. He sported a gray Fu Manchu mustache that was broad and full. Nance was a compact man who wore a wide-brimmed, black Resistol cowboy hat, which he had removed and placed on a nearby chair. He took his right hand, rubbed it vigorously over his scalp and claimed that his bald pate was the latest spring fashion look.

"Don't pay any attention to Charlie," Beth said. "He's the rodeo clown in and out of the arena."

Jake laughed along with the others and pulled out a chair. He noticed that their hot dogs had chili draped across the top of homemade slaw. *That's my kinda hot dog,* he thought.

"Meredith, you can sit beside me." Beth offered. Beth was dressed in jeans and the blue western shirt she was wearing reflected her startling blue eyes. She stood about five-feet-two in her boots. Those blue eyes and high cheek bones made it difficult not to gaze at her. She was hatless and her long straight hair framed her face and hung gently to her shoulders.

Meredith liked Beth instantly. "Can I sit in a big chair, Daddy?" she pleaded. "Beth asked me to."

"Sure if Beth doesn't mind watching you. You might fall off that big chair."

"Oh, Daddy! I'll be careful, won't I Beth?"

"Sure, you will," Beth agreed and helped Meredith onto the chair beside her. Wish and Jake took their seats and looked at the menu.

A pretty young waitress, with brunette hair tucked under a baseball cap, immediately appeared and said, "Hey, my name's Jennie and I'll be glad to take your order as soon as you're ready. Can I go ahead and get your drink order?"

"Sure, I'll have a Diet Pepsi and a lemonade for my little girl," Jake said.

Wish ordered a Pepsi for himself and then the enthusiastic waitress scooted off to get their beverages. "She seems awfully nice," Jake said as she walked away.

"Most people up here are nice," Charlie agreed, "except maybe for that pair of no-goods that just left right before y'all came in."

Beth grabbed Charlie's arm. "Now, Charlie, be nice."

He grimaced. "She's always reminding me to be nice, but those damn good-for-nothings are always causing trouble."

"Take a sip of your Pepsi, Charlie, it'll cool you down."

"Sounds like my wife," Jake said. "You'd better listen to her, too." They all laughed and Jake said, "Let's order. I'm starved." Inwardly, his thoughts were still focused on Marci and the veiled threat. *What would I do to someone who harmed the most important person in my life?*

Jennie reappeared with their drinks and set them down. "Ready to order?"

"You betcha," Jake said, snapping back to the present. He put on his happy face and ordered. "I'll have two hot dogs all-the-way with no onions and an order of fries for me and just a plain hot dog with lots of ketchup for the young lady. What'll you have, Wish?"

"I'll have the same as he's havin'," Wish said.

"This is the hot dog eatin'est bunch of people I've ever seen," Jennie said laughing as she headed for the kitchen.

Wish could barely wait to tell the Nance's about Jake McLeod being an artist and asked if they had seen any of his work.

"Oh yes," Beth said. "We've admired his work for years. Someday Charlie is going to buy one of his originals for me, aren't you, Charlie?"

"Sure thing, darlin'," Charlie said, "just as soon as my ship comes in!"

Everyone was still laughing when a fresh breeze followed a nice looking couple through the swinging doors into the saloon.

Charlie looked up. "Well, look who just walked through the door."

The couple made their way over to their table. "Who're your friends, Charlie?" the man asked.

Wish answered before Charlie could open his mouth. "This here's Jake McLeod and this pretty little thing next to Beth is his daughter, Meredith."

"Bob Adams," the man said, extending his hand, "and this is my wife, Judy."

"Very pleased to meet both of you," Jake said to the couple.

Charlie joined in. "Bob and Judy own the Silver Spur and have made it a really nice place."

"Thanks for the compliment, Charlie," Bob said. "Jake McLeod. I've heard that name somewhere."

"I guess you should have," Beth said. "His paintings hang just about everywhere. He has a gallery in Mooresville."

"That's where I've heard the name," Bob said. "You'll have to forgive our ignorance, but we just moved here a few years ago from California. You're that artist from Mooresville."

Jake laughed, "That's quite alright. There are a lot of people in my own hometown that aren't familiar with my work. Sometimes, I feel like I'm the Rodney Dangerfield of the art world." The group remembered Dangerfield as the comedian who always complained that he never got any respect and laughed at Jake.

The Adams pulled up chairs and joined them.

Jennie Foster, their attentive waitress, kept their glasses filled. Meredith kept hers drained and before long announced to Jake, "Daddy, I gotta go."

"I'll take her," Beth offered, and off they went.

"I got started into this fatherhood thing a little late," Jake said, "but I wouldn't have missed it for the world. Meredith has brought so much joy into our lives."

"She seems awfully precocious. How old is she?"

"She's almost five," Jake said. "She keeps us on our toes. She's a smart girl and funny, too, like her mother."

Beth and Meredith returned to the table just as the batwing

doors of the saloon swung open and Deputy Floyd Alexander and Detective Marci McLeod strode inside.

CHAPTER 13

"HEY, MAMA!" Meredith squealed at the sight of Marci.

"Hi, sweetie," Marci said. She went over to give her daughter a hug and then gave Jake a questioning glance. "What are you two doing up here?"

"We're ridin' horses!" Meredith interrupted.

"You're what?" Marci asked.

"No harm done, honey," Jake said, "I just thought Meredith and I would spend some quality time together. She wanted to see some horses and what better place to do that than Love Valley."

"You're right, honey, it sounds like fun. It just caught me by surprise finding you two sitting here."

"And you, little girl," Marci said turning to Meredith, "you be careful around those horses. They're just like men. You never know what they're gonna do next."

Beth laughed, "You got that right, ma'am!" Everyone joined in the laughter and she, Charlie, and Wish were introduced to

Marci and Deputy Alexander.

"What are *you* doing here?" Jake asked Marci. "Does your visit have anything to do with those break-ins you told me about?"

In almost a whisper, Marci said, "I'm afraid there's been more than a break-in this time. Floyd and Leroy Ingle were canvassing area residents about a gunshot that was reported last night and came upon a mobile home where they found an old hound dog whining and scratching at the front door."

"A hound dog?" Jake asked.

"Yes. They said the dog was really persistent, so they knocked to see if any one was home. That hound wouldn't quit scratching at the door, so the deputies thought somebody might be in trouble. The door was unlocked so they entered the dwelling."

Not sure whether to go any further with the story, Marci hesitated.

"Well, what happened?" Jake asked.

Marci gazed at the crowd sitting around the table and finally felt she had to tell them what was going on, they were going to hear it on the news tonight anyway. "I'm sorry to tell you folks, but Love Valley had a murder last night."

"You can't be serious," Beth said with disbelief.

"I'm afraid I am," Marci continued. "We found the victim lying face-up across his bed. His skull had been crushed with a blunt object."

"Do you know who the victim is?" asked Charlie.

"No, we don't at this time. There was no identification on the body; it looks like the assailant took his wallet. The deceased is an elderly man, I'd say in his eighties. The crime scene techs should be there now working the site."

Beth's., blue eyes welled with tears. "Why would anybody kill an old man like that?" she asked.

Marci replied, "It looks like a robbery gone bad. We can't

find anybody at home near there who might know the victim's name. I wonder if one of you folks who live around here could accompany us back to the trailer and possibly identify the victim?"

"Sure, I'll go," Charlie volunteered. "Where's the trailer?"

"Not too far from here, off Mitchell Trail."

Marci gave Meredith a hug, blew Jake a kiss, and told everyone goodbye before leaving with Charlie and the deputy.

All was quiet at the table for a moment until Meredith broke the silence. "Where'd Mama go, Daddy?"

"She and Charlie had to run an errand. Charlie will be right back, but Mommy has to work. We'll see her tonight."

"Okay, Daddy."

"I thought I heard something that sounded like a gunshot last night," Wish said. "It was a good ways up the hill and it was hard to tell where it was comin' from. I didn't pay too much attention. It could've been a car or truck backfirin' for all I knew."

Bob Adams joined in the conversation. "Anyway, she said the man's head had been bashed in. She didn't mention anybody being shot!"

"That's true," Wish said.

"I hate to hear about somebody getting killed," Beth said as she stirred her Diet Pepsi with a straw.

Meredith listened intently to their conversation, but said nothing.

"Why can't people get along? Love Valley is a loving place," Beth said.

"I know!" Wish agreed. "Andy and Ellenora have worked so hard to make this a special place and it'd be a shame to have it ruined by just a few no-account people."

"The only trouble Love Valley ever had was when they put on that darned ol' rock concert back in the '70s," Beth offered.

"That was a mess, wasn't it?" Wish chuckled.

"Yeah, it sure was, but that was way back then. Now all the rodeos go on without a hitch. It's been great living here," Beth said as she looked up to see Jennie coming through the kitchen door.

The pretty young brunette sat down the tray on a nearby table, "Okay everybody, here's your hot dogs." Jennie began setting their meals before them with a flourish.

"Thanks," Jake said smiling at her. "They look delicious."

"Mine's got plenty of ketchup. Just like I like 'em," Meredith exclaimed.

"What do we do before we eat?" Jake asked her.

"We say the blessin'," Meredith said with pride.

"That's right."

Beth Nance reached over and grabbed Meredith's hand. Then everyone followed her lead and joined hands in a circle around the table before she led them all in grace.

"We'll let you folks enjoy your meal," Bob said after the blessing. "Judy and I had better go help in the kitchen. The way hot dogs are flying out the door, it looks like they might need some help back there." He turned to Jake and Meredith before entering the kitchen. "You two come back and see us anytime."

"You can count on that," Jake said. "We'll be back."

"Good hot dog," Meredith said with ketchup smeared all over her chin.

They all laughed at the precocious little girl with green eyes and red hair who looked so much like her mother.

As the conversation slowed down, pictures of the bearded cowboy, Dewayne Allison, came to Jake's mind. Being married to a detective had made him a more suspicious person and a pretty good judge of character. He couldn't help but wonder if Allison had any part in the Love Valley murder.

CHAPTER 14

MARCI LISTENED INTENTLY while Charlie Nance pointed out who lived along Mitchell Trail. When Deputy Alexander swung the Charger into a long winding driveway lined with native cedar and scrub pine, Charlie said, "This takes us to old Bud Beckett's place."

"Do you know the man that lives here?" Marci asked.

"Sure, everybody up here knows Bud. He's a kind old coot, but he keeps to himself most of the time. I see him up at Andy's hardware store every day or so."

Three deputies had joined Ingle and were standing guard at crime scene tape. An old blue-tick hound came from behind the trailer, but didn't bark as they parked and stepped out of the vehicle.

"Take it easy," one of the deputies said to the dog as he knelt and scratched behind the hound's ears. "Everything's gonna be alright."

"That's Rounder," Charlie said, "Bud's old hound." The dog wagged his tail desultorily as they proceeded to the open door of the mobile home.

Nance had a sick feeling in his stomach as he followed Marci into the kitchen. "This way," she told him. She led the way down the narrow hallway and cautioned Charlie not to touch anything. "The body's back here," she said.

Charlie's legs were shaking as he followed her to the back bedroom. There on the rumpled bedspread lay his friend. There was a severe gash across his forehead, just above the brow of his right eye. Blood from the wound had run down his face and soaked the spread.

"Good Lord!" Nance said. He quickly turned his head away from the brutal scene and quietly confirmed the deceased's identity to Marci. "It's Bud, alright." Tears welled in Charlie's eyes and he suddenly felt as if he was going to be sick. "If you don't need me for anything else, I'll be outside"

"Sure," Marci said. "Get some air. We'll be out in just a minute."

Charlie fled out the door, down the steps, and over to some dried grass next to a flower bed, where he fell to the ground and lost his lunch. *God, why would anybody hurt old Bud? Bud wouldn't harm a flea.*

A young deputy walked over to him and asked if he could get him some water. "We keep some in our cars," he said. Charlie noticed the young deputy's name bar had Chambers written on it. He declined the water, but took a breath mint from his pocket and put it in his mouth. "If there's anything I can do for you, let me know," the deputy said.

"Thanks, I'll be fine," Charlie said. "I just wasn't ready for that. Heck, I've seen worse looking wounds than that in my years on the rodeo circuit, but never on an eighty-year-old innocent man who was a friend of mine. That was just too much."

"I understand, sir," Chambers responded.

As Marci and Deputy Alexander approached them, Chambers said, "The ME's on his way. Are the crime boys havin' any luck?" he asked.

"It looks like a robbery. The man's wallet is missing and the bedroom was tossed. You know them, they're thorough," Marci said. "Maybe we'll get lucky and find some prints to run through AFIS."

"What's that?" Charlie asked.

"AFIS is an acronym for the Automated Fingerprint Identification System. Now, even local law enforcement agencies have access. If the perpetrator has ever committed a crime, been in military service, or had a government job, their prints will be in the system. Iredell County now has its own AFIS and Crime Lab."

Marci added, "Chambers wait out here with Leroy and Floyd for the medical examiner and help keep the press away. Word'll get out soon and we'll be bombarded with questions we don't have answers for."

Turning to Charlie, Marci asked, "You okay?"

Nance nodded with no comment.

"Come on, I'll take you back to town."

"Well?" Beth asked, as Charlie and Marci walked through the door. "Was it anybody we know?"

"It's...it's...old Bud Beckett," Charlie finally stammered.

"Bud! Oh no," Beth said. "Why in the world would anybody hurt that old man?" Her eyes filled quickly and tears ran down her cheeks before she could stop them.

Meredith looked up at Beth and asked, "Why you cryin'?"

Beth grabbed Meredith and hugged her fiercely. The four year old looked at her father and mother helplessly for some sort of answer as to why Beth was crying. Sensing Meredith's discomfort, Beth said, "It's all right, honey, we just lost an old friend."

"I'm sorry," Meredith said, "maybe we can help find him."

"No, darlin', he passed away. He's already in Heaven."

"Oh. I thought you said he was lost."

"Well," Beth began, "he is lost from us. That's what I meant."

"You mean he's dead?"

"Yes, sweetheart, he's dead."

"I know what dead is," the little girl said with understanding beyond her years.

As Marci reached down to take Meredith from Beth's grasp, she said, "Meredith understands much more than the average four year old."

"She is a special child," Beth said. "I already love her and I just met her."

"Thank you," Marci said, "but maybe Jake should take her home now."

"Sure, I understand."

Jake rose from the table and asked Meredith, "Ready to go angel?"

"No, I wanna stay and ride Applejack."

"Meredith," her mother said firmly and handed her to Jake.

The little girl added quickly, "But we can go if you want to."

From across the table, Wish said to Meredith, "You can come back and ride Applejack any time you want to."

"Thank you," Meredith said sweetly, "we'll be back, won't we, Daddy?"

"Sure we will," Jake said. "But we'd better get you home now."

Marci waited for Jake and Meredith to leave, pulled up a chair, and sat down at the table with Charlie and Beth Nance and Wish Phillips. "Can you think of anyone who may have had a grudge with Mr. Beckett?"

"No," Beth said, "he was a kind old man."

"Anyone up here you know who has been in trouble with the law before?"

"Oh, maybe a couple," Charlie said.

"Any names you can give me?"

"Well, the only one that comes to my mind right now is that good-for-nothin' Dewayne Allison."

"Now, Charlie, you don't know if he had anything to do with this," Beth said.

"I know that, but she asked if we knew anybody who'd been in trouble before. Besides that, I just don't trust the man."

"Why's that?" Marci asked.

Well, he stole a friend of mine's horse one time."

"That was a long time ago, Charlie," Beth reminded him.

"I didn't say he was a murderer, I just said he stole a horse and I didn't trust him, that's all."

"Thanks folks." Marci rose to go, "This is somewhere to start."

Charlie told Marci where Allison lived, so she drove down the street to his trailer and knocked several times on his door, but he was not home. "I'll come back to you later, Mr. Allison," Marci said aloud to herself and climbed back into her cruiser and drove away.

CHAPTER 15

JAKE AND MEREDITH returned to Mooresville to relieve Joanie. Since Meredith slept almost all the way back, Jake knew a proper afternoon nap would be out of the question.

"Y'all are home early," Joanie said as they entered the gallery. "How was Love Valley?"

"It was fun! I got to ride a horse," Meredith said, "and somebody got killed, too! I heard them talkin' about it."

"What?" Joanie asked incredulously.

"A man was murdered last night or early this morning," Jake explained. "Marci was there working the case and came into the restaurant and asked one of the men who was eating with us to identify the body."

"Somebody was murdered in Love Valley? That's hard to believe," Joanie said. "I really hate to hear that."

"The victim was an elderly gentleman. Marci said it could have been a robbery."

"Is that the reason ya'll got home so early?"

"Yes, I suppose so."

"Well, did you still have some fun?"

Jake was grateful to change the subject. "Oh, we really had a good time," Jake said. "You should have seen this little cowgirl ride a horse."

"Aw, Daddy, I ain't no cowgirl," Meredith said laughing.

"I am not a cowgirl," Jake corrected.

"Well, I ain't a cowgirl, either."

"I give up," Jake said.

"Why hellfire and da...oops, I almost forgot. Sorry, Jake. Heck, I ain't never learned proper English yet and I'm...well you know about how old I am," Joanie laughed.

"That's okay, Joanie. I appreciate you watching your language around Meredith. She picks up on just about everything."

"Hell, don't I know it. She's one smart kid if I ever saw one."

"You just did it again," Jake said

"Did what? Did I? Oh, Jake, I'm sorry as h...oops. I almost said hell."

"You did say it again," Jake chided her.

"Dammit, Jake. I try, I really do."

"I know you do, Joanie. I'm not fussing at you. Just try to remember when Meredith is around."

"Okay," Joanie promised. "When's Marci comin' home?"

"I have no idea. She's the lead detective on this murder case. It's no telling when we'll get to see her."

Jake was right, it was after dark when Marci drove into their driveway.

CHAPTER 16

"OKAY PEOPLE, here's what we have," Detective Marci McLeod said the next morning to the homicide unit that was seated before her. "I hope you've all had your coffee, we have a lot to do today. The victim's name is Walter "Bud" Beckett. He's lived in the area for years. No known enemies. He wasn't known for having much money or flashing any around; though it does-n't mean he didn't have some stashed. We gotta canvass everyone in and near Love Valley and I mean everyone. Ask if they have seen anyone suspicious hanging around the area."

"Several folks have reported they heard a gunshot that night," a deputy offered.

"We're checking on that, but it appears the victim was killed by blunt force trauma to the head. The techs did find a single bullet hole in the wall of the bedroom, but no gun. The bullet hole appears to be from a large caliber gun, probably a forty-five. Mitchell Trail is a dead-end road, so somebody must have seen the perp when he came back down the road."

"I've talked with a couple of folks who live in Love Valley year round and I was given a name that needs to be followed up on. He wasn't home when I went there earlier."

Marci asked one of the deputies and her partner, Detective Jamie Campbell, to follow up on Dewayne Allison and told them where he lived.

After a brief silence, Marci spoke again. "Okay, we're all on the same page and you all know what to do, so let's get started."

Marci drove the Charger to Love Valley after the early morning briefing and stopped at Andy Barker's hardware store to have a chat with the mayor.

"Hey! Come in and make yourself at home," Mayor Barker said to Marci as she entered the store. Even though there were some flowers blooming on the Brushy Mountain hillsides, the morning air still had a chill. "This old woodstove really puts out the heat. We need it early in the morning, but doggoned if it don't get a little hot in here by lunch. Danielle stoked it pretty good this morning. She must have thought it was gonna be cool all day long."

"It feels good," Marci said, as she rubbed her hands together before the stove. "Mayor Barker, my name is Marci McLeod. I'm a detective for the Iredell County Sheriff's Department."

"I know who you are," the good mayor said, his blue eyes sparkling. "I know every deputy and detective in the county and I even know your husband. I want him to paint my town some day."

"You seem to be a well-informed man."

"I try to make it my business to keep up with nearly everything that's goin' on in my town," he said proudly.

"Well, I wanted to talk to you about an incident that happened near here two nights ago," Marci asked.

"You're talking about the murder of old Bud Beckett?"

"Why yes, as a matter of fact, I am. If there's any way you could help me, I'd appreciate it very much."

"Damn shame," Barker said. "I always thought Bud could take care of himself."

"What makes you say that?"

"Well, Bud had an old forty-five he kept under his pillow just in case anyone broke in on him. He always bragged that he'd be ready for any SOB that'd try to rob him."

"We didn't find a gun at the scene."

"It was common knowledge that he had one and wouldn't hesitate to use it."

"Well, thank you very much for your help, Mayor. I'll be back in touch and keep you informed."

"We don't take it kindly when one of our citizens gets murdered," Mayor Barker exclaimed. "We'll do anything we can to help you find the person who did this to Bud." Tears welled in the man's eyes. "Bud's been my friend for over fifty years."

"We'll catch him. Don't you worry, Mayor," Marci vowed. "We'll catch him."

CHAPTER 17

DEWAYNE ALLISON and Shorty Parsons had spent most of the day drinking. Late in the evening Allison went home for more beer money in case they would need it.

Early the next morning, he sat at Shorty Parson's kitchen table counting a stack of money that consisted of ten and twenty-dollar bills. "Where'd you get all that money?" his friend asked.

"None of your business!" Allison bellowed.

"Well, you don't have to yell at me. I thought maybe you got it from your old lady or sumpin'."

"Maybe I did, but it ain't none of your business. I ain't seen that woman since the divorce. Anyway, she never gave me no money when we was married."

"Okay, alright. Just don't yell at me."

The big man quickly changed the subject. "Hey, look here at what I got," he said, holding up a large pistol he withdrew from under the table.

"Boy, that's a nice'un. Where'd you get that thing?"

"Damn, you're gettin' nosy these days."

"Sorry. I just didn't know you had a gun, that's all."

"Well, I got one now and I've had it for a while. I just didn't want you to know it."

"I'm okay with that," his friend said hesitantly. "You don't have to tell me everything you do. I was just askin'."

Eager to change the subject, the smaller man asked, "Hey, we gotta get somethin' to eat, I'm hungry. Wanna run down to the service station and get a ham biscuit?"

"Might as well," his sullen friend agreed.

They piled into a battered pickup truck and headed out Mountain View Road in search of breakfast.

Allison stopped the battered pickup at the intersection of Highway 115 and then turned left.

"Where we goin? I thought we wuz just gonna get a ham biscuit down at the station."

"I changed my mind. We go there all the time," Allison snorted.

After a few miles, he took a right onto Highway 901 toward Union Grove.

"Are we gonna eat at the Cook Shack?" asked Parsons as they neared the heart of Union Grove.

"No, we're gonna eat at one of them places near the interstate." After another two miles he pulled into the parking lot of a truck stop near Interstate 77 and switched off the motor of the truck.

"I'm gonna buy you a big breakfast, Short Stuff," the tall man bragged. "I got some money, might as well spend some of it."

"I just can't believe you got all that money."

"I told you not to ask so many questions, didn't I?"

"I wadn't askin', I just said I can't believe it. I'm glad you got it, I'm real hungry."

"Okay. Just don't bring it up again."

"I won't. Can I order bacon and eggs and grits, too?"

"Sure you can, little buddy. Order what you want, I'm buyin'."

CHAPTER 18

"HARD DAY, HONEY?" Jake asked as Marci wearily came through the door.

"It was indeed. It's been two weeks since the murder in Love Valley and we're still sorting through the information we have. Mr. Beckett lived in such a secluded place, no one saw anything."

"What do you know so far?"

"Well, it looks like he took a shot at the intruder, but missed and sent a slug into his bedroom wall."

"Maybe Mr. Beckett knew the person who attacked him."

"That's what we're thinking, too. He must have known the perp or he wouldn't have let him into his bedroom. And there was no sign of forcible entry into the trailer. We'll get him, it's just a matter of time," Marci said with determination.

"I know you will. You always do."

"Thanks for having faith in me. You're always the one to

cheer me on when I need it most. We made a good team once before tracking down those missing women, didn't we?" she said smiling.

"We sure did. Maybe I can help on this one, too, just as a sounding board." Jake paused before continuing. "You know, I could go back to Love Valley, just visiting mind you, and keep my ear to the ground. I might pick up on some things that law enforcement officers don't hear. Sometimes, the average person is reluctant to talk to the police because they're afraid to get involved."

"I know that, but this is a murder case and I think the killer is someone who knew Mr. Beckett, possibly someone who lives up there. I don't want you to get hurt."

"Nobody would even know what I was doing. I could take Meredith with me. She really likes Beth and Charlie Nance and Wish, too. Wish would probably let her ride Applejack again. You know she'd like that. Who'd expect an old white-headed artist and a four-year old of being covert spies for the sheriff's department?"

"You really enjoy the challenge, don't you?"

"Well, maybe just a little," Jake said grinning.

"It's just too dangerous, Jake. Leave it to us, okay?" Changing the subject, Marci said, "Right now, I need a glass of wine and a little TLC."

"You came to the right place for both things, Detective!" Jake headed to the kitchen and soon returned with two glasses of Shelton Vineyards' Cabernet Sauvignon.

Jake turned on the gas logs in the den and they sat on the couch together and sipped their wine before the fire. Marci gradually relaxed and asked, "Where's Meredith?"

"Sleeping," Jake said, with a twinkle in his eye.

Marci kissed him and then eased up from the couch. "I'll check on her and meet you in the 'playroom.'"

Jake was waiting for Marci and had already turned the covers down on the bed. She quickly undressed and joined him in their king-sized bed. "Hold me for a while," she said, "I need some loving reassurance."

"They don't call me 'Dr. Jake, the-feel-good-man' for nothing," he said as he wrapped her in his arms and kissed her.

"Ohhhh," Marci sighed. "That's nice."

"Are you starting to feel a little more reassured yet?"

"Maybe just a little," Marci said. "Why don't you do that some more?"

"Like this?" he said and kissed her again.

"Just like that," Marci whispered, "now let's make love slowly."

"I just love the way you think," Jake said.

CHAPTER 19

"**I** FEEL SO MUCH BETTER," Marci said, stretching and yawning as the early morning sun streaked through the bedroom window.

"Good morning, darling," Jake said smiling at her from the doorway.

"I really slept well. Lord knows I needed that. What time is it?"

"A little past seven thirty," Jake said. "You were right, you needed that, so I just let you sleep."

"Seven thirty! Why didn't you wake me up, Jake McLeod?"

"Like I said, you needed to rest. I have breakfast ready for you, so get your robe on unless you want to go for another round. You know what seeing your bare breasts does to me," Jake said grinning.

Marci reached beside the bed and picked up a bedroom slipper and threw it at him. "Get outta here and let me get some clothes on."

"I'll be glad to help, but that'll just make you a little later," Jake said.

She threw the other shoe at him and laughed. "You're something else for an old man."

"I wasn't too old last night, was I?" Jake countered.

"No, you were just right. Now let me get dressed. Go check on Meredith."

"Yes, ma'am," Jake said and closed the door.

CHAPTER 20

"WANNA GO BACK to Love Valley?" Jake asked Meredith later that morning.

"Sure," she responded with eagerness. "Can we go today?"

"I'll bet that old Applejack's been wondering where you've been," Jake said.

Meredith was so excited at the prospect of returning to Love Valley she could barely eat her breakfast. "I bet Applejack has really missed me," she said taking a big bite of Cheerios. "Let's go see him and Wish and Beth and Charlie and have a hot dog."

"Slow down, slow down," Jake told her. "Love Valley and your friends will still be there after you finish your breakfast."

Jake watched with amusement as Meredith tried unsuccessfully to get an overloaded spoonful of cereal into her mouth. Cheerios spilled onto the table and milk ran down her chin. "I'm going to introduce you to someone very special today," he said as he took her napkin and wiped her chin.

"Who, Daddy?"

"Mr. Andy Barker. He's the man who built the town over fifty years ago."

Marci caught part of the conversation between Jake and Meredith as she came into the kitchen. "What are you two so excited about?"

Meredith, dribbling Cheerios on her shirt, looked up at her mother. "We going back to Love Valley," she said with milk once again streaming down her dimpled chin.

"You are?" Marci said and took the napkin from Jake and wiped her daughter's face.

As soon as the cleaning job was done, Meredith eagerly plunged her spoon into her bowl, brought up another heaping spoonful of cereal, and shoved most of it into her mouth. "Uh-huh," she said through another mouthful of Cheerios. "Daddy said I was going to meet Mr. Barker."

"Well, I guess that'll be okay," Marci agreed.

"We'll be fine," Jake assured her.

"You will take care of Daddy today for me, won't you?"

"Of course, Mama, I always do."

"Well then, kiss me bye, honey, I gotta run," Marci said as she leaned down to her daughter.

Meredith planted a slobbery kiss on Marci's cheek and said, "I love you, Mama."

"And I love you, too," Marci said and wiped her own face with a napkin.

"You gonna kiss Daddy goodbye, too, ain't you Mama?"

"You bet I am," Marci said. "And please try not to say ain't, Meredith."

"Joanie says it all the time. What's wrong with ain't?"

Jake decided not to bring Joanie into the conversation and asked Marci, "Do you have to leave already?"

"Yes, somebody made me late and I really need to get going now. Kiss me goodbye so I can go."

Jake kissed her on the lips and then Marci said, "Follow me out to the cruiser."

"Sure, what's up?"

No sooner than they were out the door, Marci said, "I thought we agreed that you weren't going back to Love Valley asking a bunch of questions."

"Me, ask questions?" Jake said, looking hurt.

"Yes, you, Sherlock."

"Honestly, I was just taking Meredith back to meet Andy Barker and maybe see Beth and Charlie and Wish."

"Is that all?"

"Well and maybe ride Applejack while we're there."

"Okay, if that's all you do. You just let us handle this investigation, okay?"

"Yes, ma'am," Jake said faking shame.

"Kiss me again," Marci said, "I gotta run."

Jake opened the door of the cruiser and kissed her goodbye one more time. Marci climbed into the Charger, closed the door, and headed for a day filled with uncertainty.

CHAPTER 21

I N HER OFFICE at the Iredell County Sheriff's Department in Statesville, Marci studied the autopsy and forensic report, crime-scene photographs, and notes and interviews from the other detectives. She went over the facts again that she had personally gathered and written in the murder book.

- *Gunshot heard. Happened sometime late, Friday night, March 16.*
- *Two witnesses thought they heard a truck backfire.*
- *Victim, Walter "Bud" Beckett, found Saturday morning.*
- *Techs retrieved slug from bedroom wall of trailer.*
- *Slug was a .45 caliber.*
- *Beckett's pistol missing*
- *Appears that the victim knew the perp. He let him into his home. No signs of forcible entry.*
- *Blunt force trauma to the head from possibly a hard metal*

object. No wood fibers found in wound.
- *Why did Beckett let the perp into his bedroom?*
- *Most prints found at scene were Beckett's. A few smudged prints on front door were not good enough for identification.*
- *One partial on front door sent to AFIS.*
- *No one suspicious seen hanging around Beckett's trailer.*
- *Follow up on Dewayne Allison. Have not located him yet.*

"Oh my aching back," Marci groaned as she stretched her arms over her head. She removed the reading glasses that she had been using lately and rubbed her eyes with her knuckles. "Damn, I hate being over forty," she muttered.

Jamie Campbell walked into her office as Marci was rubbing her eyes and pointed to the murder book, "You find anything in there you haven't seen before?" he asked half-joking.

"Nothing I didn't already know. I just thought that something might jump out at me this time. We need a real break in this case."

"We can always hope," Campbell said.

CHAPTER 22

SPRING WAS DEFINITELY in the air as Jake and Meredith headed for Love Valley. *The groundhog may have seen his shadow,* Jake thought as he drove down Mountain View Road, *but winter's gone for good 'til November. Hallelujah.*

"Are we 'bout there, Daddy?"

"Just a couple more miles."

"I hope Beth's there and we can get a hot dog," Meredith said with anticipation.

"We're going to stop at the hardware store first to meet Mr. Barker, remember?"

"Is he a cowboy, too, like Wish and Charlie?"

"Yes, he's a real cowboy. You're gonna like him, I promise."

Jake turned onto Love Valley Road and pulled the Jeep to a stop in front of the hardware store.

"We're here!" Jake said.

"Are we goin' in that old buildin'?"

"We sure are," Jake said as he helped Meredith out of the Jeep and then up the rock steps that led into the store.

"Well, hello there. You folks come in and sit a spell," Andy Barker said, as Jake swung open the door. "And who is this pretty little lady?" Before they could answer, Barker teased, "Now let me guess. I'll betcha you're that little Miss Meredith McLeod from Mooresville."

Startled, Meredith looked up at Jake. "How'd he know my name, Daddy?"

"I know everybody," Mayor Barker bragged and patted Meredith on the head as he rose from his chair beside the woodstove and extended his hand to Jake.

Jake admired the firm grip of the tall, slim mayor. Dressed in his denim jeans, shirt, and jacket and his tan Resistol hat, Andy Barker was the perfect personification of a western cowboy. From his western belt all the way down to his worn boots, this man, Jake thought, was about as authentic as they came.

With a friendly smile and a twinkle in his merry blue eyes, he said, "It's mighty good to see you again Mr. McLeod. You've done well since I last saw you. It's been years."

"Thanks, Mr. Mayor. I've been pretty busy since I opened the gallery," Jake said with modesty.

"Just call me Andy, everybody does. What brings you folks back to Love Valley? I heard you were here the other day."

"Meredith likes the horses very much and she wants to see her new friends, Beth and Charlie Nance, again and Wish Phillips, too."

"She's a smart girl. They're good people. Come here and sit beside me," he said to Meredith.

Meredith wasn't quite sure yet about this man her father brought her to meet. She quickly gazed up at Jake and then climbed up onto the chair beside Love Valley's affable mayor.

"You know, if I had a little girl like you, I'd be the proudest daddy in all of Iredell County," the elder Barker said to her.

"Daddy's proud of me, too, ain't you Daddy?"

"Yes, I am," Jake agreed. "Remember though, we aren't supposed to say ain't, Meredith."

"I'm sorry, but what am I 'posed to say?"

"She's got all the time in the world to learn her schoolin'," Barker said. "Sit down for a spell, Jake. I've been wantin' to talk to you for a long time."

"Talk to me?" Jake asked. "About what?"

"About paintin' my town."

"Wish said something about that, too, but I thought he was kidding."

"I'm not kiddin'. I'm gettin' up in years," the mayor said as he pushed his battered hat back on his head and looked Jake in the eye. "I really would like for you to paint a scene or two from around here. That'd tickle Ellenora to death."

No sooner than the words were out of his mouth, the door swung open and in walked a spry woman who appeared to be about the same age as the mayor. She smiled broadly when she saw Meredith with Andy.

"Well, look here," the woman said. "You got another new girlfriend, Andy?"

"Ellenora, I'd like you to meet two of my special guests from Mooresville, Miss Meredith McLeod and her daddy, Jake.

"It's certainly nice meeting you," Jake said as he politely rose from his chair to greet her.

"Meredith just brought her daddy along to keep her company," the mayor said with a grin.

"That's not right," Meredith exclaimed, "Daddy brought me."

"Is that the way it was?" he teased.

"Yes. My daddy brought me here to see Beth and Charlie

and Wish and to eat hot dogs with ketchup."

Barker leaned down to Meredith and said, "I have a gift for you."

"You do?"

Barker took Meredith's hand in his and placed a silver dollar in it.

Meredith's eyes grew wide when she saw the coin. "Look Daddy, a big quarter."

Mayor Barker laughed when Meredith stood up, hugged him, and said, "Thank you for the quarter."

They were all still laughing when Jake said, "Thank you for your kindness, Andy. It certainly has been nice meeting you, Miss Ellenora."

"Don't be in a big rush," she replied.

"Oh, we're not," Jake explained, "but we'd better go find Beth and Charlie."

"Don't forget Wish!" Meredith chided him.

"Oh, and Wish, too."

They opened the door to leave when Mayor Barker called out, "Don't you forget about the paintings now."

"I won't," Jake promised as Meredith ran back and reached up to give Mrs. Barker a big hug.

"Please come back and see us again soon," Ellenora said.

"We will, won't we, Daddy?"

"We sure will."

Jake helped Meredith down the stone steps, buckled her into her car seat, and drove to the small parking between the blacksmith shop and Tori Pass.

Meredith gripped Jake's hand as they walked toward the main street. The mayor and his wife lived in the first building on the left. A pear tree, in full bloom, stood at the entrance to the Barker's home and honey were bees darting from blossom to blossom.

"Look, Daddy! Bumble bees!"

"No, sweetheart, those are honey bees."

"Honey bees?"

"Yes, they make honey from the pear blossoms."

Meredith scrunched her eyes in confusion, but let it drop when she saw Wish riding toward them on Applejack.

"Hey, Wish!" Meredith squealed when she saw him.

"Hey there, yourself, little girl, did you come up for another hot dog?"

"I did and to ride Applejack!"

"Well we'll just have to see what we can do about that, won't we?" Wish reached down and in one swift motion, swung the happy little girl up onto his saddle.

"Okay if I ride her up the street and back a couple times?" he asked Jake.

"Sure, that's fine. Want a hot dog when you get back?"

"You betcha," Wish said. "But this time, I'm buyin'."

CHAPTER 23

Wish trotted Applejack up and down the dusty street a few times before he stopped in front of the Silver Spur. "I hope I didn't ride her too long. She was really havin' a great time."

"I was watching. She was having a ball," Jake said.

"You're gonna end up havin' to buy her a horse. She's takin' to it mighty quick," Wish said with a grin.

"You're probably right," Jake agreed. "I just don't know what her mother would say about that."

Wish laughed and handed Meredith to Jake.

"Thank you so much for letting her ride with you. I really appreciate it," Jake said.

"No problem. I enjoy it," Wish said, "she's a lot of fun. Now, how about them hot dogs?"

Jake and Meredith followed Wish into the Silver Spur and there were Charlie and Beth Nance sitting at the same table as before. Charlie raised his hand in greeting and motioned for

Jake to join them.

"How you doin', Princess?" Beth asked Meredith.

"I'm doin' good. I just rode Applejack."

"That's great," Beth said and tickled Meredith under her chin. "Are you gonna sit with me again?" Without asking her father, Meredith climbed up onto the chair beside Beth.

Their conversation included everything from the murder of Bud Beckett to riding horses, but they were constantly being distracted by two cowboys talking loudly on the deck at the rear of the restaurant. The cowboys' language was not only loud, but sometimes vulgar.

Beth kept reaching over and placing a calming hand on Charlie's leg. She knew it wouldn't be long before he confronted the inconsiderate men. Nance admitted that he sometimes had a short fuse and an intolerance of people with no manners.

After listening to the harsh language as long as he could stand it, Wish finally said, "Y'all excuse me for a minute, I'll be right back."

"I'll go with you," Charlie said.

"Charlie, let Wish handle this please," Beth said. "He's very capable."

The soft-spoken cowboy opened the door to the deck and approached the two ill-mannered men. He immediately recognized one of the men sporting a scruffy beard as Dewayne Allison. It appeared that he and his diminutive friend, Shorty Parsons, had been drinking for a while by the amount of beer cans strewn about the deck.

"What do you want?" asked Allison.

Wish stared the man straight in the eye. "Could y'all please hold it down a bit? There're some women and a little girl inside and it's upsettin' to hear such foul language in their presence."

"Well, lah-te-dah," Allison mocked.

"I wish you wouldn't have done that," Wish said.

"Why's that, Bub?"

"I didn't want those nice people in there to see me kick your ass and throw you off the deck."

"What?" Allison asked not believing he had heard Wish correctly.

"Either you shut your filthy mouth or walk down those steps and out of sight so we can finish this conversation behind the saloon."

"You're serious, ain't you?" said the hardcase cowboy.

"I sure am!" Wish said boldly. "Well. What's it gonna be?"

"There ain't no need to get uppity about it," the crude man said. "You just go back in there and eat with them women."

"That's what I'm plannin' on doin' if you can keep the noise down." Having said that, Wish turned his back to the two rowdies, closed the door quietly behind him, and returned to his seat beside Jake.

"What was that all about?" Jake asked.

"Did you not hear the language those eggheads were using out there? There ain't no sense in talkin' so loud and usin' language like that where there's womenfolk and children present."

The more Jake learned about Wish Phillips, the more he admired the man. "Who are those guys?" Jake asked.

"That big one with the beard is Dewayne Allison. He's the same no-good your wife arrested years ago. The other one is a poor, dumb cowboy that had his head kicked in by a mule a few years back. He just follows Dewayne around because Dewayne'll buy 'im beer and food sometimes. His name's Fred Parsons, but everybody up here just calls him Shorty."

"This Allison fellow's name seems to keep popping up everywhere I go," Jake said, a little concerned.

"Oh, don't worry about them two," Charlie said, not to alarm Jake, "if they keep up with their loud talkin', I'll go out there myself."

"Now, Charlie," Beth said, "I don't hear them right now, so why don't we go ahead and order our hot dogs. You want a hot dog, Meredith?"

"Sure, with lots of ketchup."

CHAPTER 24

"DID YOU SEE THE WAY that ol' Wish Phillips acted?" Dewayne asked Shorty. "That son of a bitch thinks he's better than we are just because he don't drink or cuss."

"I always thought he was a pretty good guy," the small man said.

"Damn, Shorty, don't you know nothin'?"

Shorty didn't have an answer for that outburst. He just wanted to get out of there before any trouble started. "Why don't we go ridin'? We ain't been on our horses in a couple of weeks. We can catch the Ridge Trail and ride all the way over to Fox Mountain."

"I don't wanna go up there. That's where ol' Bud was murdered."

"What's that got to do with us?" Shorty asked. "We might even see some real detectives up there still poking around his property, lookin' for clues and stuff like that. You know, like they do on TV."

"I done told you, I ain't ridin' up there. C'mon, let's just take a ride in the truck and go down to Statesville a little bit."

"What for?"

"Just to see the sights or go to Walmart or somethin'."

"Sometimes, Dewayne, I just don't understand you at all," Shorty said in exasperation.

The two cowboys bounded down the stairs that led off the deck of the Silver Spur, crawled into Dewayne's old pickup truck that was parked at the bottom of the hill, and struck out for the county seat.

"They must have left the back way," Wish noticed. "It sure is quieter with them gone, that's for sure."

"It's definitely a lot better now," Beth said. "Let's just enjoy our meal. Here it comes now," she said, watching the waitress coming from the kitchen.

"Are y'all ready for some good old hot dogs?" Jennie asked as she sat down a big oval tray filled to the brim with plates of hot dogs and French fries.

"I am," Meredith chimed, "but we gotta say the blessin' first, right, Beth?"

"That's right," Beth said as she took Meredith's hand in hers. Everyone around the table joined hands, too, as Beth led them in prayer.

"Can I say the blessin' next time?" Meredith asked.

"Sure you can. Don't forget everybody. Next time Meredith is going to say the blessin'."

"That'll be great," Charlie said, "now let's eat. I'm hungrier than a woodpecker with a headache."

Meredith said, "You're funny, Charlie."

Everyone laughed at the two of them but soon the conversation around the table died down as they dived into their food.

CHAPTER 25

THE PHONE ON HER DESK was ringing when Gail Caldwell returned from lunch. She said, "Hello," and her Midwestern accent was still recognizable even after the many years she had lived in North Carolina.

"Hey, Gail, it's me, Joanie."

"Hi, Joanie, you are coming tonight aren't you?"

"It's Wednesday night, ain't it? I'll be there with bells on."

"Oh, I thought that you may be calling to say you couldn't come."

"Heck no, nothin' like that. Listen, Gail, I have a great idea. I've been shop sittin' at the gallery for Jake a couple of times lately so he and Meredith could spend some time together. Do you know where he's been takin' her?"

"I have no idea," Gail said.

"To Love Valley, that's where!"

Having no clue where the conversation was going, Gail

asked, "Are you making this up, Joanie?"

"I knew it. You ain't been there before; have you?" Before Gail could answer, Joanie charged ahead. "Well, I think it's time for us Wednesday Night girls to have another adventure and I think Love Valley would be the perfect place."

"I don't know, Joanie," Gail said. "Isn't that where Marci is investigating a murder?"

"Yeah, she is. She could show us all around."

"But, Joanie…"

"Don't be like that. It'll be a blast and I need you to help me convince the others tonight."

"But, Joanie, I can't…"

"See you at six-thirty," Joanie said and ended the call.

Gail Caldwell just stood there for a moment staring at the phone.

CHAPTER 26

THE WEDNESDAY NIGHT CLUB met that evening at the Crimson Cape on North Main Street in Mooresville and everyone was there: Joanie Mitchell; Gail Caldwell; Debbie Seacrest Wells, and Marci Meredith McLeod.

As soon as the waitress brought their salads, Joanie could stand it no longer. She took her fork and rapped the side of her glass a few times to get their attention. "Girls, girls!" she said. "Listen up! I've got a great idea for a day of fun?"

"Oh, no," chorused the group. "Not again."

"What do y'all mean, not again? Have I ever steered you wrong?"

They all laughed. "Okay, Joanie, what do you have in mind this time?" asked Debbie.

"A trip to Love Valley."

"Love Valley?" Debbie said, "You must be kidding. There can't be a real town called Love Valley in North Carolina."

"Well, according to little Miss Meredith McLeod, there is."

Marci broke in, "Joanie, you know that's where I'm investigating a murder?"

"Yeah, I know that and I also know that's where Jake has been taking Meredith. That's all that youngun talks about when she comes back. She tells me about the mayor and his wife and somebody named Charlie and Beth and Wish. That girl don't forget a thing. She even rides a horse named Applejack."

"But, Joanie…," Marci started.

'Now, dammit, Marci, this'll be fun. We ain't gonna bother your investigation. We're just gonna ride some horses, that's all."

Marci had to admit she didn't have an objection to just riding horses. "Well if you promise to have an experienced guide take you along the trails and not go off on your own," Marci warned.

"We promise, don't we, girls?"

"Joanie, are you sure you want to do this?" Debbie asked timidly. "I've hardly seen a horse before, much less ridden one."

"What's wrong with you girls? Even Gail agrees with me. We talked about it earlier today, ain't that right, Gail?" Before Gail could respond, Joanie quipped, "Aw hell, it'll be a blast."

They all looked at each other…each one, for a brief moment remembering another Wednesday Night Club outing when the three of them, Debbie, Joanie, and Gail, had spent several terrifying days and nights lost in the woods of Wilkes County. After the death of their friend and captor, Carmen Romano, and her failed ransom attempt, they had been rescued with much of the credit going to Detective Marci Meredith, now Marci McLeod.

"Come on girls, let's don't dwell on what happened five years ago," Gail said, breaking the silence.

"You know, it might be fun," Debbie said, warming up to the idea.

"You know it will," Joanie said. "Y'all meet me in the First

Baptist Church parking lot in downtown at 8:30 Saturday morning...I'll drive."

It was a lost cause trying to talk Joanie Mitchell out of anything so Marci finally gave in. "I'll tell you what girls, I'll meet you in Love Valley and introduce you to Jake and Meredith's friends. Jake and Meredith can handle the gallery."

"All right!" Joanie said, "Now you're talking!"

Marci knew the girls would have fun in Love Valley, but she could not help being concerned for their safety and the safety of the town's residents until the murderer was caught.

CHAPTER 27

Aᴼᴼᴼᴼ**FTER ANOTHER NIGHT** of drinking, Dewayne Allison dropped Shorty off at his driveway and grunted, "See ya later, I'm gonna catch up on some sleep." It was late, but sleep was not what Dewayne had on his mind. He had been troubled all evening and wanted to be alone and think. Even though Allison had told Shorty that he did not want to go near Beckett's place, something was compelling him to make that drive up Mitchell Trail. Fifty yards from the Beckett driveway, he spotted an Iredell County Sheriff's cruiser parked at the driveway's entrance.

He hurriedly pulled into the nearest driveway, turned around, and eased back down the gravel road toward Love Valley.

Since he'd been drinking, Dewayne drove the truck slowly as he headed down the mountain. He often glanced in his mirror and hoped he would not see a flashing, blue light following him. That was the last thing Dewayne needed—a DWI.

Allison rounded the last curve coming down the hill and

for some unexplained reason, pulled into the driveway of the Love Valley Presbyterian Church. He turned his truck around and parked behind the building so he could see if the deputy had followed him.

Dewayne had never been a religious person and had not been in a church since he was a child, but strangely found himself praying and asking for God's help. It didn't make sense…what was happening to him? Dewayne's heart was pounding in his chest. The events of the last few weeks were weighing heavily on his mind.

Still sitting in the cab of his truck; he thought once more of Bud Beckett. *Why'd Bud have to die? He was a crotchety old man, but he never bothered anybody. What if that Detective McLeod interviews me? She might even suspect me of the murder since I threatened her when she arrested me.*

Childhood memories came flooding back as he sat there behind the church. He could barely remember his father who had left his mother and him when he was only five years old. His mother's inability to show her love to him had hurt Dewayne very deeply. He remembered her now and how she shared herself with all those men. He could not understand why she couldn't love him. *If only she'd told me one time that she loved me,* he thought. He remembered not shedding a tear when she was buried behind the little Baptist church in Alexander County.

The emotionally scarred man had spent most of his adult life drinking and lashing out at everyone with whom he came in contact. His drinking had become even heavier since his bitter divorce. For the first time, he realized how lonely he really was. If it were not for Shorty Parsons, he'd have no friends at all. Since coming to Love Valley all he'd done was make enemies. Most folks steered away from him. Even Mayor Barker, Charlie Nance and Wish Phillips had tried to be friends with him, but Dewayne kept them at a distance.

Dewayne opened his eyes and realized where he was. Convinced now that the deputy had not followed him, he turned the ignition off, rolled down his window, and listened to the sounds of the night. From down the hill near the arena, he heard one of Charlie Nance's horses snort. An owl in the distance hooted two times and flew to a tree nearby. He could even hear the sound of voices wafting through the late evening breeze as couples were drifting back to their homes after an evening at the Silver Spur. Dewayne Allison had forgotten what it was like to just listen to the sounds of a peaceful evening.

Dewayne climbed out of his truck, quietly closed the door, and walked around to the front of the church in the crisp night air. Inexplicably, he found himself gazing up at the cross that was mounted to the top of the steeple. Security lights from down the road illuminated the cross against the black night. He could look at nothing else. He stood there in the dark, almost in a trance, gazing upward at the cross until his neck hurt. He remembered what his grandmother had told him the cross represented. Dewayne Allison was shaken to the core as he recalled many of the things he had done in the past. He'd never been ashamed of them before, but tonight, he felt shame for the first time in his life. Clearly moved by the occurrence, he quickly got back into his truck and headed toward his trailer.

Dewayne was shaking by the time he arrived home, but sat in his truck thinking about what had just happened to him. After sitting alone in his truck for over two hours, praying and thinking, another realization finally came to Dewayne Allison. *I'm an alcoholic.*

For the first time in his adult life, Dewayne Allison cried.

CHAPTER 28

"OKAY, GIRLS, here we are," Joanie said. "Ain't this place somethin'?"

"It looks like we just stepped back in time!" Debbie said. "I've never seen anything like this in my life."

"I told you it was a western town. See, there ain't any cars on the main street, just horses. How neat is that?"

"Well, it surely is different. I'll have to say that," Gail observed, as they walked up the dusty street.

"Marci, this is your day off, so act like it," Joanie ordered. "Just have a little fun. You can't work all the time."

"I'll try, but I'm keeping my eyes and ears open. I desperately need a break in this case."

Andy Barker stepped out onto his porch just as the four women approached the Love Valley sign that spanned the entrance to the town's main street. Never missing an opportunity to speak to pretty women, he called out, "Howdy, ladies.

Welcome to my town."

Marci spoke first, "Good morning, Mayor, how are you today?"

"Well, well. How are you Detective McLeod? Any leads yet on the case?"

"We're working on it, but this is my day off and I thought I'd bring my friends up here to do a little riding. And maybe do a little detecting, too, while I'm at it," Marci added.

When Marci introduced the mayor to Gail, Debbie, and Joanie, he gave them each a welcoming hug and a kiss on the cheek. "I sure hope y'all enjoy the day and come back as often as you can."

"Boy, he's a friendly sort, ain't he?" laughed Joanie as they walked up the street.

"He is for sure," Marci said.

It didn't take long for them to walk to the end of the street and back. When they arrived in front of the mayor's house, he was just getting into his truck.

"Well, that didn't take long," Barker said grinning at them.

Joanie spoke first as usual. "Do you have a place around here where we can rent a horse?"

The mayor laughed. "We sure do." He directed them to Love Valley Stables. "Tell Pete I sent you. He'll treat you right." He then bade them goodbye with a twinkle in his eye. "Y'all enjoy yourselves now, y' hear."

"I really like him," Gail said. "He is so down to earth."

About that time, a lone man came walking from behind one of the buildings, saw them and stopped. "Look at that cowboy," Debbie said. "This really is a western town."

The man sported a straggly beard and wore a cowboy hat and jeans as did most men at Love Valley. He quickly pulled is hat down further to hide his face even more and then resumed his unsteady pace toward them. The cowboy never looked up.

He concentrated on walking and chose not to speak as he made his way down the main street and past the women.

They watched the cowboy amble down the street until Joanie broke in. "Come on, girls. Are we just gonna stand here gawkin' at some cowboy or we gonna ride a horse?"

I wonder who that man is, Marci thought. *He looks awfully familiar.*

CHAPTER 29

D EWAYNE ALLISON SAT on the edge of his bed using his
fingertips to gently rub his temples. He felt different this morning, but he wasn't sure why. His lifelong feelings of anger and
resentment seemed to have melted away during the night. He'd
slept well and woke up thinking, *this is the first day of the rest of my
life and I want to make the most of it.*

He rose from his bed, walked to the small window in his
tiny bedroom, and looked out upon a sun-filled morning.

Who is that? Dewayne thought when he saw a strange man
walking down the street outside his window. A chill ran through
him as he stared in disbelief. *That man looks like me!*

Dewayne quickly slipped into his dirty jeans, pulled on his
boots, and hurried out the door in search of his look-a-like. He
looked up and down the street, but only saw a cowboy saddling
his horse for a morning ride. *Nobody can get gone that quick. Where'd
he go!*

Dewayne ran around to the back of his tiny trailer and found nothing but a pile of beer cans that had spilled from an overflowing trash can. Confused, he walked back to the front of his mobile home and looked up and down the street one more time, scratched his head, and went back inside.

Twenty minutes later, showered and dressed in clean clothes, Dewayne walked up to the main street and down to the hardware store.

"Good morning, Andy," Dewayne said to the mayor as he walked in and grabbed a chair by the stove. "How's it goin'?"

"I'm doin' fine, but how are you doin, Dewayne? You look like you're walkin' pretty straight this mornin'."

"Andy," he began, "I'm quittin' my drinkin'."

Speechless, the mayor just looked at Dewayne and waited for him to continue.

"You know, Andy, I'm forty years old and ain't got a dang thing to show for all my years of bein' here but a pile of beer cans behind my trailer. To tell you the truth, I'm ashamed of the mess I made outta my life and the way I treated people all these years, 'specially Shorty. He's a good old boy and I've been pretty mean to him a lot of times."

Allison had Andy's attention now. "What in the world brought this change about?"

"Well, it's the strangest thing. I drove up toward Bud's trailer last night just to see what was going on, but when I saw a sheriff's car parked at his driveway I got scared. I'd been drinkin' a little bit and I didn't want to get a DWI.

"So what happened?"

"Well, I turned my truck around and drove back down the hill and did something strange. I don't even know what made me do it."

"You're talkin' in riddles, Dewayne. What'd you do?"

"You ain't gonna believe this Andy, but I pulled into the

church driveway and sat in my truck for a while, waitin' to see if the deputy was following me."

Andy was getting a little impatient waiting for Dewayne to go on. "That was all you did, just sit in your truck?"

"That was what was so strange, Andy. I don't know what made me do it, but I got out of the truck and walked around to the front of the church and somethin' made me look up at the cross. You know the one on top of the steeple."

"Yeah, I know. Go on."

"Well, I got the chills and I hightailed it outta there. When I got home, I just sat in the truck for the longest time and did a little prayin', like my granny taught me."

"That's not so strange, Dewayne, sounds like to me you just might have met the Lord and didn't know it."

"Met the Lord? What're you talkin' about?"

"Let me ask you something, Dewayne. Do you feel different?"

"I sure do. I reckon that's why I'm givin' up drinkin'. I don't even feel like I want a drink right now. And I don't ever remember not wantin' a beer."

"Well, Dewayne, all I can say is, congratulations. I'm sure proud of you. Now, if you can just get Shorty to do the same thing, Love Valley will be a much better place for everybody."

"What'll I do now, Andy? I know I made a lot of people mad at me over the years and I know they have a right to be mad. But I want to make things right."

"The Good Lord really must have spoken to you last night, Dewayne, for you to make this kind of change."

"You know, I guess maybe he did. I know I ain't never felt like this before."

"This is the answer to a lot of prayers, Dewayne. There's been a heap of folks prayin' for your hide and Shorty's, too, for a long time. I guess the Good Lord still saw some good in you and figured you were worth savin' after all."

"You know," Dewayne said, "maybe I'll go and apologize to some of the people I wronged. That'll be a good start, won't it?" he asked the surprised mayor.

"That sure would be a great start, Dewayne. Find yourself a full-time job and stay on the straight and narrow path they talk about in the Bible. You'll do fine."

"I'll try my best, Mayor, I really will and thanks for listenin' to me. You just don't know how much better I feel!"

"Yes I do. I know exactly how you feel," Barker said.

"By the way, have you seen a fellow around town that looks like me?" Dewayne asked.

Barker wrinkled his brow and pushed his weathered, sweat-stained hat back on his head as he pondered the question. "Now that you mentioned it, I have seen somebody that looks a lot like you. I just saw him yesterday. I do remember sayin' to myself at the time: 'Lord knows we don't need another Dewayne Allison around here.'"

They both laughed and the cowboy replied, "That's the danged truth, if I ever heard it!"

They talked a little more before Dewayne said, "Well, Andy; thanks again for listenin'. I guess I'd better get out there and get started on the new Dewayne Allison."

The mayor grinned. "You do that now. If you feel like you want another beer, come and see me first and we can talk."

Dewayne extended his hand and Andy shook it heartily.

With that, the new Dewayne Allison walked through the door of Andy's Hardware Store, down the stone steps, and out into the beautiful sunshine.

CHAPTER 30

THE COWBOY WALKED into the Moonshine Gift Shop and looked around briefly, but didn't seem interested in the merchandise. "May I help you find something?" shop owner, Tori Callanan, asked him.

He turned and stared at the young lady for a moment with piercing, black eyes and then without saying a word, quietly stepped out onto the boardwalk.

Tori dropped what she was doing and walked over to the door to get a better look at him, but he was nowhere to be seen. She looked up and down the dusty street. He was just gone.

Now that's strange, she thought as she stepped back inside her shop and continued stocking new merchandise on the shelf.

A noise outside the door caught her attention and she looked up to see Beth Nance entering her shop. "How's it going?" Beth asked.

"Hi, Beth, I guess everything is going pretty well, but the

strangest thing just happened."

"What's that?" Beth asked; her interest aroused.

"Did you see the guy who just left the store right before you came in?"

"No. Why?"

"Well, this tall man with a beard man came into the store and looked around for a little bit, didn't say a word mind you, and when I asked if I could help him, he just up and left."

"Have you ever seen him before?"

"No, I haven't, but you know what was so strange about the whole thing? At first I thought it was Dewayne Allison, but there was something different about this guy."

"Are you sure it wasn't Dewayne?"

"It couldn't have been. He had a beard like Dewayne's, but his eyes—they were dark and seemed to look right through me." Tori paused and said, "To tell you the truth, it was very unsettling."

"I can imagine," Beth agreed.

CHAPTER 31

THE WOMEN OF the Wednesday Night Club walked down to Love Valley Stables and found Pete saddling a beautiful roan.

"Howdy, ladies," he said touching the brim of his hat as they came through the door. The stable smelled of fresh hay, horse manure, and leather. Several stalls were filled with horses munching on hay. The roan stood patiently, switching his tail while Pete tightened the cinch.

When he had finished, the elderly cowboy turned and said, "Andy said to expect some pretty ladies coming by soon, so I went ahead and started saddling up some horses for you."

"That's great," Gail said and introduced the women to Pete. "We'll need some instructions before we can ride."

"These horses are so gentle and used to tenderfoots ridin' them, they won't give you a bit of problem. You want 'em to go, just squeeze 'em with your legs a little bit and they'll take right off. You want 'em to stop, just pull back on the reins and say whoa. Pull the reins in the direction you want them to turn. They're pretty smart animals and they'll do fine for you."

"Hell, is that all there is to it?" Joanie asked.

"Yep, that's about it. Let me get the last one saddled up and you'll be ready to go."

Debbie glanced over at Gail and smiled. "This is going to be fun, right?"

"Sure," Gail said, "it'll be fun."

They each led their horses outside and Pete instructed them on how to mount safely. Sitting astride the animals, each woman wore a wide smile as they nudged them forward and up the street of Love Valley.

"Hot dang!" Joanie shouted back to the rest of the ladies. She had already gone ahead and was enjoying every minute. "Is this fun or what?"

Gail agreed and kneed her horse to catch up with Joanie just as a cowboy headed toward them. Gail whispered to Joanie, "Isn't that the same man that passed us earlier and didn't say a word?"

"He looks like the same guy," Joanie said, "but I think that the man we saw earlier had on a different shirt. Besides that, this one smiled at me!"

"You think every man smiles at you, Joanie," Debbie said laughing.

Joanie studied the big man a little more as he headed down Tori Pass and shrugged, "Maybe they're twins!"

"Could be," said Gail.

Marci and Debbie caught up with Joanie and Gail and rode four abreast for a while. Debbie said, "Let's turn these horses around if we can and go down that little street beside the parking area."

They all agreed and with little difficulty got their mounts turned around and headed down Tori Pass.

Joanie was heard saying, "I finally got the hang of steerin' one of these things and now I can't find the damn brakes."

Marci laughed at Joanie's frustration and trotted her mount alongside Gail. "What were you and Joanie talking about a while ago?"

"Oh, you know Joanie. She's already noticed a couple of cowboys that looked alike. She thought that was funny."

"What was so funny about it?"

"They both had beards and were wearing a cowboy hat and jeans. They were also about the same size. Joanie thought they might be twins."

"That Joanie," Marci said. "She's always looking at men. Why don't the three of you enjoy your ride? I saw the mayor get into his truck and head toward his hardware store. I think I'll go pay him another visit."

"Okay. See you in a bit," Gail said as she rode off to join the other women.

Marci turned her horse around and urged it back up the incline, turned and headed to the mayor's store.

When Marci rode past the blacksmith shop, she waved to the men standing near the door and the cowboys touched the brims of their hats in acknowledgement. *I really like this place,* she thought. *It's a shame that one individual can disrupt the lives of these nice folks.*

When Marci arrived at the hardware store, she tied the pinto she was riding to the hitching rail, climbed the steps and opened the heavy door.

"Hi again, Mr. Mayor," Marci said as she entered the store and neared the woodstove. "I thought I saw you heading this way and figured you'd be coming to the store."

"Well, well, it's good to see you again, Detective; are you havin' fun?"

"Just getting started," Marci responded.

"That's quite a nice group of friends you have with you," Barker said.

"Yes they are," Marci said. "The four of us usually meet together on Wednesday nights for dinner and have a good time."

"Wednesday nights, you say. But this is Saturday," Barker reminded her.

"Oh, this is just a special outing. It was Joanie's idea and a very good one, I'd say."

"I thought at first this might be a social call, but it 'pears to me you got somethin' on your mind, Detective. Can I help you?"

"Well, maybe so," Marci said.

The mayor pointed to a chair, "Why don't you sit a spell?"

After taking her seat, Marci said, "You told me that you tried to make it your business to keep up with everything going on in your town."

"I try my best," Barker said. He nodded, pushed is hat back on his head, and waited for her to continue.

"Tell me about Dewayne Allison," she said.

The mayor arched his brow. "Why the interest in Dewayne?"

"His name has come up several times in our interviews with local residents, but we haven't been able to interview him yet. The deputies can never catch him at home."

"Yeah, he's a hard one to catch sometimes. He stays up at Shorty Parsons' a good bit. I've know Dewayne for years." Barker continued, "He has the reputation of being drunk most of the time. And he can get pretty rowdy and loud sometimes, but all-in-all he's never been in any serious trouble that I know of."

"Do you think he's capable of committing murder?" Marci asked.

"Dewayne? No, I don't think so. He's always been an ornery cuss, but when he came to see me this morning he seemed like a different person."

"Allison was here?" Marci asked incredulously.

"Yes he was," Barker said. "Dewayne told me he's quit drinkin' and he's gonna make it up to the folks of Love Valley for the way he's been behavin' all these years. He said he's ashamed of some of the things he's done and that he was gonna be a different person from now on."

"Do you think he was sincere?"

"Yes, I really believe he was."

"I wonder what brought all that about?" asked Marci.

"He told me, but I think it'd be better if you ask him, Detective."

"I'll do just that," Marci said. "How long has he been gone?"

"Oh, I'd say he left about an hour ago. He lives in a little trailer down the hill from the parking lot. You can't miss it. It has a big pile of beer cans behind it."

"Yeah, I know," Marci said. I tried to catch him there earlier, but he wasn't home. Can you describe him to me?"

"Well, Dewayne's tall like me, well over six feet. There aren't that many men in Love Valley as tall as Dewayne and me. He's usually wearin' a cowboy hat, jeans, and boots like most of the cowboys in town. One thing that sets him apart from everybody else is that straggly beard he has. You know, I just remembered something else Dewayne said this morning."

"What's that?"

"He said he saw someone in town that looked just like him. That's hard to believe...one Dewayne Allison is enough for any town. That's what I told him," Barker said. "We both got a good laugh out of it, but Dewayne seemed really bothered by this lookalike."

"Now isn't that something?" Marci said.

"What's that?" the mayor asked.

"Well, the girls were just saying they saw somebody that fits that description. In fact, Joanie said there were two cowboys who looked like that. She even thought they might be twins."

"There are no twins in Love Valley," the mayor said, "or I

would know about it."

"Hmmm," Marci said. "That's interesting. Will you let me know if you hear anything else about this person who looks like Dewayne?"

"I sure will," the mayor promised. "You goin' to talk to Dewayne?"

"I'm headed that way now. Thanks for the information, Mayor," Marci said.

"Come back anytime. You're always welcome. Talk to ol' Dewayne. He might wanna unload some of his past sins."

"I will and thanks again," Marci said as she was leaving.

She stepped down to the street, untied her horse, swung onto the saddle, and sat there for a few minutes thinking about the conversation she'd just had with the mayor. *Dewayne Allison. Why does that name sound so familiar to me?* Marci sat in the saddle staring back toward town for a few minutes more and eventually turned her horse and went in search of her friends.

"There you are!" yelled Joanie. "Can't you quit workin' a little bit?"

"I'm sorry, girls, but there's one more thing I need to do first. I have to pay a little visit to someone if I can catch him home. It won't take long, he just lives right down that hill there," Marci said, pointing toward a small trailer at the bottom of the hill.

"We just saw a man there a few minutes ago," Debbie said.

Joanie butted in, "It's one of them cowboys we saw this morning."

"You sure?" Marci asked.

"Sure, I'm sure. He's the one that smiled at me earlier. Right now, he's in his backyard pickin' up beer cans and puttin' 'em in a sack; you can't miss him."

"Do all men smile at you, Joanie?"

"Well, I would hope so," she replied, a twinkle in her eye.

"Why don't you girls ride around for a while, I'm gonna pay this fellow a little visit while I'm here."

CHAPTER 32

MARCI HEARD THE RATTLING of cans long before she
made it down the hill. A bearded man behind a small trailer was
stuffing beer cans into a sack, just like Joanie had said.

He straightened up and rubbed his back as Marci reined
in her horse. "Hello, Mr. Allison?"

"Yep, that's me alright. Can I help you?"

"I'm Detective Marci McLeod with the Iredell County Sheriff's Department. I'd like to ask you a few questions, if you have
time?"

"Sure," Dewayne said. He removed his hat, took his handkerchief out of his back pocket, and wiped the sweat from his
hatband. "I figured you'd get around to me sooner or later."

"Why's that, Mr. Allison?"

"You don't remember me, do you?"

"I'm afraid not. Refresh my memory for me."

"Why don't you get down off your horse and let's sit on the

steps. I need to take a break anyway."

Marci dismounted, tied the reins to a small bush, and joined Dewayne at the front of his trailer. "Can I get you something to drink?" he asked as they sat down.

"I'm fine," she said, "but thank you." Marci studied his face with interest. She finally said, "You look so familiar, Mr. Allison."

"That's what I was getting ready to tell you, ma'am. I got a confession to make."

The word confession got Marci's heart thumping. "Would you like an attorney present, Mr. Allison, before you say anything else?"

"Oh! No, ma'am, it's nothin' like that! I ain't done nothin' wrong this time. It's just about you knowin' me."

The man definitely had Marci's attention. "Go on," she coaxed.

"Well, the whole thing happened about seven years ago. I was drunk and took off on somebody else's horse without askin' and one thing led to another."

"That's it! I do remember you now!" Marci said. "You got real sassy with me and I had to arrest you! Whatever happened to that case?"

Chagrined, Allison admitted, "Well, the charges were dropped. The horse belonged to a drinkin' buddy of mine and he knew I did crazy things when I was drunk."

"Well, I certainly remember you giving me a hard time," Marci said with a half-grin, not really sure why he was telling her this.

"That's right, ma'am, I did. And I'm sure sorry for the way I acted," Allison said. He continued before Marci could say anything else. "And I said some things I wish I could take back, but I know I can't, so all I can do now is apologize. I hope you'll forgive me."

That was certainly not what Marci had expected to hear.

"Why, thank you, Mr. Allison."

Dewayne relaxed, smiled, and then heaved a big sigh. "I'm sure glad that's over with," he said.

"Why's that?" Marci said, warming up to the man in spite of herself. "Having to apologize wasn't that bad was it?"

"No, I guess not. It's just something I ain't done very often."

Marci nodded knowingly and forged on. "Mr. Allison, I still need to ask you some questions. As you know we're interviewing everybody in Love Valley about Bud Beckett's murder."

"I knew you were. I was wondering why nobody had been by to interview me yet."

"Someone has been by here a few times, but were unable to catch you," Marci said. "How long have you lived in Love Valley?"

"Oh, about ten years or so, I'd say."

"Did you know Mr. Beckett?"

"Sure, just about everybody did."

"Where were you the night Mr. Beckett was murdered?"

"M…me…?" Dewayne stuttered. Marci picked up on the hesitancy in his voice. "Why me and Shorty was drinking at his house."

"Were you there all night long?"

"Well," he thought, "I came back here for a little bit to pick up some more beer money."

"How long were you gone from Shorty's place?"

"Maybe half an hour or so, I don't really know. I remember usin' the bathroom while I was here and checkin' on things."

"What kind of things?"

"You know, just things. I was checkin' to see if anybody had broke into my trailer. I guess you know about all them break-ins we been havin'?"

"Why were you so worried about a break-in?"

"Well," he stammered, "the lock ain't worth nothin' and lots of people have been broke into."

"Yes," Marci said and paused longer than necessary to give him a chance to think about what he was going to say next.

"Aw hell, ma'am," Dewayne finally said and broke into a sweat. He took his hat off and wiped his forehead with his arm.

"Go on," Marci encouraged.

The cowboy put his hat back on and looked pleadingly at the detective. "You gotta believe me. 'Cause, I ain't done nothin' wrong."

"Nobody said you've done anything wrong, so what's to worry about unless…"

"Unless what? Oh, no. You can't even think I had somethin' to do with killin' Bud. I liked the old man. Everybody up here liked him. I hope you find who done it. I really do."

"Then why are you so reluctant to tell me why you came home?"

Allison took a deep breath before answering. "The truth is, ma'am," he tentatively began; "I was worried about the pistol I got hid in my bedroom. Guns and cash are the first things people steal when they break into somebody's house, so I took the pistol and my money back to Shorty's 'cause I knew I was gonna be up there all night."

Marci arched an eyebrow. "A pistol?"

"Yes, ma'am, I got an old forty-five Colt revolver. I traded for it off this feller that needed some work done."

"Is the gun registered, Mr. Allison?" Marci said, reverting back to a more formal interrogation.

"You see, ma'am, that's the problem. It ain't registered and I knew if that thing got stole I'd never get it back. You can see why I was so worried?" Allison swallowed hard and his Adam's apple bobbed up and down.

Marci looked at him with a fixed gaze for a moment. "You said something about money, too. How much are we talking about?"

"Just a couple of hundred dollars," Allison said. I've been squirreling some back and it's took me two years to save that much. I guess I woulda had a lot more saved if I hadn't been drinking so much."

After an extended pause, Marci said, "I see."

"Do I need to get a lawyer, ma'am?"

"That's up to you. You are not under arrest, yet. Is the pistol in your home now, Mr. Allison?"

"Yes, ma'am, I brought it back the next day. You want me to go get it?" he offered.

"No. I will accompany you inside, but you will not touch it. Do you understand?"

"Yes, ma'am."

Marci glanced around at his meager belongings when they stepped inside the tiny mobile home and suddenly felt sorry for the man. Getting to the business at hand, she asked with a rather stern voice, "Okay, where is the firearm, Mr. Allison?"

"In the top drawer of the nightstand beside my bed."

"Take me to it," she instructed.

He led her into his small bedroom and pointed beside his bed. "It's over there in the nightstand, just like I told you."

"Okay, Mr. Allison; stand over there against the wall," she ordered. "Keep your hands where I can see them at all times."

"Yes, ma'am." Allison removed his hat again and stood silently against the bedroom wall while the detective opened the drawer. The forty-five was there just as he had said, wrapped in an old undershirt.

Marci carefully removed the gun from the drawer, partially un-wrapped it from the undershirt, and smelled the barrel for any scent of burnt powder. "Has this gun been fired recently?" she asked the nervous Dewayne.

"No, ma'am. I ain't never fired it. Them bullets are so expensive, I can't afford 'em."

Marci couldn't help but smile when she heard that admission. She took a portion of the shirt and held the firearm by the grips and then spun the cylinder. "This gun doesn't have any bullets in it," Marci said, perplexed.

"That's what I've been tryin' to tell you," Dewayne sighed with relief. "Am I gonna go to jail 'cause of the gun?"

"I don't know yet," Marci said keeping the heat on. "But I will have to run ballistics on it. I'll take it with me now and bring you a receipt right back. They're in my car."

"Ma'am," Allison said, "you're really a nice person and I'm real sorry for them unkind things I said about you."

"That's alright, Dewayne," Marci said, getting back on to a first name basis with him again. "How about you and I just starting over and forgetting about what happened back then?"

"You mean it?"

"Sure I do. The mayor told me that you're trying to get your life straightened out now."

"That's right, ma'am. That's the reason I was pickin' up all them beer cans. I'm gonna clean the place up and I ain't drinkin' no more. I get kinda crazy when I drink."

"Good for you," the detective said. "I'll get a receipt for the pistol right now and bring back it to you. Are you gonna be here for a while?"

"I'll be right here, I promise. And, ma'am..."

"Yes, Dewayne?"

"Thank you for not still bein' mad at me."

"Get back to picking up your cans, Dewayne. That's all forgotten. I'm going to ride up to my car and get you a receipt, so don't go anywhere."

"No, ma'am, I won't. I'll be right here when you get back. I promise."

Marci swung up onto her horse and rode up the hill. Her thoughts were with Dewayne Allison as she rode. *He'll be there when*

I get back. I know he will. Maybe he is a changed man.

CHAPTER 33

WHEN MARCI REACHED her car, she tied her horse to a
small bush, opened the passenger door and crammed the
revolver, still wrapped in the undershirt, inside the glove com-
partment. She walked around to the driver's side and retrieved
her briefcase, rifled through its contents until she found the
appropriate form. She locked the car before she swung up onto
her horse and trotted back to Dewayne Allison's trailer.

Dewayne was sitting on his front steps when she rode up,
but he stood and removed his hat when he saw her approach.

"Here you are, Dewayne," Marci said. "This is a receipt for
your pistol."

"Thank you, ma'am," Allison responded. "Was Bud shot,
ma'am?" he asked with sincerity.

"There was a shot fired at the scene. That's all I can tell
you."

"Do you think I'll ever get my gun back?"

Marci laughed. "That's the least of your worries. Please don't leave the area. We'll want to talk with you again."

"Okay, ma'am," he agreed.

"Now tell me Shorty's real name and where I can find him."

"Sure," Allison said and told her how to find Fred Parsons, better known as Shorty.

CHAPTER 34

SHORTY PARSONS WAS SITTING on his porch enjoying the morning sun when Marci rode up. "Fred Parsons?" she called down to him, still astride her horse.

He rocked forward in his chair when she called his name. "Yes, ma'am, that's me. Do I know you?" Shorty asked squinting up into the bright sunlight.

"No, Mr. Parsons. I don't think so. I'm Detective Marci McLeod with the Iredell County Sheriff's Department and I'd like to ask you a few questions."

"Ask me questions, about what?"

"Do you mind if I join you on your porch, Mr. Parsons? It looks mighty comfortable there in the shade."

"No, ma'am, I don't mind at all. You can sit right here," he said pointing to an old rocker that had seen its better days.

Marci climbed down and tied the reins to the porch post and joined Parsons.

"What's this about, ma'am?" Shorty asked with concern.

Marci got right to the point. "Did you know Bud Beckett?"

"Sure, everybody knew ol' Bud. That was a shame what happened to him."

"Where were you the night he was murdered?"

"Me? Why would you ask something like that?"

She pressed on. "Do you remember where you were and what you were doing that night?"

"I guess so," he stammered. "Me and Dewayne was probably drinkin' as usual," he said.

"Oh," the detective said, suddenly remembering that the young man had been kicked in the head by a mule. Marci decided to take it a little slower. "This is really important, Mr. Parsons."

"Okay, but could you just call me Shorty, everybody does?"

"Think hard, Shorty; try to remember where you were drinking that evening."

He took a deep breath and exhaled before answering. "Yes, ma'am, I remember. We was both here almost all night long."

"You said almost all night. Did you or Mr. Allison leave at some point during the evening?"

"Well, Dewayne left for a little bit," Parsons said. "He said he had to run home and get some more beer money."

"Did he come back with a lot of money?"

"I saw him countin' some on the kitchen table."

Marci thought she was finally getting somewhere. "Did it look like a lot of money, Mr. Parsons?"

"Well, any money looks like a lot of money to me. I don't ever have much. I'm on disability. I got kicked in the head by a mule one time."

"I'm sorry," Marci said but continued with her questioning. "Mr. Parsons, do you know if Dewayne Allison owns a .45 caliber revolver?"

The question visibly disturbed the cowboy and he paused before answering Marci's question. "I don't wanna get Dewayne into no trouble, ma'am, but I gotta tell you the truth, don't I?"

"Yes, it would be in your best interest if you told me the truth. You could get into trouble yourself if you lied to a detective in a murder investigation."

"How do I know that you're a real detective?" the cowboy asked her point blank.

"I know I am not dressed like one today, but I am definitely a real detective." Marci reached in the back pocket of her jeans and withdrew her gold shield mounted in its leather case and showed it to him.

"Good gosh amighty," Shorty said. "I ain't never seen one of them in real life before."

She took a good look at the small man dressed in worn blue jeans and a western shirt. His hat was pushed back on his head while he examined her shield. *He seemed so innocent,* Marci thought, *but yet had enough presence about him to ask for proper identification before continuing the interview .Go figure.*

"Okay, Shorty," Marci said, "let me ask you again. Do you have any knowledge of Dewayne Allison owning a gun?"

Without hesitation, Parsons answered, "Yes ma'am. He showed me a big pistol that next morning."

"Did he tell you where he obtained the firearm?"

"No, ma'am. He just told me to mind my own business. Dewayne gets like that sometimes when he's been drinkin'."

"Had he been drinking that night?"

"I'd say! We drunk a huge case of beer, just the two of us."

"I see," Marci said. "Well, thank you for your help, Mr. Parsons. I'll be in touch if I have any more questions, so please don't leave the area."

"Ma'am," Shorty said, "I ain't goin' nowhere, I don't even know how to drive."

CHAPTER 35

MARCI PULLED UP beside her friends in the parking lot. "It's about time," Joanie said.

"I know, but I just couldn't help it. Some things just fell into my lap and I had to go with it while it was there."

"Well whatever trips your trigger," Joanie said with a wry smile.

Debbie chimed in, "I'm starved, let's get something to eat."

The suggestion sounded good to all four women.

"Where does Jake take Meredith to eat?" Gail asked.

"The Silver Spur," Joanie said, "and I hope to God they have somethin' to eat besides hot dogs."

"I'm sure they will," Marci assured her, "it's a regular restaurant. Hot dogs are just what Jake and Meredith like."

"Good," Joanie said, "I could almost eat this damn horse I'm ridin'." They all laughed at Joanie's way of putting things.

After a satisfying lunch, they were ready for an afternoon

ride. Since Marci had spent most of the morning working on her day off, she was anxious to spend time with her friends. Pete had told them about Ridge Trail, so they decided to venture out of town and enjoy the afternoon riding through the hills of the Brushy Mountains.

CHAPTER 36

SHORTY PARSONS WALKED down Tori Pass to Dewayne's trailer to tell him about the visit from the detective. Allison was cleaning up the remainder of the beer cans and loading them in his truck when he saw his friend ambling down the hill. Dewayne threw the last bag into the back of the truck and sat on the rear bumper.

"Hey, Shorty, I was just comin' to get you as soon as I finished loadin' up these beer cans. I thought you could ride with me to the landfill."

"Dewayne," Shorty began, "I got somethin' to tell you. I hope you won't get mad at me, but I couldn't help it."

"Why would I get mad at you, Shorty? You're my friend. Anyway, things are gonna change now. Wait and see."

Perplexed, Shorty said, "You ain't even heard what I'm gonna tell you yet."

"It don't make no difference," the big man said. "I ain't

gonna get mad at you no more.

"You mean that, Dewayne?"

"I sure do, Shorty. You're about the only friend I got and I ain't been the kind of friend you deserve."

Almost in tears, Shorty asked, "Are you alright, Dewayne? You ain't never talked like that before."

"To tell you the truth, Shorty, something happened to me after I left your house the other night. I started up Mitchell Trail just to see if anybody was at Bud's place."

"What happened, Dewayne?"

"Well, I turned around and started back home when I saw a sheriff's car parked in the driveway. But, when I got to the church something made me turn into the driveway."

"You pulled into the church's driveway? What for?"

"I wanted to see if that deputy was coming down the hill after me. I was scared he was goin' to get me for driving drunk, so I turned the truck around and just sat there in the truck watchin' for him."

"What happened?"

"Nothin'," Dewayne said. "I don't guess he saw me, so after sittin' there for a few minutes, I got out and walked around to the front of the church."

Parsons was listening intently as Dewayne continued, "I don't know what it was, but something made me look up at that cross on top of the steeple and it was like somebody was talkin' to me."

"Talkin' to you?"

"Shorty, it was like no other thing I ever experienced. It was like I heard the Lord talkin' to me. It scared me."

Wide-eyed and in awe of Dewayne's story, Shorty said, "Gosh amighty!"

"Well, after that, I got back into my truck, drove down to the trailer, and sat there for a while thinkin' about it all and then went to bed and slept like a baby. The best sleep I've had in a long. I'm tellin' you now, Shorty, I ain't drinkin' no more!"

"Honest?"

"Honest. And I'll tell you somethin' else," Dewayne said, "I'm sorry for the way I been treatin' you all these years." The big man started to cry and huge tears coursed down his cheeks.

Shorty looked at the penitent man before him and was at a loss for words. He reached out and placed his hand on his friend's shoulder and said in a quiet voice, "It's okay, Dewayne."

Allison's crying eventually subsided and he wiped his face with his sleeve. "Thanks, Shorty, you're a good friend."

"You are, too," Shorty said. "Don't cry no more, Dewayne."

"I'm okay now. What was you gonna tell me?"

The little man was relieved to change the subject. "I was gonna tell you that that detective woman came to see me. She kept on askin' questions. She wanted to know if you had a gun and if you had any money."

"What'd you tell her?"

"I told her the truth, Dewayne. You know I can't lie as good as you can. People always know when I'm lyin'."

"That's okay, Shorty. I'm glad you told her the truth."

Surprised, he said, "You are?"

"Yep, that's the way it's gonna be from now on, the truth all the way."

Shorty was really confused now, he'd never known Dewayne to tell the truth when a lie would do just as well.

He asked, "But where did you get the gun and the money?"

"I traded some work for the gun, but I didn't have any bullets for it. I've been saving my cash from the odd jobs I've been doing. I decided I was gonna see how much I had before I blew it all on beer. I'm sure glad I didn't do that now."

"Gosh amighty, Dewayne. You mean you ain't in no trouble?"

"I don't think so. The gun's not registered though. I might be in some trouble over that, but I told the detective the truth, too, Shorty. She knows everything. I even apologized to her for the way I acted when she arrested me years ago."

"Dang, you sure have changed, Dewayne. Are we still gonna be friends?"

"You betcha, little buddy, but I ain't drinkin' no more. From now on, I'm gonna try to be an upstandin' citizen."

"Doggone, Dewayne. I never thought I'd hear you talkin' like that."

"Me neither. Ain't it a hoot?" Allison said, as got up and looped his arm around his little friend's shoulder.

CHAPTER 37

RIDGE TRAIL BEGAN at the end of the main street and ran behind Charlie and Beth Nance's house. Their home sat precariously on the side of the hill that overlooked the arena and their barns. Charlie and Beth managed the arena where they hosted junior rodeos and professional rodeo events.

After working around the arena for most of the morning, Charlie went to the barn where they kept their miniature horses and donkeys.

He was tossing hay in the corral for the animals when he thought he heard the sound of women's laughter. The cowboy paused, removed his hat, and then took out his handkerchief to wipe his brow. After listening carefully, Nance decided the laughter was coming from up on Ridge Trail. He hurriedly climbed the hill to see who was having such a good time and saw the women from the Wednesday Night Club plodding slowly along on their horses.

"How y'all doin', ladies?" he said with a gallant wave of his hat. I hope you're enjoying Love Valley."

"Oh, we are," said Gail. "This is fun."

"Where does this trail go?" asked Debbie.

"Oh, it'll circle around north of Love Valley and all the way over to Fox Mountain Road," Charlie said.

Joanie chimed in, "It ain't too far, is it? My butt is already gettin' sore."

Charlie laughed, "No, it's not too bad. You'll enjoy it. Just be careful on this trail. It winds a little ways through the woods before coming back out on the road."

"Thanks, we'll be fine," Gail said. "Pete told us all about it when we got our horses."

"Good ol' Pete," Charlie said smiling.

"Ladies," Marci said, "let me introduce you to Charlie Nance."

"Charlie! Hey, that's Meredith's friend," Joanie added.

Charlie gave a graceful bow and said, "Charmed, ladies, I'm sure."

"Ain't you somethin'," Joanie said laughing.

"I do my best, ma'am," Charlie countered with a big grin. "By the way, Detective McLeod, how's the investigation goin'?"

"Actually, I learned some interesting things this morning. It's been very enlightening, to say the least. I may even have made a new friend."

"You don't say? Do I know them?" Charlie asked.

The detective's horse snorted, reared his head, and tried to turn around, but Marci held him in check. "You do indeed," she said smiling, "Dewayne Allison."

"Dewayne Allison! Are you kiddin' me?"

"No, sir, I am not kidding and would you believe he even apologized to me for the way he acted when I arrested him years ago?"

"Well, I'll be damned! 'Scuse me, ladies, but if that don't beat all, I don't know what does!"

Marci laughed. "I must say I was as surprised as you are."

Nance took off his hat again and rubbed his shaven pate with a handkerchief he'd taken out of the back pocket of his jeans. "You can't tell me there ain't no such thing as a miracle. Wait
'til I tell Beth."

"Be sure to tell Beth hello from me. Right now, we'd better get moving," Marci said.

"Have a good ride, ladies," Charlie said and once again bowed.

CHAPTER 38

HIS PIERCING EYES followed the women as they rounded a bend along the heavily wooded trail. The bearded stranger darted behind a large oak and watched them intently and listened to their conversation. He watched them until they had ridden out of sight.

Not wanting to arouse anyone's suspicions, he had spent much of the last two weeks in the cabin alone and only went to town occasionally.

He believed there was a lot more money hidden somewhere in his uncle's trailer. *The old man shoulda had more money, the bastard. He never spent it on nothing. The ol' fool was holdin' out on me, I know he was.*

The stranger's head began to hurt as his mind raced. *Why'd he have to go and pull that damned gun on me? The son of a bitch coulda killed me.*

The more he thought, the madder he got. He pulled his hat down over his forehead and set out through the woods, taking what he hoped was the short cut back to Mitchell Trail. As he tromped through the dried leaves on the floor of the heavily forested hills, he wondered, *Why in hell, anybody would want to live in this Godforsaken place.* He kicked at a stick lying in his path as he started down into a ravine. *I'm gonna get back inside that trailer and find out where the old man stashed the rest of his money.*

The stranger stopped at the bottom of the small ravine where rainwater had eroded a path to lower elevations. He paused and removed his hat and listened. *I must be hearin' things.* But he remained still and once again heard the faint sound of a hound baying in the distance.

CHAPTER 39

THE WOMEN CONTINUED along the trail as it wound its way up and down hills and through the woods. Now from a new vantage point, hidden behind an ancient hickory tree, the bearded stranger could see them again. He watched as they laughed and joked with each other. *If they knew that I was watching them, they wouldn't be so damn happy.*

That thought brought a wicked smile to his lips.

Mitchell Trail came into view and the women stopped their horses to give them a break before deciding which way to turn. After a brief discussion, they turned left and headed back south.

After a short ways, Marci pointed to a gravel lane among the cedars and pines. "There's the driveway that leads to the trailer where Bud Beckett lived."

"It looks so peaceful," Debbie said. "You would never think that a murder could have been committed in such a beautiful place as this."

"Violent crime knows no boundaries, nor does it take a vacation," Marci said sadly.

"Well, it's just a damn shame if you ask me," Joanie added.

Gail was quiet for a while, sitting astride her dappled mare. She was thinking about what had taken place just a few weeks earlier down the tree-lined lane. "Is there anywhere that people can be safe these days?"

"Sadly, there isn't," Marci said. "Quite often, murders are committed by someone the victim knew. That's what we think happened here. Otherwise, Mr. Beckett would never have let the perp into his home, much less his bedroom. So far, we have little to go on," she added.

"Do you think the murderer is still around here?" Debbie asked.

"It's a possibility, there's really no way to know for sure."

"Are there no witnesses at all, Marci?"

"Not one," she said. "So, now you can see what we're up against." Marci nudged her horse down Mitchell Trail and the other ladies followed close behind.

The eavesdropper had overheard one of the ladies call the redhead Marci. *Looks like she's the one who knows what's goin' on. She must be the detective I heard about. Sure glad to hear her say there are no witnesses.* Silently, he sneaked further back into the woods. He had only been able to hear bits and pieces of the conversation, but he had heard what he wanted to hear.

CHAPTER 40

DEWAYNE ALLISON had borrowed a rake from Mayor Barker and was cleaning up trash in front of his trailer when the four women from the Wednesday Night Club approached him on horseback.

He looked up from his task as the women reined up in front of his trailer. Dewayne smiled, removed his hat, and then leaned on the rake. "Well, howdy, Detective McLeod," he said. Noticing the other women, he added, "I hope y'all are havin' a nice ride."

"Yes we are; thank you, Dewayne. These are my friends, Gail, Joanie, and Debbie."

"Howdy," Allison said and nodded to each one. "Didn't I see y'all earlier?"

"We've seen you a couple of times today," Joanie said, "but didn't you have a beard then?"

"Yes, ma'am, I did, but I saw somebody this mornin' that

looked a lot like me and it gave me the willies. I didn't like that at all, so I just shaved it off."

"I remember seeing you coming out of the Silver Spur this mornin'," Joanie said.

"I ain't been in the Silver Spur today, ma'am. You must have me mixed up with that cowboy I was tellin' you about."

"Maybe so," Joanie said.

"I see you're cleaning up around here," Marci said pointing to the rake in his hand.

"Yes, ma'am, I don't know how in the world I used to live in this mess. I guess when you're half-drunk most of the time, you just don't notice."

"Well, I'm proud of you, Dewayne," Marci said, using his first name again. "Taking the first step is always the hardest. Keep your nose clean and we'll see you later," she added grinning down at the cowboy.

"Yes, ma'am, I sure will," he said with pride and added, "me and Shorty, too."

The women waved bye to the newly clean-shaven cowboy and nudged their horses toward the barn where they had rented them for the day.

"Don't you think he looks like Robert Redford in a country sort of way?" Joanie asked.

"Kind of," Gail said. "I wondered why his face was so red."

"I suppose it was because he just shaved off his straggly beard. He had it this morning when I interviewed him," Marci said. "He doesn't even look like the same man."

"Well, ain't you gonna tell us about the interview?" Joanie asked.

"I'll tell you what I can," Marci said. "We sat down together and had a good talk and now I'm convinced he's innocent."

"Why is that?" Gail probed.

"Well, because of his drinking, Dewayne had a reputation as a troublemaker, but he has vowed to turn his life around and remain sober. He was afraid he may be considered a suspect because of his past."

"What did he do in the past?" Debbie asked.

"I'm not at liberty to say. Let's just say, I knew him before and leave it at that."

Gail said with her usual sincerity, "We all need to pray for him. Pray that he has really turned his life around."

"We can do that," Joanie said. "Hell, I pray every day."

The women laughed. She seemed to never change and they really wouldn't want her to. She just wouldn't be Joanie if she did.

"What'd I say that was so damn funny? That's what I'd like to know."

"Come on, Joanie, we're almost back to the barn," Marci chuckled.

Joanie turned to Gail, "What'd I say, Gail?"

"It doesn't matter. We were just having a little fun."

"Good, I thought I'd said something bad there for a while. I'm gettin' better with my language after being around Meredith. You have to watch everything you say around that youngun'. She don't forget anything. Smart as a whip, that little girl is."

After the women returned their horses, they walked around the lot stretching their aching bodies. Joanie was rubbing her behind with both hands. "Damn, my butt's gonna be sore tonight. I guess Ed'll have to give it a good massage."

"Since when did you need an excuse for a butt massage?" Debbie asked, laughing.

"Well, I don't reckon I did, come to think of it," Joanie said joining in the laughter.

"I'll see you girls later," Marci said. "I want to hang around town just a little longer and ask a few more questions. You all go ahead and I'll catch up with you back in Mooresville.

CHAPTER 41

Afraid he might be seen walking down the long drive-way, the stranger made his way silently behind the row of pines and cedars that lined both sides of the graveled lane. He stopped behind a cedar tree that had spread its prickly branches almost to the ground and waited and listened. Hearing nothing but his heart beating, he continued until he could see the deserted mobile home sitting forlornly in the weed-infested yard. Today, no sheriff's car was parked in the driveway.

The yellow crime-scene tape was still draped across the door and it twisted slightly in the gentle breeze. He waited for a few minutes in silence and watched as the sun turned a brilliant orange and disappeared behind Fox Mountain.

I don't want to rush across the yard, out in the open. Just because a vehicle's not there, don't mean that an officer ain't there. I ain't that damn dumb.

He wrapped his arms around himself in an effort to ward

off the cold mountain air as he waited. He could not stop thinking about his uncle's money. *I know Uncle Bud had more money. The bastard never spent much from what I heard Mama say about him. There's gotta be some more hidden somewhere inside that trailer.*

A noise in the woods behind him diverted his attention. He turned and saw nothing, but couldn't help thinking about Beckett's dog. Sweat trickled down the back of his shirt even though the air was cool and getting colder.

I wonder what happened to that old, worthless hound dog? I don't want him to start barkin' loud enough to wake up the dead. Maybe somebody took him. I hope so; I don't want to have to shoot the son of a bitch.

While standing alone in the cold, many thoughts raced through his mind as he waited for darkness to settle over the valley. *Why am I even worried? Hell, I doubt anybody even knew the old man had any kin.*

Having just thought that, he remembered the letters his mother had written to her brother. *I wish Mama hadn't wrote him and told him them lies about me. Hell, I worked some. I just didn't like it. She didn't have to go and tell him I wadn't workin'. Mama didn't have a pot to pee in when she died and she worked her ass off. Where'd it get her? I'll be damned if I'm gonna do that.*

He thought back to that fateful night and wondered if it could have turned out differently. *If the damned old fool would've just gave me some money without pullin' that gun on me, I could've been long gone from this place. But no, he had to act macho like he was Clint Eastwood or somebody. Hell, he was eighty-two years old.*

Having waited until total darkness had fallen, the desperate man inched his way to the mobile home. He looked to his left and then to his right before he climbed the same steps he had stumbled down on his last visit. With a violent jerk, he tore the crime-scene tape in half and attempted to pry open the door with the ill-fated tire iron.

"Come on, come on, dammit!" he said aloud. *I always heard*

these cheap-ass trailers were easy targets. Just push the end of a tire iron between the door and the jamb and the sucker was supposed to pop wide open.

No sooner than he thought it, the door popped open with a snap. He wished he'd brought a flashlight, but decided that no one was around to see the light anyway, so he turned the light on in the kitchen.

Every surface was covered with fingerprint dust. *They can dust all they want to, but the bastards ain't gonna find my prints anywhere,* he laughed to himself.

He began systematically tearing open the cabinets, one by one. He found the flour canister and emptied it first, then the sugar canister, and then the coffee. He took the corn flake box and poured the contents out onto the kitchen table. He tore open ad emptied every package he found. He went to the refrigerator and swung open the freezer.

Damn, they don't have this much trouble on TV finding money that's hid in peoples' houses.

Getting more frustrated, he flung packages of frozen food across the room with pent-up fury. At the very back of the freezer, he noticed a package wrapped in white freezer paper like his mother used to get from the butcher. He grabbed the package and discovered that it was not as heavy as a frozen piece of meat would be. He took the package to the kitchen sink and nervously ripped off the tape and began stripping the layers of paper away.

"Hot damn," he said aloud when he saw the green, rolled bills. "I knew it. I knew the old bastard had to have more money." He unrolled three stacks of hundred dollar bills. He began to tremble, not from fear or from the cold, but from the excitement. His nerves were wound as tight as a watch spring. "Hell, I'm rich!" he said as he danced around the kitchen.

Suddenly, he grew quiet. Was he imagining things? Had he heard a noise outside the door? He thought he'd heard someone coming up the steps to the trailer. The thief drew his uncle's pistol from his pants and aimed it at the door. He quickly turned off the light and waited.

Another sound came from the deck. "Who's out there?" he asked nervously.

No response. He aimed the gun at the door and said one more time. "You better show your face or I'm coming out there shootin'!"

Rounder, Beckett's old blue-tick hound, whimpered and ambled inside the trailer and sniffed around, paying no attention to the burglar.

"Damn, you almost got shot, you worthless dog," he told the orphaned hound.

Rounder sniffed at the thief's leg and then slowly walked out the door and into the night. The thief watched the dog enter into the woods and then he heard a mournful howl that sent chills down his spine and bristled the hair on the back of his neck.

CHAPTER 42

"JAMIE?" MARCI CALLED out to Detective Campbell in his nearby office, "have you found next of kin for Mr. Beckett?"

Campbell rose from his desk and walked over and stood in Marci's doorway. "I'm working on it," he said. "By the way, the ballistics came back on Dewayne Allison's gun and it is not the weapon that was fired in the trailer."

"I didn't think it would be," she said and grinned. "He didn't even have bullets for the thing."

Jamie laughed out loud. "What about the registration? You gonna push it?"

"I don't think so," Marci said. "Dewayne got that old pistol as payment for some work he'd done. I'm not going to tell him he's off the hook quite yet. I still might need him. When this is all over, I'll probably give the thing back to him."

Jamie laughed, "You're mean."

"Who, me?"

"Yes, you. Remind me not to ever make you mad."

"I just can't help it sometimes," she said laughing. After a brief pause, Marci wrinkled her brow in deep thought. "You know, Jamie, it'll really help if we can find Mr. Beckett's next of kin. Why don't you work on that from this end and I'll go have another fireside chat with Mayor Barker."

"Will do," Campbell agreed, "something's bound to break soon."

"You would think," Marci agreed.

Marci parked the cruiser in front of Andy Barker's hardware store, climbed the rock steps, and let herself inside. The mayor was leaning back in his chair listening to a group of men talking politics and telling jokes.

"Well, hello there detective," the always-charming Andy Barker greeted her.

"Good morning," Marci said and walked over to receive her hug from the mayor.

"Fellows," Andy said to the crowd of men who had gathered around the stove. "This is Detective Marci McLeod of the Iredell County Sheriff's Department. She's investigatin' Bud Beckett's murder. If any of you know anything at all, saw anything or anyone suspicious, this is the lady to tell."

"Why thank you, Mr. Mayor," Marci said.

"Danielle, get Detective McLeod a chair," the mayor said to the young lady behind the counter.

The detective took the proffered chair and sat down near the stove and unbuttoned her jacket. Getting down to business, she said to the group, "We could really use your help gentlemen. So far we don't have a whole lot to go on."

One of the men asked, "When do you think ol' Bud's gonna be buried?"

"We're trying to locate his next of kin so we can notify them. So far, we haven't had anyone come forward to claim the body. Do any of you know if Mr. Beckett was ever married or had any other family?"

A man in his seventies, wearing a pair of faded overalls spoke up. "I heard him say that he had a sister livin' up in Virginia somewhere."

"A sister, thank you," Marci said. "By chance, did he tell you her name?"

"Nah, I just heard Bud mention his sister a couple of times. He did say she had a no-good son. Said the boy wouldn't work in a pie factory." That brought a few chuckles among the men.

"Do you know his first or last name?" Marci asked.

"No, I sure don't, sorry," the man said apologizing.

The men grew silent, thinking, trying their best to remember something, anything that would help. For a short time, the sound of wood crackling and hissing in the stove was all that was heard.

"Wait a minute," the man in overalls said, "I believe the nephew's name is Bart or maybe Jerome. I got no idea why I get those two names confused. They don't even sound alike. But I do remember Bud talking about how good-for-nothing he was. Dang it, I just can't remember like I used to. If it comes back to me, I'll tell Andy."

Marci waited a few minutes more, but no further information was forthcoming. "Thanks for your help," she said, "that's certainly more to go on than we had before. If you think of anything else that might have a bearing on this case, please get in touch with me or let Andy know."

Marci rose, thanked them, said her goodbyes, and quietly closed the door and then made her way down the steps to the waiting cruiser. She was just opening the door to get in when she saw a bearded man watching her from a distance. *He reminds me of Dewayne Allison, but that can't be Dewayne; he shaved off his beard.*

Her thoughts were interrupted when the door to the hardware store swung open and the man in overalls called out, "Wait a minute, Detective, I just thought of somethin'."

Marci turned toward him. "Yes, what is it?"

"I think Bud's nephew's name is Jerome. The Bart's what had me messed up. I think his name is Jerome Barton. I knew it would come to me sooner or later."

Marci was grateful for the first real lead. "That's great, sir. Thank you so much. This is a big help."

"If I think of anything else, I'll be sure to tell Andy. I want you to find who killed our friend."

"We'll do our best and what you have just told me will bring us one step closer."

CHAPTER 43

MARCI WAS IN HIGH SPIRITS when she climbed into her car. *Now, at least, we have a name to go on. If we can just find out where in Virginia these people live, we can notify them and lay Bud Beckett to rest.*

"Jamie," she said into the mic, "it seems that Bud Beckett has a sister and a nephew living in Virginia. I don't have a name for the sister, but we're pretty certain the nephew's name is Jerome Barton. Go ahead and run him into the system and see what you can come up with. Get back to me as soon as you can."

"Will do," Campbell said.

She switched on the ignition and the Charger roared to life. Before Marci put the cruiser in gear, she noticed that the same bearded man was still up the road and he appeared to be watching her. *I think I'll go have a talk with this guy. I don't know if he's been interviewed yet and there's no time like the present.*

Marci pulled onto the road and headed toward the main

street, but before she got to where she had seen the man, he had disappeared behind a horse barn. She pulled the cruiser over to the side of the road and got out, quietly closing the door. She stepped out onto the dust-laden street and quietly slipped around to the back of the barn only to discover the stranger had completely vanished.

Where could he have gone in that short time? Marci stepped inside the barn, looked into each stall and then the feed room. Puzzled, the detective went back outside and saw a man and a woman riding toward her on two beautiful buckskin horses.

The pair reined up at Marci's request. The man, who appeared to be in his early sixties, was dressed like a weekend cowboy in snakeskin boots and a brand new Stetson. "Anything wrong?" he asked. The woman, who appeared to be at least twenty years younger, let her riding companion do the talking.

"Did you just see a bearded man duck behind this barn a minute ago?"

"No, we were talking to each other and not paying attention," the man answered.

"I was hoping you had seen him," Marci said. "He's tall, over six feet, has a heavy beard, and was wearing a black hat and jeans."

"No, I'm sorry," the man said, "I wish we could help you."

"Uncle Henry," the young woman suddenly spoke, "I think I saw him. He ran into the barn, came right out the back, and then ran down the hill toward Mitchell Trail."

"I didn't see him," the man apologized. "I was looking at you," he said to the young lady.

"Are you with the sheriff's department?" the woman asked.

"Yes, ma'am. I'm Detective Marci McLeod," she said and showed them her badge. "Are you folks just visiting Love Valley?"

"Yes, we're from Charlotte. We just come up on weekends. What's the trouble?"

"A man was murdered here a couple of weeks ago and we're questioning everybody. It gets confusing sometimes because of all the visitors." Marci asked, "Were you folks up here that weekend?"

The man answered, "We were as a matter of fact. We've heard about the murder. Any leads so far?"

"A few," Marci replied. "Did you folks see or hear anything that Saturday night that seemed suspicious?"

"Well, we'd just stepped out onto the back deck of the Silver Spur and were talking to our friends. Jack Little said he'd heard a backfire. Nobody thought too much about it." The man continued, "I was leaning over the back rail when I saw a beat-up looking truck coming down Mitchell Trail and thought it could have been responsible for the backfire. You know how those old trucks are?"

"Yes, sir," Marci said. "Can you tell me anymore about the truck?"

"No, I'm afraid I don't know much about old trucks. I have a new Ford F-150 myself. I do remember the thing was rattling like it had a loose tailpipe or something and it had a lot of rust on the driver's door."

"That's great, anything else?"

"No, I guess that's about it."

"Well, thank you very much for your help. What are your names?" Marci asked pulling a notebook from her jacket pocket. "Just so we can get in touch with you again if we have any follow-up questions. Also, so we can mark you off the list of people we have already questioned."

"My name is Henry McDonald and this is my niece, Marcia McDonald, my brother's daughter," the man said. "Marcia's the only one in the family, other than me, who likes to ride. I guess we're kind of kindred spirits."

"I love coming here with Uncle Henry on Saturdays and

getting out of the city, too," the young woman said. "My friends think I'm crazy for coming up here to Love Valley."

"Why's that?"

"Well, there are lots of other places to ride horses, but none of them have the atmosphere we find here. I know it's a little rough around the edges, but we still love it." She laughed and added, "And what would a Saturday be without a hug from Andy Barker?"

Marci nodded smiling. "Thanks again and please let me know if you think of anything else," she said and handed the man her card.

"We certainly will and good luck with the investigation," he said.

Marci's cell phone rang as they headed their buckskins down the street. "Yes, Jamie. What do you have?"

CHAPTER 44

DETECTIVE CAMPBELL FINALLY had some good news for Marci. "You remember Sid Bellman, don't you?"

Marci had fond memories of Deputy Bellman. He had worked with her on the case of the missing women, the case where she had met Jake McLeod.

"Of course I remember Sid," she said. "What's the old man up to since he's retired?"

"He fishes a lot more now," Jamie said. "In fact, he's become good friends with that sheriff in Wilkes County, Phil something or other."

"Sure, I remember him, Phil West.

"Anyway, getting back to why he called. He said he remembered that you couldn't stand having loose ends in your cases."

"He's right about that," Marci agreed. "Get on with it, Jamie."

"Well, he said that he and West were fishin' on Kerr Lake

yesterday when the sheriff got a call."

"Yes, go on." Campbell was milking the news for all it was worth and Marci was becoming more anxious with each passing minute. "Would you just tell me what the call was about?"

"Okay, do you remember searching for those lost ladies a few years back?"

"Of course, I do."

"Well, it seems that the body the ladies found when they were lost in the woods had never been identified until now. Wilkes County finally got a positive ID on the woman."

"That's terrific," Marci said. "Anybody we know?"

"She was Willene Colebrook."

"That name doesn't ring a bell."

"To me either, but here's the thing that got me excited," Jamie said. "She's from Love Valley."

For a moment, Campbell heard nothing on the other end of the line but Marci's breathing. Finally, she said, "You gotta be kiddin'?"

"No, ma'am."

"Well, I'll be damned," Marci said. "You know we've interviewed some Colebrooks this week. I wonder if they're related?"

"I don't know, but knowing you, you're gonna find out."

"You bet your ass, I will," Marci said and ended the call. *Yes sir, you can bet your ass, I'll find out,* she thought. *Ol' Sid is right, I hate loose ends.*

CHAPTER 45

WHEN MARCI ARRIVED back at the sheriff's office in Statesville, she went over the list of people who had been interviewed pertaining to the murder of Walter (Bud) Beckett. There were three Colebrook families living in or near Love Valley. She pondered the list for a minute, closed her eyes, and drew a deep breath. She wondered if the missing woman's name was ever reported in Iredell County.

"Jamie," she called out, loud enough for him to hear from his office across the hall. "Did you check to see if we had a Missing Persons Report on the Colebrook woman filed in Iredell County?"

"I checked again this morning just to make sure, but I can't find one," Campbell replied.

She walked over to his office and stood in the doorway thinking for a moment before speaking. Detective Campbell looked up at her from his desk and knew what was coming next.

"Jamie, I've got to go back to Love Valley and find her family. Can you handle things here while I'm gone? I should be back this afternoon."

"Sure," Campbell replied. "You go do what you gotta do. I figured you'd want to handle this yourself. I'll work on the interview file while you're gone. Here's the list of the Colebrook addresses."

On the drive to Love Valley, Marci tried to prepare herself for the upcoming interviews with the Colebrook families. Thankfully, there were only three.

Marci soon stood on the cinder block steps of an aging mobile home that looked as if had been manufactured in the seventies. There must have been a problem with a leaky roof in the past; a gabled roof had been built over the top of the trailer. She had noticed that many mobile homes in Love Valley had been outfitted with roofs of the same sort.

She took a deep breath and knocked tentatively on the door. Marci waited for a long moment before she heard footsteps inside.

The door was opened by a woman who appeared to be in her late seventies. A pink towel was wrapped around the top of her head like a turban. With a surprised look on her face the woman asked, "Can I help you?"

"Mrs. Colebrook?"

"Yes."

"I'm so sorry to interrupt you, ma'am, but I'm Detective Marci McLeod from the Iredell County Sheriff's Department. May I have a few minutes of your time?"

"What's this about?" the woman asked, adjusting the towel on her head.

"It's really important, ma'am," Marci said seriously and

forged ahead before the woman could ask any more questions. "The remains of a woman were discovered five years ago in a wooded area north of Highway 421 in Wilkes County. My office just received notification of her identity today."

The woman's face drained of all color. "They found her, didn't they?"

"Found who?" Marci asked.

The woman did not answer, but instead, invited Marci into the small trailer and asked her to sit down. "I'm sorry for my manners," she apologized, "but I was washing my hair in the kitchen sink when you knocked."

"That's quite all right."

After gaining her composure, the woman asked Marci, "Would you like some fresh coffee? I just put a pot on."

"Yes, thank you, that would be nice," Marci said. While Mrs. Colebrook was getting the coffee, the detective took her short time alone to look around at the home's meager furnishings. A threadbare recliner, with barely enough room to recline, sat near a small bar separating the den from the kitchen. The sofa was covered in brown vinyl and had been duct-taped in several places. Evidently, the woman got by on just her social security.

"Do you live here by yourself?" Marci asked when she returned with the coffee.

"Yes, I do now," she said as she sat down. "Harlan, that was my husband, died late last year. He really loved it here. Sometimes I think he loved his horse more than he did me," she said with a half-hearted chuckle. Mrs. Colebrook poured and handed Marci her coffee in a chipped mug. "Do you need cream or sugar?"

"No, this is fine, thank you."

Marci took a sip of her coffee and looked at the elderly Mrs. Colebrook. "This woman found in Wilkes County several years ago, you knew her, didn't you?"

Mrs. Colebrook drew in a breath and hesitated before speaking. "You said they identified her. What's her name?"

"I know this is difficult for you, Mrs. Colebrook." Marci paused briefly and then went on. "The woman's name was Willene Colebrook of Love Valley."

An audible gasp escaped from the elderly woman as she dropped her coffee cup to the floor and buried her face in her hands. The pink towel unraveled and fell from her head as she bent forward with her hands still covering her face and cried softly.

"I'm sorry. I truly am." Marci rose from her chair, set her cup on the bar, and sat down beside the grieving woman. She tried to console Mrs. Colebrook by wrapping her arms around her as she cried.

After gaining some composure, the woman wiped her face with the towel and looked up at Marci.

"They said she was from Love Valley?"

"Yes, ma'am. That's how I knew to come here. There aren't that many Colebrooks in this area and you are actually the first place I came. How do you know her, Mrs. Colebrook?"

"I just knew she had to be dead. Willene was my only daughter and she never got in touch with me after she left. She was always such a thoughtful girl."

"Yes, ma'am," Marci said, letting the woman talk about her child.

"She would have never left like that and not called me."

"Why did she leave?"

"Well," the heartbroken mother began, "Harlan was a hard man, Mrs. McLeod. He told Willene that she'd have to leave home if she didn't straighten up."

"Were there any particular problems?" Marci probed.

"No, not one in particular," she said. "You see, Willene was a pretty young woman, a beautiful child," the mother said wistfully. "Her looks made her very popular with the men and she started running with the wrong crowd."

"Yes, ma'am," Marci said. "That happens a lot."

Mrs. Colebrook continued, "That crowd she hung out with was pretty wild and she got took in by their ways."

"And you never heard from her again?"

"No, and that's what bothered me so much."

"Why didn't you report her missing, Mrs. Colebrook?"

"Harlan didn't want me to. He said Willene made her bed and she'd have to lie in it. I told you he was a hard man. We figured she'd just run off somewhere and was afraid to come home." The woman bowed her head again and cried into her towel.

When she had composed herself again, Marci went on to explain where the young woman had been found and that her murderer had since been killed in the mountains of northwest Wilkes County.

"Is there anything I can do to help you, Mrs. Colebrook?"

"No, I don't think so, but thank you so much for coming to tell me about Willene. Now I can lay her to rest. Please come back and see me, won't you. I don't get many visitors."

Before Marci left, she asked Mrs. Colebrook one last question. "Do you know why your daughter was in Wilkes County?"

"I really don't know for sure," she said, "but some of that crowd drank an awful lot of moonshine and I think they went down there to get it. Willene might have even gone to get it for them. She could be talked into just about anything."

Marci thanked Mrs. Colebrook and again offered her condolences. She promised to see her again when she was in Love Valley.

Then Detective Marci McLeod got into the cruiser, drove up to the little church on the hill where Dewayne Allison had met God, and sat alone in the car and cried.

CHAPTER 46

THE BEARDED STRANGER, Jerome Barton, walked into the woods off Fox Mountain Road onto an overgrown lane that had once been used to haul timber. Carrying a small flashlight, he walked directly to what looked like a forgotten brush pile. He knew the way well—he had made the pile himself. A smile formed on his lips when he saw that it was still untouched. It looked just like he had left it. He propped the flashlight on a stump, removed his lightweight jacket, and tossed it onto a bed of dry leaves. Barton then began pulling limbs off one-by-one and setting them aside to use again.

A battered, 1983 Chevrolet pickup with a rusted driver's side door slowly materialized amid the tangled limbs. After brushing away the detritus from the top of the cab, he grabbed his jacket and flashlight and climbed in.

The old truck had been sitting under the brush pile for a few days. Barton hoped it would still start. He stuck the key into the ignition and gave it a twist but a grinding sound was all he heard. He tried again. Barton felt a trickle of sweat run down his back as he turned the ignition again; luckily it started on the third try. He let out a sigh of relief and then steered his way through the discarded limbs, through the woods, and down Fox Mountain Road toward Love Valley.

Barton drove slowly down the mountain, carefully maneuvering around the curves. The starlit sky and the dim headlights of his old truck barely illuminated the gravel road.

As he drove, he began formulating a plan. In the short time he'd been in Love Valley, Barton had noticed a lot of older folks living alone on the back roads. The fact that wealthy people came up just on the weekends had not slipped by him either. He was going to take advantage of his good fortune while he was here.

All I need are a few more good hits and I can go down to Mexico. Hell, I could live it up down there with one of them pretty senoritas.

CHAPTER 47

AFTER CRYING FOR A FEW minutes, Marci wiped her eyes and sat in the patrol car with the windows down. She inhaled the springtime air deeply and then laid her head back on the head-rest. *Sometimes I wish I were in some other kind of work.* She found herself praying for Mrs. Colebrook and then after a time, collected herself and called Campbell.

"I'm coming back to the office, Jamie, be there in a bit."

"That was fast," Jamie said.

"I'll tell you all about it when I get there," Marci said and signed off.

Later, Marci sat across from Campbell at his desk and filled him in on the notification. She did not elaborate; she just gave him the facts. Having worked with Marci the last four years, Campbell realized something was bothering her. Offering encouragement, he said, "You did good finding the Colebrook woman's mother so quickly." He continued, "I couldn't believe it when you called me back so soon. The very first place you checked—how often does that happen in this business?"

"Not very often, that's for sure," Marci agreed. Filled with emotion, she said, "I don't think I will ever get used to notifying the next of kin. This one really got to me, Jamie."

"What was so different about this one?"

"Oh, I don't know. Just seeing the hopeless state of Mrs. Colebrook's existence, I guess. The poor woman lives alone in an old trailer with no visitors, hardly any money, and now she has lost all hope of ever seeing her only daughter alive again."

"That sure is a sad state of affairs," Campbell agreed.

"But, I was the one who dashed the remaining hope she had," Marci said and then broke down in tears.

Campbell sat there, not knowing what to do. Should he reach across the desk and pat her hand, hug her, or just let her cry it out? Marci McLeod rarely showed her emotions when involved in a case.

He sat there in silence for a minute and then passed her his handkerchief. She took it gratefully and after a while, blew her nose. "Thanks," she said as she handed it back to him, "and thanks for listening. Maybe it's because I have a daughter of my own now," she said. "I don't know what I would do if anything ever happened to Meredith. I can't even think about it, it makes me so sad."

"I think I understand," Campbell said. "I don't have any children of my own, just nieces and nephews. I know that ain't the same."

Marci looked at him through red-rimmed eyes and said weakly, "Thank you, Jamie, for letting me melt down for a little bit. I'm sorry I lost it."

"Hey, no problem," he said not knowing what else to say. He thought for a moment and finally reached over and grabbed her hand. "What are friends for?"

Marci dried her eyes and looked at her partner sitting across the desk and gave his hand a hard squeeze. "I owe you one, Jamie, but I will have to shoot you in the knee if you tell anybody about this."

Campbell let go of her hand and laughed. "Now that's more like the Marci McLeod I know!"

CHAPTER 48

JAKE WAS POURING a cup of coffee when Marci got home. "Hey, honey," he said as she dropped her purse on the kitchen table. "How was your day?"

Without saying a word she walked over and placed her arms around his waist and leaned into him.

"Hold me please," Marci managed to say.

"What's wrong, sweetheart?" Jake said as he set the cup on the counter and wrapped his arms around her. "Are you okay?"

"I'm alright, I just had a very bad day," she said and began crying into his chest. Jake patiently placed his chin on the top of her head and tenderly rubbed her back while she gained control of her emotions.

"Maybe we need to talk about it," Jake suggested. "Sit down here at the table and have a cup of coffee with me. It's better than that stuff you get at the sheriff's department."

Marci smiled, "Okay."

Jake poured her a cup and sat down across the table from her. They sipped their coffee in silence for a while. "You're right," Marci finally said.

Surprised, Jake said, "I am, about what?"

"The coffee," Marci said smiling.

"You want to tell me about it now?" Jake asked.

After a while, she sighed heavily and looked up from her cup into his understanding eyes. "Thank you," she said. "You always know just what I need."

Jake gave her a sympathetic smile and waited patiently for her to tell him what was bothering her.

Marci took in a deep breath before continuing. "Do you remember when Gail and Debbie found that woman's body in the woods when they were kidnapped?"

"Of course I do," Jake said. "Her head had been separated from her body and was lying across the road."

"That's the one," Marci said. "Well, we finally got an ID on her."

"After all this time! That's great, isn't it?"

"It is, as far as tying up loose ends go," Marci said. "The victim's name was Willene Colebrook and she was from Love Valley. I went there this morning and talked to her mother."

"You've made plenty of notifications before and I've never seen you upset like this."

"It was so sad, Jake."

"How in the world did she end up in the woods of Wilkes County?"

"Her mother said that, on occasion, her daughter went down there to buy moonshine for her male friends."

"Well, I guess that explains the connection with Yancey Darwood," Jake said.

"It looks that way," Marci agreed. She took another sip of coffee and he could see tears welling up in her eyes again. "Oh,

Jake, it just broke my heart. Mrs. Colebrook's husband was a hard case. Willene was involved with a rough crowd, so he gave her the option to either straighten up or get out."

"So she left home and never went back," Jake said.

"That's right. She never saw her folks again. Her father's dead now and the poor mother lives alone in a little trailer in Love Valley and now she's lost her only child."

Jake reached across the table and took her hands in his.

"Thanks for listening," Marci said as she rose from the table. "I need to look in on Meredith. I just want to see her and make sure she's okay. That poor woman lost her only daughter years ago and today I dashed all the hope she had of ever seeing her again. That was the hardest thing I've ever had to do. I would die if anything happened to Meredith or to you."

Jake understood what she was feeling. He rose, took her by the arm, and they walked down the hall to Meredith's room.

Marci opened the door quietly and peeked in at their peacefully sleeping daughter. "Isn't she beautiful?"

"She looks just like her mother," Jake said smiling.

They stood there for a moment admiring their sleeping child. Marci took the back of her hand and gently touched the cheek of the sleeping girl. She then turned and looked up at Jake. "Let's have another baby," she said with tears in her eyes.

"Are you sure?"

"Neither one of us is getting any younger, Jake. I'd love for Meredith to have a brother or sister. I can't bear the thought of losing an only child."

"Well, when do you want to start?"

"How about right now?" Marci said.

CHAPTER 49

Hazel Colebrook put off going to bed as long as she could. Sitting up and reading the Bible seemed like the thing to do. The elderly woman had finally fallen asleep in her recliner with the Bible lying across her lap. A knock on her door awoke her with a start. She sat up straight and listened. There was another knock, louder this time. She was confused when she saw the time on her clock. *Who could be knocking on my door at this time of night?*

"Open up it's an emergency!"

Confused at first, but finally answering; "Oh my Lord." She lowered the leg rest on the recliner, got up as quickly as she could, and hurried to the door.

Always willing to help a stranger in need, she lifted the security chain and opened the door to Jerome Barton.

CHAPTER 50

"WHAT'S UP, JAMIE?" Marci said, answering the phone beside the bed.

"There's been another one."

"Another one, what?"

"I hate to tell you this, Marci, but there's been another murder in Love Valley," Campbell said.

Marci threw back the covers and swung her feet to the floor. "Do you have an ID on the victim yet?"

"I'm afraid we do," Jamie said, "Mrs. Hazel Colebrook."

Marci, silent for a moment, said softly into the phone, "Oh my God, the poor woman."

"Are you okay, Marci?" Campbell asked.

"Yes, thanks," she said, "I'll be alright. What time is it?"

"It's ten after seven. I'm already on my way up there."

"I'll meet you there," Marci said and hung up.

Jake, awakened by the ringing of the phone, asked, "What's

wrong, honey?"

"Remember, I was just telling you about the mother of the woman we found in Wilkes County?"

"Yes. What about her?"

"She was murdered last night."

CHAPTER 51

WHEN MARCI ARRIVED at the scene, Jamie Campbell and two deputies were standing outside by the yellow crime scene tape. She was sick to her stomach at the thought of Mrs. Colebrook lying dead inside the trailer.

"I'm sure sorry, Marci," Jamie said when she walked up.

"Thanks, Jamie, I am too," she said sadly. "Who discovered the body?"

"Willard Hollifield. He's a local cowboy who was out for his morning ride. Said he saw Mrs. Colebrook's front door standing wide open about six-thirty this morning. It was cold outside and he couldn't imagine her having the door standing open like that."

"Thanks, I'll want to talk with him in a minute, but first I want to see Mrs. Colebrook."

Marci tentatively stepped inside the trailer and noticed the cushions on the sofa were turned upside down. A half-empty coffee cup, with a chip on the rim, was still sitting on the counter. A lamp was overturned on the small table beside the recliner where a bible lay open to the Gospel of Matthew.

"Where's Mrs. Colebrook?" Marci asked.

"Back here," Campbell said and led Marci into a small bedroom at the rear of the trailer.

Hazel Colebrook lay across the bed face down with a large gash in the back of her skull. Blood from the wound had made a dark stain on the bedspread.

Marci was tempted to turn away. She could hardly believe she had coffee with this woman less than twenty-four hours before. "Any idea what time this might have happened?"

"The ME's on his way," Jamie said.

Marci pulled on a pair of latex gloves and bent over the body. She gently turned Mrs. Colebrook's head slightly and examined the wound. "Bud Beckett had a head wound very similar," Marci said, "could be the same perp."

"That's what I thought, too," Campbell agreed. "Look like another robbery to you?"

"Sure does," Marci said.

Marci stood and took off the gloves and crammed them into her jacket pocket. "Let me talk to Mr. Hollifield now." Marci McLeod was saddened at first but now she was mad. She turned and headed out the door.

A shaken Willard Hollifield was standing next to Deputy Floyd Alexander. His hands were shaking while holding the reins to his dappled gray horse. Hollifield took a deep breath and exhaled a misty cloud in the cold air. He and Alexander watched in silence as Marci strode purposefully across the road toward them.

"Good morning, Floyd," Marci said to the deputy.

"Morning, Detective," Alexander said. "This is Mr. Willard Hollifield. He's the gentleman who called us."

"Mr. Hollifield," Marci said extending her hand, "I appreciate you calling this in and waiting for us."

"I was just riding by…" he said choking on his words.

Marci gave him time to compose himself before continuing.

"Please tell me what happened, Mr. Hollifield."

"Well, there was a good frost on the ground this morning," he started and hesitated again for words. "I…I just saw her door standing wide open," he stammered.

Marci waited and let him continue at his pace. "I knew something wasn't right," he said. "Mrs. Colebrook lived alone in that trailer and I'd never seen her door standing wide open like that before, not even in the summertime."

"Did you go inside the trailer, Mr. Hollifield?"

He hesitated and then admitted, "Yes, ma'am. I didn't know what else to do, so I stepped inside and called for her, but she never answered."

"Then what did you do?" Marci asked.

"Well, I thought I'd better see if she was alright, you know, so I looked in the bedroom and there she was."

"Did you touch any thing?"

"No, ma'am. I never touched her or anything," Hollifield declared. "I just ran outside and called the sheriff's department on my cell phone."

"You did the right thing, Mr. Hollifield. We appreciate it very much. You've been a big help. Please give your statement to Deputy Alexander and you can go on with your ride."

"Thank you," Hollifield said. "I can't believe this is happening in Love Valley. This is a peaceful place."

"I know," Marci agreed, "but trouble will find a way to make itself at home just about anywhere."

CHAPTER 52

BARTON THOUGHT KILLING the woman would have bothered him more than it did. Each time was getting easier. After all, he'd killed his own uncle and a man in Virginia. The death of the man in Galax had been ruled an accident, but he knew better. There was one more death, too, but Jerome tried not to think about that one.

It had been like taking candy from a baby, he thought. *I can't believe that old woman had all that money hid in her dresser drawer under her ratty underwear. The things these old people do just amaze me.*

Barton counted and recounted the money and put it in neat stacks on his small kitchen table. He figured a few more hits like the old lady and he'd have it made. He took the stacks and put them in a dirty sack and then stuffed the sack back into the hole beneath the cabin floor and replaced the board.

Satisfied, with his success, he opened a can of pork and beans and ate them greedily along with some saltines. After satisfying his appetite, Barton laid down on his smelly cot for a nap. Sleep never came, but it was a chance to think about his situation in Love Valley.

No one knows who I am, so I can pretty much come and go as I please. Just one or two more easy marks and I'll call it quits here and go somewhere else.

A barn owl deep in the woods swooshed down in silence and grabbed his supper from the forest floor and then flew back to his perch in the ancient oak tree. The sound of a mournful howl from somewhere not far away floated through the night and life went on in the wooded hills.

CHAPTER 53

DETECTIVE JAMIE CAMPBELL stood outside Marci's office and knocked on the doorframe with the back of his knuckle, "Want some coffee?"

"Yes, thanks," Marci said as she took the proffered cup. "Any news on the Barton family yet?"

"Yes and no," Jamie said. "There are lots of Bartons in Virginia, but I only found one household with a Jerome Barton."

"Great, good work, Jamie. Where does he live?"

"He lives with his mother, Beatrice Barton, in Galax. Beatrice must be the sister of Bud Beckett the farmer was telling you about."

"Were you able to contact Mrs. Barton?"

"Not yet," Campbell said, "their phone has been disconnected."

"What about her son Jerome?" Marci eyed the detective from across the room. "I know that look, Jamie. What else do you have?"

"Well, he's had some run-ins with the law up there."

Marci arched her eyebrows, "Yeah?"

"He's had his share of speeding tickets, three DWIs, and was a person of interest in a man's death that was eventually ruled as accidental."

"Let's put out a BOLO on Jerome Barton and see if we can catch up with him. Find out what kind of vehicle he drives."

"I'll get right on it," Campbell said. "Maybe a Be-On-the-Look-Out notice will help us find Barton, so we can notify Mr. Beckett's family of his death."

CHAPTER 54

Barton FIGURED THE NEWS of last night's murder would be spreading like wildfire. He thought he could hang around in town and maybe find out what was being said. *Better to know than be in the dark.*

He slipped into downtown Love Valley on foot. A dozen or so horses were tied to the hitching rails along the main street. A couple of dogs raised their heads and looked at Barton as he walked by and then went back to their naps. *They don't seem to be interested in me, so maybe nobody else is either. Hell, I'll just go in and have myself a beer.*

Jerome walked brazenly through the batwing doors into the Silver Spur. No one seemed to take notice of him, so he sat down at one of the empty tables.

Jennie Foster, always Johnny-on-the-spot, came quickly to his table, "Hi, what can I get for you today?" she said brightly.

"Gimme a longneck and a hamburger," he said sourly.

"Comin' right up," Jennie said and headed for the kitchen.

Before she got out of earshot, "Gimme an order of fries, too," he shouted.

"Sure thing," she answered, but before going to the kitchen with his order, she came back to the table. "Excuse me," she said, "but are you kin to Dewayne Allison?"

"Who's Dewayne Allison?" he asked with contempt.

"I didn't mean to offend you, but you sure look an awful lot like Dewayne."

"Don't know him." Barton said. "Go ahead and get my order in. I'm 'bout to starve."

"You bet," Jennie said. "Sorry about all the questions, but you sure do look like ol' Dewayne. I had to ask."

CHAPTER 55

DAYS PASSED AND the sheriff's office still had not been able to contact the Barton family. They did find out that a Jerome Barton of Galax, Virginia drove a 1983 Chevy pickup, but that was all. Marci called Detective Campbell into her office. Before he had a chance to sit down, she said, "Take charge here for the rest of the day, Jamie. I'm going to Galax."

"Galax?" he asked.

"Yes. I'm goin' up there to see if I can find the Bartons or talk to some of their neighbors. I thought for sure we would have heard something by now after sending out that BOLO on the son. Somebody has to know something."

"You're probably right," Jamie agreed.

"I gotta run this by the Sheriff, but I don't think he'll give me much grief. If he approves of my little trip, I'll be back late today."

"Everything will be fine here. Don't worry about it. I got it under control."

"Thanks," Marci said and headed down the hall to the sheriff's office.

After getting clearance from Sheriff Nichols, Marci headed north on I-77. She soon sped past milepost 69 and entered into Yadkin County. Famous for its many vineyards, in recent years the area had been dubbed the next Napa Valley. Billboards dotted the bucolic countryside advertising the many wineries. Marci and Jake enjoyed visiting many of the wineries throughout the valley, but Shelton Vineyards at Exit 93 was their favorite.

She turned off the interstate at Exit 100 as planned and drove west on Highway 89. Marci knew these roads well, having driven along them with her husband. Jake loved the mountains and they would often take Highway 89 and then turn left on Highway 18 and follow the curvy mountain road. This short cut took them through Edmonds and Ennice, across the crest of the mountains, rewarding them with spectacular views.

Beautiful scenery always inspired Jake. Anytime they took one of these beautiful drives through their beloved North Carolina mountains, Jake would come home enthused and want to paint.

The miles rapidly clicked off and Marci drove past the short cut and continued on her journey. She entered the state of Virginia and soon crossed over the Blue Ridge Parkway. Galax was only a few miles ahead.

She found the police department, pulled into a visitor's parking spot. Inside, the officer on duty met her at the desk. Mayfield was the name on her identification badge and the woman's smile put Marci at ease. She introduced herself and asked to see the chief of police, Sam Kinkaid.

After waiting in the reception area for ten minutes, Marci

was ushered down a narrow, tiled hall. A husky, young sergeant was coming out of the chief's door at the same time Marci and the desk officer arrived. There was no way the two of them could pass through the door at the same time. The man must have topped the scales at two-eighty and was all muscle. The sergeant surprised her with a quick smile showing a mouthful of even white teeth. "Good morning," he said, as he turned sideways to let her pass.

"Good morning," Marci said. "Thanks. How is the chief this morning?"

"Sorta grumpy, like usual," he chuckled and lumbered down the hall.

"Come on in," the chief said as he rose with his hand extended. "My name's Sam Kinkaid. Take a seat and tell me how I can help you."

Marci noticed the large, but soft hands of the chief. She introduced herself and sized him up mentally as she took her seat. He was a big man himself sporting a head of thinning, gray hair. It looked as if he had worked out in the gym at one time, but his body was now going soft. *Too many hours behind the desk,* Marci thought.

The chief asked if she wanted coffee, but she declined. Marci took her time and shared what information she had concerning the murder of Bud Beckett and her reason for coming to Galax.

"I remember the Bartons," Kinkaid said. "The old man died and left poor old Mrs. Barton to raise that worthless, sonovabitchin' son of theirs by herself."

Marci listened intently as the chief described the young man. "He wouldn't hold down a job for a week. That boy was lazy to the bone. Stayed in trouble a lot, but poor old Mrs. Barton would talk me out of arresting him or he woulda had a rap sheet a mile long. I always said, that cuss oughta been shot with shit and then killed for stinkin'."

Marci couldn't help but grin.

"Excuse my language, ma'am, but I get kinda riled every time I think about that boy."

Marci interjected, "My office has attempted several times to contact Mrs. Barton about the death of her brother, but her phone seems to be disconnected."

"That don't surprise me none. That poor old woman probably couldn't pay the bill."

"I was hoping you could help me with the notification," Marci said.

"Sure, no problem, I'll take you over there myself. Maybe we can find her at home."

CHAPTER 56

KINKAID LED MARCI to a shiny new Dodge Charger and opened the door for her. After settling into the cruiser and buckling up, she asked the chief, "How do you like the Charger compared to the Crown Vic?"

"Oh hell, I like 'em both," he said. "But the young officers, they like the new Chargers better. They're tickled to death to drive 'em. They better like 'em," he laughed, "we've got four of 'em now."

The chief backed out of the parking place marked 'Chief Kinkaid', turned left out of the lot, drove through the main shopping district, turned right, and then drove up a hill to the left. He steered around a few small curves and drove one more block before stopping the cruiser.

"Here we are," he said. "It ain't much, but it's all Mrs. Barton can afford without help from her son."

Marci stared at the one-story house that had seen its better days. She noticed the set of rotting steps that led up to a small covered porch. Two boards were hanging like loose teeth from the wall beside the front door. Several windows were broken and one was covered with a sheet of plywood.

"Do you think they still live here?" Marci asked.

"I really don't know. I haven't heard anything from Mrs. Barton in a good while. I was hoping that son of hers had straightened out. Let's go see if anybody's home."

Kinkaid led the way up the rickety steps being careful not to fall through the rotted boards. He turned and warned Marci, "Be careful there, Detective, these damn steps ain't in good shape." She carefully followed in the chief's footsteps. Kinkaid rang the doorbell and then looked at Marci. "I can hear the bell ringing inside the house, so I know it works." He waited a few minutes and then knocked a few times and still no one came to the door.

"What do you think, Chief?" Marci asked.

"Well, it don't look like anybody's home, you want to check with her neighbor while we're here?"

"That'd be great," Marci said. "I really need to find Mrs. Barton."

"Alright, let's get started," Kincaid said. He led the way off the porch and down the rickety steps.

CHAPTER 57

KINKAID MARCHED UP the steps of the modest home next door. It was a small, one-story house covered in vinyl siding. Dark green shutters adorned each of the windows that faced the street. The yard was neat and daffodils lined the sidewalk. Marci kept a short distance behind the chief—this was his home turf.

She watched as he rang the bell and then waited patiently for someone to come. After a moment, footsteps were heard approaching the door. A woman in her late-seventies or early eighties opened the door slightly and asked in a timid voice, "May I help you?"

Kinkaid showed her his badge. "Hello, ma'am, I'm Chief Sam Kinkaid," he began. "Do you mind if we ask you a few questions about the Bartons who live next door?"

"No, I don't mind at all," the elderly lady said and closed the door enough for her to unlatch the security chain. They heard the chain rattle and the door opened wider. "Please come right in," the woman said. She seemed eager to talk to someone about her next-door neighbors.

Marci and the chief followed her inside the house and were led into a small den with décor that dated back to the fifties. Before their hostess asked them to take their seat on a brown, faux-leather couch, she introduced herself as Rachel Vanderhoot.

The chief began, "Mrs. Vanderhoot, thank you for taking time to answer a few questions. This is Detective Marci McLeod with the Iredell County Sheriff's Department in North Carolina. This has to do with a case she's working on."

"Oh, my," she said. "You came all the way from North Carolina?"

"It's not that far," Marci said anxious to get on with the questions. "Mrs. Vanderhoot, do you know the Bartons very well?"

"No, not really," she said. "I used to see her gather her mail every morning and we'd nod or sometimes speak. That's about the extent of our relationship."

"Is she not friendly?"

"To tell you the truth, I'm afraid to go around them very much. That son of hers...he scares me."

"How so?" Marci asked.

"Well, he's a pretty big man, you know. He has those dark eyes that seem to look right through you and he drinks all of the time, too."

"Is there anything else you can tell us?"

"Jerome, that's her son, he rarely works. He just lays around the house playing that awful loud music."

"Loud music," Marci said.

"Oh yes, it's terrible. He'll play it at all hours. I can barely get any sleep. But, you know, I haven't heard it lately."

"Do you happen to know where Mrs. Barton works?"

"Yes, she works down at the glass and mirror place."

"Is there anything else you can tell us about her son?" Marci asked with patience, taking her time with the woman.

"I really don't like the man at all. To tell you the truth, he's downright obnoxious."

"Can you describe him for us?"

"Well, a few months ago he started growing this straggly looking beard," she said as she brought her hand to her chin and made a gesture. "It didn't make him look any better either. And that long hair. I don't like to see men with long hair."

Marci suppressed a grin. "Did you know him very well?"

"He's never spoken to me in all the years they've lived there and I've never spoke to him." Mrs. Vanderhoot paused and then asked Marci, "Why are you asking all these questions?"

Chief Kinkaid broke in, "Detective McLeod needs to speak with Mrs. Barton about an official matter and her phone seems to be disconnected. We wouldn't be here asking you questions, Mrs. Vanderhoot, but we can't find anybody at home."

"I haven't seen Beatrice in a while, but that son of hers was over there a few weeks ago. I could hear that awful music."

"What kind of music?" Marci prodded.

"You know; hillbilly music and it suits him, too. He's always dressed like a cowboy, but as far as I know, he's never been around a horse in his life."

Marci looked over at the chief. "Do you have any questions, Chief Kinkaid? I think that's about all for me."

"No, I'm fine here," he said. They both rose and Kinkaid extended his hand to Mrs. Vanderhoot. "Thank you very much for your time, ma'am," he said and gave her his card. "Please call me the next time you see either of them at their house."

She promised them she would.

Marci thanked her as well and also handed her a business card. After saying their goodbyes, she and the chief walked down the steps to the cruiser.

CHAPTER 58

"WELL, WHADAYA THINK?" asked Kinkaid.

Marci said, "For beginners, I'd like to know where Mrs. Barton is."

"I agree," said the chief, "Mrs. Vanderhoot said she hasn't seen her in a while. I wonder what that means?"

"I was told that the only relative she had other than her son was Bud Beckett. Is it likely she went to see someone else and stayed for a while?"

"I don't know," Kinkaid said. "You wanna take another look around their house before we go back to headquarters?"

Marci said, "That sounds good to me, Chief."

Kinkaid once again climbed the steps onto the porch and this time knocked loudly on the front door. "Police!" he said. Still no answer.

Marci carefully made her way across the rotting porch, put her hands up to the window to shade her eyes, and peered inside.

"Chief, you might want to take a look at this."

Kinkaid joined Marci at the window and shaded his eyes. "It looks like there's been a struggle in there," he said. "See that overturned table and broken lamp on the floor? Maybe we'd better go in and see if Mrs. Barton is okay."

"I think that's a good idea," Marci agreed.

The chief took the butt of his Glock-40 and tapped the glass in the front door. Shards of glass shattered and fell mostly inside the house. Kinkaid carefully reached in and unlocked the door. They entered slowly, with the chief leading the way. He called out to see if anyone was home. The temperature inside the house seemed colder than it did outside. The modest furniture was adequate, but looked like it had been well taken care of. Marci noticed that part of a braided oval rug in the center of the room had been pushed up under the sofa.

"Something has gone on here, that's for sure," Kinkaid said. "I think I'll call in for a couple of officers to help us out. In the meantime, let's check the other rooms."

They spread out, Kinkaid taking the rooms on one side of the house and Marci the other. When she searched the master bedroom, she called for him to join her.

"A woman would never leave all her things here," she said pointing to the open closet. "All her clothes look like they're still hanging in there." She added, "Her toiletries are still in the bathroom and even her dresser drawers looked untouched. Something is not right with this picture. I have a bad feeling about this, Chief."

"Listen, Marci," Kinkaid said, "just call me Sam. My name's not Chief."

Marci laughed. "Fair enough."

A noise outside caught their attention. "Looks like a couple of my officers just got here," Kinkaid said, holding the curtain aside to peer out the window. He motioned for them to come inside. The officers entered the living room and nodded to Marci.

Kinkaid asked them, "One of you go see if there is an out-building or a door to a basement."

"Yes, sir," one of the young men replied, mock-saluting as he went through the kitchen door that led onto the back porch and the backyard.

Before long, the officer reappeared in the kitchen door-way. "Sir, I found a basement door."

CHAPTER 59

MARCI AND KINKAID followed the officers to the rear of the house to a set of slanting doors that led under the kitchen. The doors were secured together by a padlock that was threaded through a strong steel hasp. Kinkaid ordered the officer to retrieve some bolt cutters from the cruiser.

The young man returned quickly, *not even out of breath,* Marci thought, and attempted to hand the bolt cutters to the chief.

"I don't want 'em," Kinkaid said. "Give 'em to Henry." Henry, the other young officer on the scene, took the bolt cutters and with two tries, cut the lock. The two officers pulled the doors open exposing a set of steps that led into the basement.

The entrance reminded Marci of her grandmother's home. It had an outside basement entry just like the Barton's. She remembered the smell of potatoes, apples, and onions that her grandmother kept in the cool, dark basement beneath her house. Scores of quart jars filled with green beans, beets, pickles, boiled potatoes, and corn filled the shelves along the wall.

Her reminiscing was short lived. "Damn!" Kinkaid said as he reached for his handkerchief.

Marci recognized the odor immediately—the unforgettable smell of death. She quickly handed the chief some Vick's VapoRub she kept in her jacket pocket. The menthol scent kept the strong odor of a decaying body from penetrating their nostrils. Chief Kinkaid readily took the offered jar and spread a dollop under his nose. "Thanks," he said and handed it back to Marci.

"I always have it handy just in case," she said and placed a dab under her nose. "I'm ready when you are, Sam."

Kinkaid reached in and felt around for a light switch. He found one to the right of the door, flipped it up, and suddenly the basement was awash with light provided by two overhead, 100-watt bulbs.

There were no canned vegetables, no potatoes, no onions, and no apples on shelves along the wall. A discarded sofa was stashed in one corner of the basement along with some storage boxes. A chair was turned upside down on one end of the sofa. An antique iron bed frame leaned up against one wall. A blue tarp lay in a rumpled heap in another corner.

"Smells like it's coming from over there," Kinkaid said pointing to the tarp.

He tentatively walked over and lifted one corner of the tarp and peered at the still, pallid body beneath it. The victim's skull had been bashed in.

"Oh man," Kinkaid said.

Marci took a quick look over his shoulder. "Is that Mrs. Barton?" she asked.

"It sure as hell is," Kinkaid said. He then gently placed the tarp back just as he had found it. He turned, visibly shaken and

Marci waited until he had composed himself.

"I'm so sorry, Sam. How do you want to handle this?"

Kinkaid took charge. He told his officers, "Let's get a search warrant from a superior court judge and do this thing by the book. I don't want anything to come back and bite us in the butt when we get to court."

They climbed the basement steps and walked outside into the fresh air. Kinkaid posted an officer by the door to secure the scene until he could obtain a warrant.

Marci waited around for the preliminary coroner's report. It was early evening when she headed home. Her mind was consumed with the details surrounding the death of Mrs. Barton in Galax and the two murders in Love Valley.

According to the preliminary report, Beatrice Barton had been dead for over three weeks. Her body had been hidden in the cellar of her home to avoid discovery. And where is her son, Jerome? Is he capable of killing his own mother?

When she had put that question to Chief Kinkaid, he told her that Jerome was a perpetual troublemaker. He had been, at one time, a suspect in the death of a man in Galax a year or so ago, before the death had finally been ruled an accident.

After seeing Mrs. Barton's fatal wound, Marci was convinced that her death was related to the two deaths in Love Valley…each of them were caused by blunt force trauma to the head and the common denominator in these murders was Jerome Barton.

Kinkaid alerted his force to be on the lookout for Jerome Barton, but Marci's instincts told her they would not find him in Galax, Virginia.

CHAPTER 60

BARTON'S LUST FOR BLOOD and money was increasing at an alarming rate. He felt no remorse for the killing of his victims, not even his own mother.

After one of his forays into town, Barton had discovered, not too far from his dilapidated cabin, a stately two-story house near the end of Fox Mountain Road. The house stood on the top of a high, wooded hill and was home to an elderly couple. A long, winding driveway led visitors through stands of maple, oak, and hickory trees to the beautifully landscaped property. The house dated back to the 1960s and sported a wrap-around porch with four, white rocking chairs.

It had been several days since he had robbed and killed Hazel Colebrook and the desire to experience that thrill again consumed him. Low-hanging clouds blocked out the half-moon as Barton approached the home in the cool night. The single light from the den window emitted a warm glow that spread across the lawn and to the edge of the woods.

Jerome Barton walked brazenly up the tree-lined gravel driveway to the front lawn. He paused beside a scarlet red maple tree to finish his Marlboro while he studied the premises. Satisfied with his plan, he took one last drag on his cigarette and then flung the rest of it down with authority like he had seen John Wayne do in the movies. He blew out the last of the smoke he had been holding in his lungs into the dark night and then began making his way to the side yard. From that vantage point he could see the faint glow that came from the downstairs window.

Looks like somebody's awake, he thought. *But, hell, that don't make any difference.* He hefted the tire iron in his right hand, testing the weight. It had served his purpose well in the past and he felt that it would again. He unconsciously shifted the iron from one hand to the other. A bead of perspiration slowly tracked down his brow and he wiped it away with his sleeve. *These people are bound to be loaded. Look at this place. Man, I've struck gold here.*

So far, his crime spree had been very profitable. He'd had no idea how easy it would be to gain access to the homes of his victims, kill and then rob them, and get away without a trace. He left nothing behind that could connect him to the crimes. No one had seen him in the area. No one could recognize him. He'd been smart, he thought, and the key to his success was leaving no witnesses.

The only thing that gnawed away at him was that female detective who had been asking questions around town. She had gotten a glimpse of him near Andy's Hardware, but he had been able to get away before she got a good look at him. He'd always been one step ahead. But, there was one more incident that bothered him—the waitress at the Silver Spur who'd caught him off guard when she asked him if he was related to some Dewayne person.

Who in the hell is this Dewayne?

There was nothing he could do about that right then, so he pushed the thoughts to the back of his mind, stepped onto the front porch, and knocked on the door.

CHAPTER 61

JEROME PEERED THROUGH the narrow windows that flanked both sides of the door and saw a man in his late seventies coming down the hall to answer his knock. *Good,* he thought, *get the man out of the way first and the rest should be easy.*

"May I help you?" the man asked as he opened the heavy wooden door.

Without a single word, Barton withdrew the tire iron from behind his back and swung it in a long sweeping, overhand arc that crushed the man's forehead before the victim could utter a sound. The pajama-clad man fell to the hardwood floor with a thud. Walter Cameron now lay silently where he had fallen, staring back at nothing.

Almost immediately, Barton heard someone open a door above him and come out to investigate the noise. "Honey, are you alright?" Maudie Cameron called from the top of the stairs. With apprehension, she called out again, "Walter! Is everything okay? Answer me!"

Barton slipped behind a large ficus tree at the foot of the stairs and remained silent, waiting. Mrs. Cameron inched her way down the stairs, calling for a response from her husband with each step. She made the turn at the bottom of the stairs and screamed when she saw her husband lying motionless on the floor. "Walter! Oh, no! Walter."

She rushed to the side of her dead husband, but never heard another sound, not even the swish of the tire iron as it crashed into the back of her skull.

The old lady didn't even know what hit her, Barton thought.

He walked over to the front door, closed it, turned the lock, and then calmly stepped over the two bodies lying on the foyer floor as if they were objects that were just in his way.

He never gave them another thought as he methodically began searching the entire house for anything of value. When he entered the study, the lamp was still on by a chair near the window. An Elmore Leonard novel lay on the table next to the chair. A bookmark protruded from between two pages halfway through the hardback; saving the place for the elderly Mr. Cameron. Jerome walked over to the window and with gloved hands, closed the blinds, and then went to the large mahogany desk that butted against one wall. When Barton found the desk drawers locked, he swore to himself. *Dammit!*

He reached into the pocket of his jeans and brought out a large jackknife and began picking the lock on the middle drawer. A small part of the knife's blade broke off and fell onto the floor, but Barton kept at it. The lock soon gave way to his abuse and the drawer slid open when he pulled on the knob. He found nothing of value in the drawer, only pens, paper clips, and other detritus usually found in desk drawers. He discovered that when he opened the middle drawer, it released the locks on the drawers along the sides of the desk. Barton yanked one of them open and began rummaging through it. He then repeated the search until he was satisfied that all the drawers in the desk held nothing but the old man's business papers.

After finding nothing inside the drawers he sat down in the leather desk chair. He thought for a minute and then pulled out the middle drawer again and began feeling underneath it. *What's this?* His fingers touched a small piece of paper taped to the bottom of the drawer. He pulled it loose and smiled smugly when he saw the numbers 4L-8R-16L and 12R scrawled on the paper. *Damn! They got a safe here somewhere. I hit the jackpot for sure!* Barton exclaimed to himself.

He got up from the desk chair and began looking behind the pictures on the wall, the proverbial hiding place for a safe. Not finding one, he then went to the bookcase and began throwing books onto the floor searching for a safe hidden in the bookcase wall.

Frustrated, he sat down at the desk again and thought for a minute and then hurriedly ran upstairs to find the master bedroom. Barton looked behind pictures, in dresser drawers, and finally in the walk-in closet. He threw the hanging clothes aside and there between the old man's suits and sport coats was a wall safe staring back at him.

With adrenalin flowing, Barton fumbled in his pocket and found the crumpled piece of paper with the handwritten numbers and letters. Sweat ran down his back as he nervously began turning the dial on the safe. He set it at 0 and then 4 to the left, 8 to the right, 16 back to the left, and finally 12 to the right. Nothing! He tried again and still nothing. *Maybe I'm not doing it right,* he thought. *I'll do it slower this time.* He set the dial to "0" and began again, slower this time. He concentrated on each number as he carefully turned the dial and finally heard an audible click as the lock gave. Barton licked his lips as he gripped the handle of the safe and pulled open the door.

Stacks of 100 dollar bills and 50 dollar bills stared back at him. He rubbed his eyes with his knuckles in disbelief. "Hot damn! I'm glad old people don't trust banks."

He ran to the king-size bed and grabbed one of the pillows and tore off the pillowcase. His breath was coming in short gasps as he began stuffing the stacks of bills into the pillowcase. Behind the stacks of currency were a coin collection and a .38 Smith and Wesson revolver. He stashed everything into the pillowcase and ran downstairs.

The victim's bodies still lay where he had left them and as Barton stepped over their motionless forms, he turned and said, "Thanks a hell of a lot," and left by the way he came in.

CHAPTER 62

CARRYING THE PILLOWCASE on his shoulder, Barton hiked through the woods by the light of the half-moon back to his cabin. He was giddy with excitement when he saw the dark cabin awaiting him as he emerged from the trees. *Man, the way it's goin', I'll have enough money so I can leave this stinkin' cabin.*

He threw open the door, stepped into the dark interior, and lit a match. By the faint glow of the small flame, he carefully laid the pillowcase on the table beside a kerosene lamp. The match he was holding quickly burned out, so Jerome grabbed another one and swiped it across the surface of the table, lifted the chimney, and lit the wick on the lamp. Soon the interior of the cabin was aglow from the flickering flame.

Barton sat down heavily on a homemade chair and began emptying the contents of the pillowcase onto the small table until piles of money slid off onto the floor. He grinned with self-satisfaction at the fortune he had amassed in his short time in Love

Valley.

Barton had come to Love Valley thinking he could live off his Uncle Bud for a while after killing his mother. He hadn't meant to kill his mother, but she just wouldn't stop nagging at him about getting a job. He was a grown man, why did she think she could tell him what to do?

He really hadn't planned on killing anyone, but one thing had led to another. After killing his uncle, Jerome realized that he really had no feelings toward his victims. They were just a means to get the money he needed. *Oh well, what's done is done,* he thought. *Anyway, I'll soon be a rich man. Just one or two more hits and that oughta do it.*

Jerome got down on his hands and knees, took the knife out of his jean pocket, and opened the blade. "Damn"! he said when he saw that the point was broken off the blade.

What the hell! I can still use it for what I need. He knelt and began prying up the board from the cabin floor. When that was accomplished, he set the board to the side, reached into the hole and retrieved the sack of currency that he had stashed there. Barton stood up and arched his aching back. *Hell, before long I'll get one of them Mexican cuties to rub my back,* he said to himself.

He emptied the sack's contents onto the table to join his latest ill-gotten gains. Barton took his seat again and just sat there for a while staring at the pile of bills on the table and the stacks that had fallen to the floor. He picked up a stack and thrust it to his nose.

Damn, that smells good! It won't be long and I'll never have to work again. I ain't wasting my time working my ass off like my mother and her selfish brother did. I'm gonna enjoy myself and when I die, I'm gonna die rich!

Barton then took all the stacks of bills and put them all into the pillowcase. The small sack was now too small to hold all the money.

CHAPTER 63

JAKE LOOKED AT MARCI sleeping soundly next to him and gently moved her arm from his chest. They had lain together all night—holding each other—not wanting to let go. They were extremely compatible when it came to lovemaking. Marci was always eager and often the instigator in the foreplay. Jake had no problem with that and had told her often that she could take the lead anytime she wished.

Marci had indeed taken the lead last night. Jake was exhausted. *This woman's going to kill me,* he thought, *but Lord what a way to go.*

The bedside phone rang and Jake quickly grabbed it hoping it would not wake Marci. He was too late. "What a night," Marci said grinning up at Jake. "Who's on the phone?"

"It's the department," Jake said and handed the phone across his chest to her.

"What's up?" She held the phone to her ear listening

intently and then said, "Where is it?" She listened a moment for directions. "Give me forty minutes," she said.

"No real big hurry," Detective Campbell said. "The scene's secure and the ME's on his way. I'll see you when you get here."

"What's going on?" Jake asked as Marci hung up the phone.

"Another murder," Marci said, "this time a double one."

"Where?"

"Love Valley again."

"You gotta be kiddin'."

"I wish I was," Marci said as she climbed out of bed. She grabbed her gown on the way to the bathroom and added, "We've got to find Jerome Barton. I think he's responsible for these murders and we have to stop him. It's like he's gotten used to killing and it doesn't bother him any more. It might have been about the money in the beginning, but now, I think the bastard's enjoying it."

Jake called out to her as he heard her turn on the shower, "Do you not have a picture of this guy you can show around?"

"No we don't. Can you believe it? There was not a single photo of him or his mother in their house. Not one. That's just not natural," Marci said from the shower.x

"His neighbor gave you a vague description of him, right?"

"Yes, she did. She said he is a large man with a straggly beard and wears western clothes. Do you have any idea how many men in Love Valley look like that?"

"Quite a few," Jake guessed.

"You're right," Marci agreed. "Could you jump in here with me and wash my back real quick before I go? No time for any hanky-panky though, just wash my back, okay? I gotta get up there."

Jake said, "Sure, what are husbands for?" The truth be told, he wasn't up for another round yet. *Maybe I'm getting old,* he thought, and then, *God I hope not!*

CHAPTER 64

THREE IREDELL COUNTY SHERIFF'S cruisers, along with the ME's and the Coroner's vehicles, were at the Cameron home when Marci arrived. Yellow crime scene tape sealed the entire area from the driveway to both sides of the house. Three detectives were walking every square inch of the lawn and driveway searching for footprints or trace evidence that may have inadvertently been left behind.

Detective Campbell greeted Marci as she climbed out of her cruiser. "Morning, Marci."

"Morning, Jamie, what do we have?"

"We have Walter Cameron, age seventy-eight lying on the floor in the foyer with his forehead bashed in. Near his body is his wife, Maudie Cameron, age seventy-three. She was hit in the back of the head with what looks like the same instrument. Same MO. Just like Bud Beckett and the Colebrook lady. Looks like the same perp."

"Sure sounds like it," Marci said, "take me in, I wanna have a look."

Campbell led Marci onto the porch and in through the front door. Her heart sank when she saw the elderly couple lying next to each other on the foyer floor. She drew in a deep breath and knelt near the two bodies. As she examined the wounds of the two completely innocent victims, a single tear ran down her cheek and she caught it with the back of her hand before Campbell saw it. *Maybe it's time for me to quit this job,* Marci thought. She finished examining the wounds on both the bodies and looked up at Jamie. "I agree," she said, "it sure looks like the same perp. We gotta stop this bastard and I mean quickly."

Marci stood and arched her back. "Man, I must be gettin' old," she said.

"Maybe this case is just gettin' to you," Campbell offered.

"Maybe so, but right now I don't have time to think about it."

"I wish we had a better description of Jerome Barton."

"Me too," Marci agreed. "Maybe we can get Barton's neighbor in Galax to work with an artist who can do a composite drawing."

"That would be better than what we have now, which is not a danged thing," he said sourly.

Marci and Campbell went through the Cameron home room by room. The crime scene techs were on the job dusting for prints and searching for trace evidence.

From the study came a shout from one of the techs. "Hey, Detective McLeod, I think I might have something here."

"What do you have?" she asked as she followed his voice down the hall.

The big, burly tech was stooped down in front of the desk. "Looks like our boy jimmied the desk drawer with a knife. There's a tiny piece of the blade lying here on the floor." He carefully picked up the point of a knife blade with a pair of tweezers and dropped it into an evidence bag and handed it to Marci.

"Good work, Don. Mark it for evidence and let's see if he left any prints on it."

"You don't really think there'll be any prints on that little piece of knife blade, do you?" Jamie asked when they stepped out onto the porch.

"Not really, but we've gotta do everything we can to find this bastard. Who knows, we might get lucky," she said.

"Detective McLeod!" yelled one of the detectives from beside a maple tree near the driveway. "Take a look at this!"

Marci and Campbell made their way over to the young detective who was holding a Marlboro cigarette butt in a plastic evidence bag. "Good job, Ben," she said to him. "Hopefully, it belonged to our suspect. I'll see if we can get a rush job on the DNA test, so when we catch the bastard we'll have some positive evidence linking him to the murders."

CHAPTER 65

THE MEMBERS OF The Wednesday Night Club were enjoying their regular outing at the Crimson Cape when Joanie remarked, "I heard they're havin' a rodeo in Love Valley this Saturday afternoon and somethin' called barrel racin'. What the hell is that? Do you race a barrel or what?"

The other women broke out in laughter at Joanie's way of seeing things.

"Well, do you race a damn barrel or not?"

Debbie spoke up. "Oh, Joanie, be serious. All I know is what I've seen on television."

"I am serious," Joanie said, but with a wide grin spreading across her face. "Are you gonna tell me what it is or am I gonna have to crawl across this table and choke it out of you?"

Debbie could barely contain herself, she was laughing so hard. When she caught her breath, she said, "No it's not racing a barrel. Women on horseback race around barrels as fast as they can, then ride back to where they started. I guess it's racing against the clock and whoever has the best time wins."

"All of 'em racin' at one time? Wouldn't that be confusin' as hell?"

"No," Debbie said, "they race around the barrel one at a time."

"Well, what in the hell do they need the barrels for?"

Gail tried her hand at explaining the concept of barrel racing. "Joanie, there are three barrels in the arena and women on horseback, one at a time, race around them in a cloverleaf pattern without knocking them over and then ride like heck back to the starting point."

"That's it?"

"That's it. Whoever has the best time wins. Simple, right?"

"If you say so," Joanie said, "but I'd have to see one for myself to understand it better."

Debbie said, "Let's all go to the rodeo. It'll be a lot of fun."

The women agreed to meet Saturday and drive up to Love Valley for their first rodeo.

"We'll see Charlie again and meet Beth, too," Gail said.

"Jake and Marci really think a lot about them and Meredith loves that Beth!" Joanie said. "Speakin' of Marci, where in the heck is she?"

No sooner than the words were out of Joanie's mouth, Marci walked through the door.

Gail thought her friend looked troubled. "Is everything alright?" she asked.

"Hey, girls, let me get a glass of wine and I'll tell you all about it."

"Wait'll you hear what we got planned," Joanie said.

"What's up?"

"We're goin' to the rodeo this Saturday!"

"That sounds fun, but I'll have to check my schedule."

Gail suggested they all take their spouses and the members

of The Wednesday Night Club agreed.

When Marci's wine came, she took a sip and began telling her friends about the murder of Mr. and Mrs. Cameron.

CHAPTER 66

M ARCI MET WITH THE homicide unit Friday morning to review the information that they had accumulated thus far. She wrote the facts on a whiteboard.

After finding the body of Beatrice Barton murdered and hidden in the basement of her home; they now had a chief suspect for the murders—Jerome Barton.

"Hair fragments from Bud Beckett and Hazel Colebrook were found on the scalps of Mr. and Mrs. Cameron," Marci said. "The only way they could have gotten there is from the murder weapon. It appears that Barton has used the same weapon to commit these murders and evidently he's not taking time to clean the thing." She had the attention of the entire unit. "He's finding it too easy now. He's not gonna stop until we stop him."

The meeting broke up after a few questions and Marci walked out of the conference room with Jamie Campbell and Sheriff Nichols. The sheriff stopped her before she could leave.

"Look, Marci, it's Friday, why don't you take the weekend off?"

"We've got four unsolved murders on our plate." Marci said. "I can't take any time off."

"Yes, you can," said Nichols. "The entire department is working on this case around the clock."

Marci thought for a moment and then said, "You know, my Wednesday Night Club has planned to go to Love Valley tomorrow for the rodeo. I'd like to go and take Jake and Meredith."

"You do that," Nichols said. "It'll do you good."

Marci would not admit it to Sheriff Nichols, but the senseless murders of five elderly victims was really getting to her. Nothing she had experienced in her career had ever affected her with such profound sadness.

She picked up her phone and dialed the gallery. "McLeod Fine Arts," Jake answered.

"What are you doin', handsome?"

"Who is this?" Jake asked.

"You'd better know who this is if you know what's good for you," Marci said.

Jake laughed. "To what do I owe this pleasure, my sweet?"

"That's better," Marci said. "The sheriff insists that I take the weekend off."

"I agree."

"Well, I agreed to take Saturday off so we could all go the rodeo at Love Valley. "

"You want to go to a rodeo?"

"Well, I hadn't mentioned it before, but the girls planned this outing on Wednesday night. I didn't think I could go, so I never brought it up. I didn't want you and Meredith to get your hopes up. Gail, Joanie, and Debbie are going, too, and taking their husbands."

"That's great!" Jake said. "We'll have a ball. Hurry home and I'll have supper waiting for you."

"You talked me into it," Marci said. "I'll finish up some paperwork and then I'll come on home."

"Sounds good, be careful, darling."

"I will."

Jake met Marci at the door and embraced her as soon as she set her purse on the table. She looped her arms around his neck and pulled him into an affectionate kiss. "That's what I've needed all day," Marci said.

"Glad I could help," Jake said as he kissed her again.

"You know you're really good at that." Marci said.

"I thought I must be pretty good. Or else you were just easy," Jake teased.

"Maybe a little bit of both," Marci said with a grin.

"Let's go to bed early tonight."

"Deal," Marci said as she nibbled on his ear and then whispered to him what she'd like to do in bed.

"You sure you want to wait?" Jake asked.

"Yeah, that'll just make it better," Marci said. "Just think about it all during dinner."

"You're a hard woman," Jake whined.

"And you're a hard man, Jake McLeod, and that's another thing I like about you," Marci said winking at him.

They both laughed and held each other for a moment longer.

Marci pulled away and asked, "Where's Meredith?"

"She's in her room playing with the model horses I bought her today."

"Model horses?"

"Yes, can you believe it? I don't know if she'll ever play with dolls again. Wait until we tell her we're all going to Love Valley tomorrow."

CHAPTER 67

THURSDAY AFTERNOON, Barton drove to Statesville and checked into a cheap motel for the night. The cabin where he had been hiding had no running water and he desperately needed a bath.

He found a reasonably priced room near Interstate 40 and paid his bill in advance with cash. The room was not austere, but it was obvious that the owners had not updated the property in years. An old, RCA television sat forlornly on the dresser. Barton plopped down on the double bed and bounced up and down a few times and noticed the mattress sagged on the left, but it was better than the cot in the cabin. The bedside lamps were fitted with low wattage bulbs and did little to dispel the gloom. The bathroom was tiled in pink ceramic. A small sink was attached directly to the wall—no cabinet hid the drainpipe. Pink polka dots decorated the plastic shower curtain that hung over the pink tub.

He took a shower and washed his hair with the shampoo provided by the motel. After drying himself, he turned down the covers on the bed and lay down. He found the remote control and began surfing the channels until he found an old B-Western movie. He fell asleep after only a few minutes.

Barton awoke refreshed, looked at the clock on the night-stand, and saw that it was a few minutes after six o'clock. The television was still on. He fumbled around until he found the remote and hurriedly switched the channel to WBTV in Charlotte. A pretty, young newscaster was talking about the grisly murders in Love Valley. "A killer is on the loose," she said and went on to describe the western hamlet nestled in the Brushy Mountains. It was kind of odd listening to the woman describe him as a cold-blooded killer. *Maybe that's what I am,* he thought, *a cold-blooded killer.* After watching the weather forecast, Barton put on his clothes and drove to a nearby Wendy's for supper.

He thought about his next move while he ate his chili and two ninety-nine cent hamburgers. He wanted to stay in Love Valley until he could pull off at least one more job. He thought that maybe it was time to get him some fresh clothes.

The next morning Jerome Barton checked out of his room and went to Walmart where he bought a new shirt, a pair of jeans, and some underwear and socks. He also purchased some food to take back with him to the cabin.

When Barton took his packages to the truck, he wished he still had his room so he could change into his new clothes. He sorted through the various plastic bags until he found the clothes he'd just purchased and put them together in one bag and went back into Walmart. Of course, he was stopped at the door by the greeter who put stickers on each item to prove he had bought them there.

Inside, Barton returned to the clothing department and had an employee unlock an empty dressing room for him. He quickly shed his old clothes, ripped the tags off the new ones and changed. He then wadded up the old ones and stuffed them into the plastic bag he was carrying and deposited them into a trash can near the front entrance. He walked out of Walmart feeling like a new man.

He noticed when he climbed back into his truck that it was already after one-thirty. A McDonald's was on the access road near Walmart, so he pulled into their parking lot and found a space. For as long as he could remember, he'd had a weakness for fast-food—the smell of hamburgers frying was just too much for him. He went inside, ordered two Big Macs, and sat down to eat among the other patrons. Nobody in McDonald's realized they were dining with a cold-blooded killer. He was the perfect gentleman and as he left, he held the door open for an elderly lady who was entering the restaurant.

Barton just drove around the area for awhile and finally pulled into the Signal Hill Mall parking lot and watched the crowd until closing time. It was late by the time he drove back to Love Valley and steered his truck up Fox Mountain Road to the large brush pile so cleverly hidden deep in the woods. He laid his groceries on the ground and began covering the truck with the aid of the moonlight shining brightly through the budding trees. Satisfied with the job, he gathered his groceries and trudged back to his little cabin hidden in the woods.

Sitting at the small table, Barton was almost tempted to get out his ill-gotten money and count it again. He derived much pleasure from feeling the bills in his hands and from smelling the aroma of the printed currency.

The pickings were good in Love Valley if he carefully chose his victims. *Those old retired people, they're the ones that's got the jack. Just one more hit and I should have enough for sure,* thought Barton.

When I got me enough money to leave, he thought, *by God, I'll trade in that old rattletrap of a truck for one of those new Ford F-150s. Of* *course, I'll do that when I get out of state. I definitely don't want to attract any attention to myself while I'm still near Love Valley. Maybe I'd better get me another used truck. I can't pay cash for a new one 'cause the dealer will have to report anything over $10,000. I ain't stupid and I ain't gonna get caught because of no damn truck.*

One more thought entered his mind before he blew out the lamp and laid down his head for the night. *Hell, I can just steal the kind of truck I want.*

CHAPTER 68

GAIL AND JAMES CALDWELL, Ed and Joanie Mitchell, and Carson and Debbie Wells were standing in the parking lot waiting for the McLeods. Love Valley was bustling with activity in anticipation of the rodeo that evening.

"Hey, y'all!" Joanie hollered when she saw the McLeods pull into the parking area. "Where'n the he…uh, where y'all been?" she said when she noticed Meredith.

"We've been down at the hardware store talking to Andy. He has a new girlfriend now, you know."

"He does?" Joanie asked.

"Yes, Meredith has become one more apple of his eye."

"He gave me another big quarter," Meredith said holding up a silver dollar. "Daddy says I have to save these quarters 'cause they're special."

"He's right," Gail said. "I'd like to have a lot of quarters just like that one. I'd save them, too."

Carson and Debbie Wells were standing to the side, holding hands and grinning at one another as they listened to the conversations being batted about. Looking at Debbie now, so happy in her new life with Carson, it was hard to imagine that she had once been a victim of spousal abuse.

Joanie caught a glimpse of the couple looking starry-eyed at each other. "What're you two grinnin' about? You look like the cat that swallowed the canary."

Debbie gazed up at her husband and then at her friends who had grown quiet. She grinned broadly. "Carson and I are expecting twins. We just found out yesterday."

"What!" Joanie shrieked. "Twins?"

"Uh huh. Isn't that great?" Debbie said.

Gail, Marci, and Joanie ran to Debbie with outstretched arms and hugged her until she could hardly breathe. Everyone cried, even Ed Mitchell. Meredith jumped up and down with excitement, not really knowing why everyone was so happy, but not wanting to miss out on the fun.

James Caldwell wiped a few stray tears from his eyes with his handkerchief and said to Jake, "I wish Gail and I could have had children. Maybe we should look into adopting. It's not too late for us, is it?"

"Never too late for happiness," Jake said. "That little girl of ours has brought so much happiness into our lives. I don't know what we would do without her. I have never laughed so much in my life. You never know what she's gonna say next."

"Gail and I should adopt a child. No sense in you having all the fun."

"I couldn't be happier than I am right now," Jake said. "I highly recommend parenthood, but, of course, Meredith is not a teenager yet."

They both laughed

A lanky cowboy rode up and Meredith squealed, "Wish!"

"How's my favorite girl?" Wish said after he had dismounted from his horse. He swooped Meredith up in his arms and swung her around.

"I'm fine. We gonna ride today, Wish?"

"You betcha, if that's alright with your folks."

"Sure it is," Jake said. "Have you met everyone here?" he asked.

"No, I haven't had the pleasure yet, but if they're friends of Meredith, they're bound to be good people," Wish said.

Introductions were made and Wish helped Meredith up onto the saddle where he joined her. "We'll be back shortly if that's okay," he said to Marci.

"Sure. Y'all go have fun," she said waving goodbye to the grinning Meredith. Marci turned back to her friends and said with a smile, "We're gonna end up having to buy a darn horse for that girl."

Everyone looked at Jake as he cleared his throat. "I, uh, looked into it already," he said.

"You what?"

"We can keep the horse here and she can ride him every time we come to Love Valley."

"What's this 'we-can' stuff you're talking about, Jake McLeod?"

Sheepishly Jake admitted, "Marci, honey, I've already bought a horse for Meredith."

"Don't you Marci-honey me, Jake McLeod!"

"It's just a little horse."

"Why didn't you ask me before you went out and bought a horse?"

"I was afraid you'd say no."

Marci's saw the look on Jake's face and she broke into laughter. "Jake McLeod, you're something else, you know that?"

Everyone laughed along with them thankful that a family

feud had been avoided.

"You're gonna love it, too. It's the prettiest horse you've ever seen. I'll go get it while Wish is taking Meredith for a ride. Then Freckles will be here when she gets back."

"Freckles?"

"Yes, that's the horse's name. And before you ask, I didn't have anything to do with naming it." Jake left them laughing and hurried down Henry Martin Trail.

He returned shortly leading a beautiful little pinto with freckles on her nose. The horse was saddled and ready for riding. Marci laughed when she saw the markings on the horse. "I can see why they call her Freckles," she said.

Wish and Meredith trotted up on Applejack. Seeing her daddy holding the reins to a little spotted horse made Meredith's eyes widen in surprise. "Get me down, get me down," she shrieked.

Ed Mitchell reached up and took Meredith from Wish's arms and stood her gently on the ground. She immediately ran over to Jake. "Wish let me drive the horse, Daddy."

"He let you guide the horse?" Jake said.

"That's what I said," Meredith retorted.

Everybody laughed at the exchange between father and daughter.

"This is a pretty horse, Daddy. What's his name?"

"The horse is not a him, it's a her," Jake said, "and her name is Freckles."

"Freckles," Meredith said. "Freckles. I like that." She walked over and reached up to pet the horse's soft nose. "I wish I had a horse just like you," she said looking into Freckle's big liquid eyes. The horse lowered her head a little more and Meredith continued petting her.

Everyone was grinning when Meredith turned around. "Ain't she the prettiest horse you ever saw?" she asked.

"She sure is," Marci said.

"Whose horse is it?" Meredith wanted to know.

"Freckles belongs to a little girl in Mooresville," Jake said.

"That's where we live. Do we know her?

"You sure do. She lives at our house," Jake said grinning.

"I live at our house, too," Meredith said and then looked at Jake and Marci with her eyes wide-open with excitement. "Is Freckles mine?" she cried.

Jake picked her up in his arms. "Yes, Freckles is all yours. Do you like her?"

"I love her!!"

"Would you like to ride Freckles?" Jake said.

"Oh boy, I sure would!" Meredith said.

Jake lifted Meredith up onto the small saddle, but kept holding the reins. "We'll have to walk beside the horse and hold onto the reins until you learn how to ride by yourself. Wish said he would give you riding lessons, how about that?"

"Oh boy," Meredith said with delight. Everyone took turns leading Freckles and Meredith up and down Main Street much to the delight of the crowd that had gathered in front of the General Store.

CHAPTER 69

JEROME BARTON WATCHED the happy crowd from a distance. An excited little girl was sitting atop a small horse that was being led up and down the main street.

What's the big deal, he thought, *just a kid ridin' a damn horse.*

Barton suddenly noticed that the female detective who had been asking a lot of questions in Love Valley took a turn leading the horse.

Damn, that's one fine lookin' woman, he thought. *I didn't know they made detectives that looked that good.* Barton was watching from a small alleyway between two of the rustic buildings that lined the main street. He pulled his hat down on his head to hide his identity, melted into the crowd, and then strolled down the hill to Mitchell Trail.

No sense in takin' chances, he said to himself and walked back up the hill past the Presbyterian Church and then headed into the woods toward his hideout on Fox Mountain.

Barton had wanted to case the crowd. It had been getting larger as the day progressed. He figured he could spot his next potential hit, maybe another couple. *I would handle them the same way I handled that couple the other night. They didn't know what hit them,* he thought with a slight grin curling his lips.

He made his way back to the cabin and retrieved his hidden stash of money, piled it onto the table, and began counting it once again. *I'm so damn close,* he thought. *Just one more job and I'm outta here.*

After carefully counting his money, he put it back into the Cameron's pillowcase and placed it in its hidey-hole beneath the cabin floor.

Barton sat at the table remembering what the waitress at the Silver Spur had said. *She'd been a little nosy askin' me about some guy named Dewayne. She even said I sure looked like that Dewayne. He must have a beard, too. I don't need to be attracting any more attention like that.*

He decided he would shave off his beard and change his appearance some. *Maybe I'll go to Tractor Supply and get me a new hat, too, and maybe even a pair of them brown overalls.*

He uncovered his hidden truck and drove as quietly as he could down the hill to Mountain View Road, and then down Highway 115 toward Statesville.

CHAPTER 70

THE RADIO IN the old truck didn't work and the quiet helped Barton think about his next move as he drove to Statesville. He soon pulled into the Walmart parking lot rather happy with himself. Inside the store, he picked up a pair of scissors, a pack of disposable razors, and a can of Gillette Foamy. The Saturday crowd slowed him down at the check out line, but he remained calm and did nothing to draw attention to himself.

Hearing his stomach growl reminded him it was time to eat. Barton decided to grab a bite at the K & W Cafeteria next to the Tractor Supply Company. The line stretched down a long, narrow corridor before it reached the serving stations. He was not expecting anything like this; he was used to fast food restaurants. His turn finally came to pick up a tray and place it on a stainless steel tray-slide that ran the length of, what seemed like to him, a mile of food. The man in front of him picked up silverware wrapped in a napkin and placed it on his tray. Barton followed suit.

When it came to the food Barton had trouble making up his mind—there were so many choices. He usually ate burgers and fries, so the huge selection of food on display confused him. A child behind him in line asked his mother, "Why don't that man make up his mind, Mommy, I'm hungry?"

Barton bit his lip to keep from saying something to the little boy; instead he quickly picked up a bowl of red Jello and some coleslaw. An array of hot vegetables came next. A lady behind the counter, wearing a hairnet, asked him if she could help him. Since Barton was not used to making all these decisions just for food, he hurriedly chose macaroni and cheese and pinto beans. The crowd behind him pushed him along to the meat choices. He was sweating by the time he got to the desserts where he chose a large piece of chocolate pie topped with whipped cream. Beverages were next and he picked up a glass of iced tea and quickly paid for his meal and found a seat.

Barton was totally out of his element. By the time he found an empty table in the corner of the dining area and sat down, he noticed he was out of breath. He sat without eating for a minute and looked around the restaurant at the large crowd of people enjoying their meals. There were scores of senior citizens, single moms trying to force-feed their squalling children, and a few men in business suits with napkins placed across their laps. He saw groups of professional women dressed in suits, farmers, and even a few construction workers who were shoveling down food like there was no tomorrow.

Barton felt as if everyone was looking at him. *I gotta get outta this place,* he thought. *I can't stand all this fancy stuff.* He picked up his tea glass and took a big swallow of the amber liquid and almost spit it out on the table. *This damn tea ain't even sweet,* he cursed. He looked around and saw a small counter loaded with several bottles of ketchup, Texas Pete, and A-1 Steak Sauce. Sugar and artificial sweetener in packets were stuffed into three small containers. Barton grabbed a handful of sugar packets and went back to his table where he summarily dumped several of them into his tea. He tasted it and found it suitable and finally began eating his meal.

Barton had always liked sweets and could hardly wait to dig into the chocolate pie. One bite of the pie made him wish he had gotten two pieces. *That's the best pie I ever ate in my life,* he thought.

Feeling calmer after eating, Barton left the restaurant and went to Tractor Supply.

Again he was overwhelmed by the large selection of merchandise. He hated making decisions. Barton eventually chose a pair of brown Carhart overalls, another pair of jeans, and a new Justin cowboy hat. His old hat was black and the new cream-colored straw hat along with the overalls would greatly alter his appearance. He paid for his merchandise and hurried to the truck.

Back at the cabin, Barton took the scissors to his straggly beard, then lathered his face with Gillette Foamy, and began scraping off the whiskers. After he finished, he studied his image in a piece of a broken mirror and said, "Hell, I hardly recognize myself now."

CHAPTER 71

THE MOORESVILLE BUNCH, as they had grown to call themselves, sat around one of the large tables in the Silver Spur, visiting with Charlie and Beth Nance and Wish Phillips.

It was the first time the ladies had met Beth and they talked nonstop while Charlie and Wish just looked at one another and smiled or nodded once in a while. Beth had often participated in barrel racing and was explaining the event to Joanie.

"Hell, didn't anybody explain it like that to me before" Joanie said. "I'll know what to look for now."

Everybody was laughing at Joanie and took no notice when a man walked up and peered over the batwing doors. He fixed his intense gaze on Marci McLeod.

Marci, caught up in the laughter, did not see him staring at her and her family.

The man drew back from the door when Jennie Foster came out of the kitchen. "Hi, Dewayne," she called out.

Marci looked up toward the door just in time to see the back of a cowboy in a cream-colored hat turn and walk away. *Dewayne looks a little different today,* she thought.

That nosy waitress had mistaken him again for that Dewayne person and it was beginning to grate on Barton's nerves. He walked briskly to the end of the main street and then made his way down the embankment toward the arena where horses were being unloaded from trailers hitched to four-door pickup trucks.

"How's it goin', Dewayne?" a cowboy wearing a black hat called out to Barton as he threaded his way through the crowd. Barton gave him a slight nod and quickened his pace toward Mitchell Trail and the woods.

Barton was sweating profusely by the time he entered the tree-covered hills. There was no actual trail to the cabin. Barton was constantly battling low-hanging limbs and spider webs as he hiked through the woods. *Hell, who is Dewayne and why does everyone think he's me? Just one more job, dammit, just one more and I'm gettin' outta here.*

After the trek through the woods, even the dilapidated cabin looked good. He threw himself on the mattress and thought about Dewayne Allison. Two times today, he had been mistaken for him. *Hell, I shaved my beard off and they still think I look like him. Who in the hell is this Dewayne?*

CHAPTER 72

DEWAYNE ALLISON WAS BUSY these days doing small repair jobs for the residents of Love Valley. He was happy in his new life and enjoyed being a positive influence around town. There was always someone needing his help. That afternoon, he repaired a leaky faucet for Angela Chapman at the General Store before walking down to the arena to see if Charlie needed help getting ready for the rodeo. He was told that Charlie had to run to Andy's Hardware and would be back later, so Dewayne decided to get something to eat.

He was passing by the stockyard when Jim Pennel, sitting on the stock pen railing, yelled to him. "Where in the hell were you goin' a little while ago?"

Dewayne sauntered over to the man and said, "What're you talkin' about, Jim?"

"You took off up Mitchell Trail like there was a ghost after you."

Caught by surprise at this accusation, Dewayne stared the cowboy in the eye and said, "Do what?"

"You mean to tell me you didn't take off like a striped-ass-ape up that hill right there?" Pennel said pointing toward Mitchell Trail.

"I swear I didn't."

"Well, you must have a twin."

"You know, you ain't the first one that's said somethin' about seein' me somewhere I wasn't. Did this guy have a beard?"

"No, he didn't. I told you, he looked just like you."

Dewayne said, "I just shaved off my beard the other day, so nobody would think I was somebody else."

"Well I'll be dogged if that don't beat all," the cowboy said as he removed his hat and wiped his brow with the back of his hand.

Dewayne replied, "It's kinda upsettin' if you ask me. Now the doggoned dude's done gone and shaved his beard off, too. I don't know what to do next."

Jim said with a grin, "You could always shave your head."

"You ain't no help a'tall," Dewayne said as he left the arena and continued walking up the hill toward town. He pushed his way into the Silver Spur and sat down heavily at the nearest empty table.

Jennie quickly came over and said, "Hey, Dewayne, why didn't you come in earlier when I waved at you?"

"Not you, too?" Dewayne was not amused.

"Not me, too, what?"

"Jim Pennel just told me that he saw me at the arena, but it wasn't me! What's happenin' here, Jennie? Has all that beer done pickled my brain?"

Jennie stared at him for a minute. "I heard you'd quit drinking and that's a good thing, but you're acting mighty strange right now."

"There's somebody in town that looks like me and it's gettin' on my nerves—people tellin' me they saw me when I know they didn't!"

"What can you do about it?"

"I got no idea."

"You want something to eat since you're here?" Jennie asked.

"I guess a hamburger and a Pepsi," Dewayne said, "maybe that'll make me feel better."

After Jennie headed for the kitchen, Marci McLeod pulled up a chair and sat down at Dewayne's table. "What's goin' on, Dewayne? You sound upset."

"Hey, Detective," he said. "I just don't know what's goin' on, that's the problem. I don't know if somebody's impersonatin' me or just happens to look like me, or what. There was somebody wanderin' around town that looked like me when I had that straggly-lookin' beard, so I shaved the thing off. Now, there's somebody that looks like me when I don't have no beard. It's gettin' on my nerves."

"Do you have any idea who it could be?"

"They ain't from around here, that's for sure," Dewayne said.

"I thought I saw you at the door earlier," Marci said, "why didn't you come on in?"

"I wasn't at the door. I was at the General Store fixing a faucet for Angela. I went down to the hardware store to get some washers. Ask Andy; he'll tell you I was there."

"Oh, boy," Marci said. "There really is a dead-ringer walking around Love Valley that looks just like you."

"That's what I've been tellin' everybody," Dewayne said.

"I tell you what, Dewayne," Marci promised, "I'll try to find the man who looks like you and ask him a few questions. Love Valley is not that big, I'm bound to run into him sooner or later.

I want to know where he's from and why, or if, he's trying to impersonate you. It may just be a coincidence that he shaved his beard off about the same time you did. If that's the case, I can't do anything about that."

"I understand," Dewayne said, "and thank you. It's just got me a little rattled right now."

"You just take it easy, Dewayne, and keep drinking those Pepsis and let the other stuff alone, okay?"

"I will and thanks."

When Marci returned to her table, Jake asked, "What was that all about? Is he still giving you trouble?"

"Oh no, nothing like that, Dewayne and I are friends now."

"Friends?"

"Yes, we have an understanding. I had him on the short list as a suspect in the murders, but he's been eliminated completely. Besides that, Dewayne's quit drinking and has gone on the straight and narrow. He's really a pretty nice guy. That alcohol was the reason I had a problem with him before. It had affected his thinking, but I think he's going to be alright now. He's rattled now because somebody in Love Valley looks just like him. I think he's afraid the lookalike might do something that he will be blamed for."

"Do you believe him?" Jake asked.

"Yes I do," Marci said. "I do believe him and I'm going to find this other man and find out what he's up to. Dewayne needs a couple of breaks and some confidence in the Iredell County Sheriff's Department. He needs to see that we don't just arrest people; we help them out, too."

CHAPTER 73

WHILE BARTON SAT in the ramshackle cabin, he pondered his next move. The pickings were so good in Love Valley, he hated to leave until he had what he thought was enough money to live comfortably without having to work.

Hell, maybe lookin' like this Dewayne feller just might be a good thing. If anyone sees me leavin' the scene of a crime, they might blame it on that poor ol' son of a bitch. Barton laughed out loud and leaned back in his chair. *I think I'll go back to town and watch a little bit of the rodeo from a distance and see what happens.*

He reached for the bottle of Jack Daniels Old #7 he'd brought with him from Galax and guzzled a few swallows. He sat up straight and grimaced as the burn went all the way down to his stomach.

Fortified, he reached for his new hat, and left the cabin. Barton thought about taking his truck, but changed his mind because he was too lazy to uncover it and cover it back up. He figured he'd have trouble finding a parking place anyway and decided to walk.

In twenty minutes, Barton stood in the woods near the windmill at the end of Henry Martin Trail watching the comings and goings of the rodeo crowd trying to be as inconspicuous as possible.

Barton decided to get a closer look at the crowd that had formed at the ticket sales tent. He inched his way down the hill and around the parked trucks and trailers until he could view the line of people waiting to pay.

Now there's some pickins' if I ever seen 'em, he said to himself when he spotted a young good-looking couple dressed to the nines. He followed the two young socialites around to the far side of the arena and sized them up as if he was buying a truck. Jerome had always thought preppies who wore their sweaters draped over their shoulders with the sleeves tied in front thought they were better than anyone else. *They might not be very old, but I'll bet they're loaded!*

Barton followed the couple and got in line behind them. When it was their turn to pay, he watched from the corner of his eye as the man extracted an expensive-looking wallet from the back pocket of his jeans and handed a $100 bill to the lady taking the money.

"Do you have anything smaller?" the woman asked handing the C-note back to him. With a look of frustration, the young man rifled though his wallet and found a $50 bill and handed it to her.

Barton saw the stack of bills in the guy's wallet and saw what looked like several twenties. *Hell he coulda gave her a twenty. That son of a bitch is just trying to act like he's a tycoon. Maybe he'll be the next one I go see. Maybe I'll just have to take him down a peg or two before I bash his brains out, too. He might think he's better than anybody else, but he ain't!*

The couple found a seat near the railing.

"Humph," Barton said as he watched the man clean off the seat for his wife, or girl friend, or whatever the hell she was. *By God, I'll take some of that rich-man-attitude out of him.* He slid in behind them so he could hear their conversation and perhaps find out where they lived.

"Honey, don't you just think this is the neatest place? Look at those two over there," the woman said pointing toward the concession stand where a lady dressed in tight jeans and a checkered shirt was buying a hot dog for a little girl.

"I certainly do see," the man said with appreciation.

She elbowed him and said, "Not her, the teenager dressed up as a cowgirl. I think she is going to compete in the barrel racing event."

"Oh, sorry."

"No you're not. You like looking at beautiful women and I don't blame you, after all, that's why you married me," she said with a seductive smile.

"When we get back to the campground tonight, I'll show you how much I appreciate you," the man said laughing.

"I'll just bet you will," she teased as she looked at him and batted her eyelids.

A sudden gust of wind blew Barton's hat off. "Dammit!" Barton swore and got up to retrieve it. When he returned, he saw the preppie woman staring at him. "Sorry" he said and quickly sat back down.

"Some people," the woman said haughtily.

"Now, Tiffany," the sweater-wearing young man said. "Don't get upset and let a little thing like that spoil our evening."

"Okay, Chip," she replied. "I won't. I promise."

No, Tiffany, you might not, Barton thought as he got up to leave, *but I sure as hell will.*

CHAPTER 74

"WHEN'S THE SHOW goin' to start, Mama?" Meredith asked.

"It's not a show, honey, it's a rodeo."

"Rodeo? What's that?"

"You just wait," Marci told her daughter. "There will be more horses than you have ever seen before and all of them right here in front of us."

"Oh boy! When's it start?" Meredith asked again.

"Right now," Marci said as the announcer called for everyone's attention. His voice was heard over the loudspeakers and the crowd grew quiet. A cowboy in a white hat announced that the parade of flags was about to begin. The spectators turned their attention to the gate at the west end of the arena.

Meredith yelled, "Look, Mama, look!"

Several young girls dressed in their best rodeo regalia rode out on their horses. Some were holding flags that represented the home states of the participating cowboys and cowgirls. The applause grew louder when the cowgirl carrying the American flag raced around the arena with Old Glory flapping in the breeze.

When the horses and riders grew still, the announcer removed his hat and asked that everyone bow their heads.

Meredith frowned and asked, "What happened, Mama?"

"Nothing happened, honey. We're going to have a prayer now."

"Just like at church?"

"Kind of," Marci said, "he's going to pray that no one gets hurt and all goes well. You'll see." Marci looked around at all the bareheaded cowboys and cowgirls who filled the arena and realized tears had welled in her eyes. Meredith grew quiet as she held Marci's hand and they both bowed their heads along with the rest of the crowd.

As soon as the crowd had said a collective, "Amen," the announcer asked that everyone place their hats over their hearts as the cowgirl carrying the American flag rode her horse to the center of the arena. The strains of the National Anthem reverberated through the wooded hills of Love Valley.

"What's wrong, Mama?" Meredith asked. "It looks like you're cryin'."

"Oh nothing, sweetie," Marci said grabbing Meredith's hand and squeezing it tight, "nothing at all."

Jake took Marci's other hand in his and said not a word. He didn't know whether the display of national pride had moved her to tears or if the ongoing murder investigation was becoming too overwhelming for her.

After the anthem, the rodeo participants rode by the stands and Jake held Meredith up high so she could see. Meredith waved at each one as they rode by. She shouted with glee when a young cowgirl rode near them dressed in a white hat and red chaps. "Look at that cowgirl, Daddy. Look! Ain't she pretty?"

"She surely is, Meredith, she surely is," Jake said. Shaking his head, he knew this was not the time to try to get Meredith not to say ain't.

The Mooresville Bunch had never seen a rodeo before and Joanie was almost as excited as Meredith. Even Gail was grinning from ear to ear.

The bareback bronc riding was the first event on the agenda and Jake winced with each gyration of the horses as they threw their hapless riders to the ground with a thud. Only three cowboys rode the required eight seconds. Then the judges, who graded the three riders, tallied their scores, and declared the winner.

Ed Mitchell came over to Jake and asked, "Are you not going to ride one of them little 'horsies' for Meredith, Jake?"

"Are you kidding? There's no way I'm even going to think about it."

James looked over Jake's way and laughed. Jake thought that James must have put Ed up to that ridiculous suggestion when he saw him nod and tip his hat. Jake laughed, too.

"Watch this," Jake said to Marci. "This is the event I want to enter." Suddenly a steer broke from a chute, running at top speed, with a horse and rider beside him to keep him in line while a cowboy dove from his speeding horse, caught the bull by the horns, and twisted him to the ground in a cloud of dust. All this took place in a matter of seconds and the crowd went wild.

Marci looked at Jake with raised eyebrows and said, "Yeah, right. Let me know if and when you're going to do that so I can make sure your insurance is paid up."

"Not to worry," Jake said.

The rodeo was good medicine for Marci. The stress lines had drained from her face.

"You know," Marci said, "these are the best hot dogs I've ever eaten."

"They're the best," Jake said. "Beth made the chili and that's what makes them so good."

"I may have to change my mind about hot dogs after eating this one."

"Will wonders never cease."

Calf roping was next. Marci watched a cowboy throw his lasso around a calf's neck and winced when the calf was jerked around so violently. Jake assured her it did not hurt the animals.

Joanie cheered the cowboys on as they jumped off their horses and quickly threw the calves to the ground and tied three of their legs together for the best time. She didn't understand all of it, but Joanie thoroughly enjoyed watching it.

Saddle bronc riding was next and then team roping where two cowboys roped a running steer. One roped the horns while the other roped the hind feet. At least that was the way it was supposed to go, but a lot of times, the young bull escaped the lassos and ran to the other end of the arena and out the gate to the stock pen.

Marci suddenly felt a chill on the back of her neck as if someone was watching her. She turned, and at first glance, saw only the crowd of happy rodeo fans. But then she looked directly behind her and saw a man in a straw cowboy hat who greatly resembled Dewayne Allison. He was scurrying up the hill behind the arena toward town.

She turned to Jake and said, "Watch Meredith, I gotta go to the bathroom."

Surprised by Marci's sudden departure, she'd just taken Meredith to the bathroom a few minutes earlier, Jake turned in time to see her racing up the hill toward the main street. *Where in the world is she going?*

CHAPTER 75

MARCI WAS PANTING for breath when she reached the dusty street of the downtown. She searched the plank sidewalk and the street. No sign of the Dewayne Allison lookalike. *Where could he have gone?* Marci poked her head in the Silver Spur and saw Jennie sitting at a table talking to the owners, Bob and Judy. She gave them a cursory wave and said, "I was just looking for somebody."

Marci continued down the sidewalk to the General Store where she found the owner, Angela Chapman, sitting with Sue Ladislaw, her cook, at one of their tables. Angela called out, "Come on in and chat. Everybody else is down at the rodeo."

"Wish I could," Marci said. "I was just looking for someone."

"Nobody here but us," Angela replied.

"Thanks, I'll be back by with the family later," Marci said and hurried down the street to the celebrated Love Valley watering hole, Jack's Place. Jack and Linda Jolly were stocking the cooler with beer when Marci walked in.

"Hi, Detective," Jack greeted. "Can I get you anything?"

"Uh, no thanks, Jack," Marci said as she looked around the empty bar. She frowned and asked, "Has anyone been in here in the last few minutes?"

"No, we're just getting ready for the rodeo crowd. We should be pretty busy tonight. Tori's comin' in to help. I don't know what we'd do without her."

"Thanks," Marci said. "See you later." She walked out onto the boardwalk and looked across the street at the Tack Shop. Mutt Burgess was sitting on the bench in front of his store and she walked over and plopped down beside him.

"What's wrong, Detective?" he asked. "You look like you just lost your best friend."

"Something about like that, I guess," Marci said. She slowed her breathing and asked, "Did you just see a man come by here a while ago that looked like Dewayne Allison?"

"Yeah, I saw Dewayne. He was moving the fastest I've ever seen him move. He looked like he was running from something or somebody. I waved at him, but he acted like he didn't even know me. I just thought he was gettin' a little stuck-up since he quit his drinkin'."

Marci turned to Burgess in all seriousness and said, "That was not Dewayne, Mutt. Somebody up here looks just like him and I'd really like to talk to him."

"You gotta be kiddin' me," Mutt said. "Why would anybody want to look like Dewayne Allison? I could think of a hell of a lot of people I'd rather look like than Dewayne."

"I know, it's a long story. I'll tell you all about it later," Marci said. "Did you see where he went?"

"Yeah, he turned the corner at Andy's house and ran down Tori Pass. I can't tell you where he went from there."

"Thanks, Mutt."

"And that's another strange thing," Mutt said. "I ain't ever seen Dewayne Allison in a hurry before. He was running."

"Sorry, Mutt, it's like I said, that wasn't Dewayne."

"Right, I forgot, but he sure as hell looked like him."

Marci walked up to Tori Pass and gave it a glance, knowing that it was unlikely she would see the imposter. He could have turned in either direction at the bottom of the hill. She returned to the dusty, deserted street and walked slowly back toward the arena thinking about what had just happened. *He just disappeared. Am I losing it or what? Maybe it is time I call it quits. I can't even keep up with one damn cowboy without losing him.*

Marci stood at the top of the hill looking over the crowd watching the rodeo. She saw Jake and Meredith laughing at Charlie Nance in his clown get-up in the middle of the arena. She drew a deep breath, exhaled, and made her way back to her seat.

"Where you been, Mama?" Meredith asked as Marci sat down.

"Oh, I had an errand to run. Did I miss anything?"

"You missed Charlie bein' a clown."

"I saw him while I was walking back. He's funny, isn't he?"

"Yep" Meredith answered laughing and turned her attention back to the action.

Jake said nothing for a minute and then turned to Marci, "Are you okay, sweetheart?"

"Yeah, I'm alright. I felt like someone was staring at me and when I turned around I saw Dewayne's lookalike running up the hill."

Jake asked, "Did you catch up with him?"

"No, I lost him."

"Please be careful, Marci. You don't know anything about this man," Jake said. "Don't let this ruin our evening. Just watch the rest of the rodeo and try to have a good time."

Marci turned her attention back to the arena, but her thoughts were elsewhere.

Barton knew the detective had been following him and he'd hidden behind horses tied to hitching rails along Main Street until he could get to Tori Pass and back on Mitchell Trail.

What is it with that damn woman? Is she some kind of psychic or what? She can't know who I am. Maybe she just thinks I'm that damned Dewayne person. He walked up Mitchell Trail toward the woods behind the Presbyterian Church.

He calmed down when he realized she was no longer following him. His thoughts returned to the sweater-wearing couple at the rodeo.

CHAPTER 76

HALF-TIME INTERMISSION was coming to a close and even though Jake had asked her to enjoy the rodeo, Marci could think of nothing but the elusive imposter. Finally, she turned to Jake. "I think I'm losing it, darling."

"What're you talkin' about, losing it?"

"I just told you that I thought I saw Dewayne Allison's imposter staring at me. I could just sense the man drilling holes in the back of my head. I turned around and there he was, high-tailing it up the hill toward town."

"Well that doesn't mean you're losing it, just because you thought a man was staring at you."

"He *was* staring at me," Marci said.

A cheer went up from the crowd and they turned their attention to the cowboy who was trying his best to hold on while riding on the back of a two thousand pound, twisting, spinning, and bucking bull. If the rider could hang on and not be thrown off for a full eight seconds, he was in the running for the prize money.

Jake jumped up when he saw the cowboy thrown high in the air and hit the ground in a cloud of dust. The snorting, slobbering bull spun around quickly and pawed the ground and then charged the prostrate cowboy who was trying to get up. The ever-ready bullfighters came to the rescue by jumping directly into the bull's path, yelling and waving their arms frantically at the angry animal.

The cowboy was helped off the field while the raging bull turned on the bullfighters and chased them toward the center of the arena where Charlie Nance, the rodeo clown, was waving wildly at the enraged animal. The bull stopped, lowered his head, and charged toward Charlie. Nance quickly jumped into the waiting barrel that he used for exactly this type of situation. From there, he made faces at the mad bull until the animal was just mere feet from him and then he ducked down out of sight. Charlie's actions seemed to make the bull even angrier and it bore down on the barrel with all its might and sent it and Charlie flying through the air.

The two bullfighters waved at the bull until it turned and chased them toward the awaiting open gate. They scampered up the railing of the bucking chute just as the bull arrived. Seeing that his tormenters were out of his reach, the animal trotted through the open gate that was quickly closed behind him.

The rodeo staff ran to the barrel just as Charlie crawled out. He waved to the cheering crowd and dusted himself off. Jake shook his head and marveled at the courage of the bull riders and rodeo clowns.

"You could always get a job like that," he said to Marci.

She elbowed him and said, "Sometimes I wish I had another job. I'm not sure if I have what it takes any more. I let one damn cowboy get away from me. One damn cowboy."

Jake squeezed her hand, "Listen, McLeod, you've still got it and don't you forget it. You're the best detective Iredell County has and they know it, or you wouldn't be the lead dog on this murder case."

"I know, but sometimes I get so frustrated. I've been wondering if this imposter has something to do with these killings. It's so strange that he keeps showing up and keeps changing his looks. I don't even know if he realizes he looks like Dewayne Allison, but it's sure grating on my nerves."

"Detective McLeod!"

Marci heard her name being called from somewhere in the stands behind her. She turned and saw Dewayne Allison and Shorty Parsons making their way down through the crowd toward her. "Right here, Dewayne. Come on down."

"Detective—" Dewayne began, trying to catch his breath. "We hoped we could find you up here."

"What can I do for you, Dewayne?"

"I saw him."

"Saw who?"

"I just saw that man that looks just like me. It scared the bejesus out of me, too."

"You haven't been drinking, have you, Dewayne?" Marci asked.

"No, I swear I ain't; I just had a hamburger and a Pepsi. Ain't that right, Shorty?"

Shorty agreed with Dewayne; neither one of them had had a drink and were cold sober.

"Describe him to me," Marci said.

"Are you not payin' attention?" Dewayne said. "I said he looks just like me!"

Marci was a little embarrassed at this and said, "I'm sorry, Dewayne, that's just one of the first things we always ask. Did you get a good look at what he was he wearing?"

"He was wearing a straw hat with a high crown, a blue shirt, and blue jeans."

Marci's attention was piqued now. "Did you see where he went?"

"Yeah, we did. Didn't we Shorty?" The little man nodded in agreement.

"Go on," Marci encouraged.

"Well, Shorty and me were down at the pens and there he came as big as life, hot-footin' it up toward the church."

"Then where did he go?"

"He kept lookin' back down the hill toward the arena, like he was checkin' to see if somebody was followin' him and then he cut in behind the church and disappeared into the woods."

"Great work, Dewayne. We're gonna get this man and see what he's up to, I promise."

"I hope so. I really hope so," Dewayne said. He was sweating heavily in the spring night and removed his hat to wipe his forehead. "I hated to bother you, Detective, but I thought you'd like to know."

"You did the right thing, Dewayne. I did want to know."

"Well, we'll let you get back to the rodeo."

"Who was that man, Mama?" asked Meredith.

"He's just a friend of ours," Marci answered.

"I like his hat," Meredith said and turned her attention back to the action in the arena.

Dewayne Allison sported a straw hat with a high crown, not unlike the one Jerome Barton was wearing.

CHAPTER 77

BARTON THOUGHT ABOUT the detective on the way back through the woods to his cabin. *She's even more beautiful than I remembered. After I get all the money from those two preppies, I'll have to see what I can do about her.*

Suddenly a terrific headache clouded Barton's thinking and he sat down on a moss-covered log to gather his thoughts. He cradled his head in his hands as his mind raced. *What's wrong with me? Why did she follow me into town. I ain't done nothin' she knows about yet.*

These things bothered him, yet he was still compelled to carry out his plan. The way he looked at it, the size of the potential score from the rich couple outweighed the risks. It was a chance he would just have to take.

He slashed his way through the woods to Fox Mountain Road and stopped at the edge of the trees. Barton looked both ways to see if anyone were coming up the dirt road. Satisfied, he continued across the road and made it safely to his cabin.

He threw himself onto the chair and panted with relief. After catching his breath, he lit the kerosene lamp that sat on the table. He then picked up the bottle of Jack Daniels and took two gulps and coughed. *Damn that's good stuff.* Barton wiped his mouth with the sleeve of his dirty shirt and thought some more about that young, preppie couple staying in the campground. *The rodeo should be over soon and I'll see if I can find them and follow them back to the campground. I hope they didn't leave the rodeo early. The way they were talkin' about what they was goin' to do to each other, got me hot just listenin' to 'em.*

Barton had never experienced any kind of meaningful relationship with a woman. He'd had a one-night stand or two, but was vastly inexperienced sexually. He often had dreams of what he would like to do with various women. He had seen some magazines during his short tenure at the glass and mirror factory in Galax where his mother had gotten him a job. But he hated it and left after only a few weeks. One of the guys he worked with had brought the magazines to work one day and let Jerome take a look at the pictures.

He was becoming more aroused just thinking about those old magazines. *Boy, I'd like to have that redheaded detective for just one night. The things I could do with her.*

A sudden noise distracted him. *What was that?* Barton jumped up from his chair, blew out the kerosene lamp, and peered out the dirty window. He saw nothing but darkness. He listened again for the sound. He then pulled the door open ever so slightly and peeked through the crack and still nothing was visible but the swaying trees. Suddenly and without warning a bone chilling sound made the hairs rise on the back of his neck and he shivered as he closed the door.

A mournful howl reverberated through the Brushy Mountain woods and Jerome Barton reached for another slug of Jack

Daniels. He sat alone in the cold, dark cabin. *That ain't nothin' but that damned old dog of Uncle Bud's.*

He took one last swallow of whiskey, picked up the tire iron, and headed out the door.

CHAPTER 78

"**I**'M TIRED OF WATCHING bull riding," Tiffany said as she reached over and massaged Chip's thigh with her ring-laden hand. She knew how much he liked that.

"So, what do you have in mind?" Chip Davenport said to his young, blond, buxom wife.

She answered him with a coy smile, "C'mon and I'll show you."

Davenport helped her up from the dusty, wooden seat and brushed the seat of her jeans off very slowly with his hand. "How's that," he said with a smile.

"Very nice," she said winking at him. She was in a good mood and could not wait to get back to their motorhome in the campground.

Barton had arrived back at the rodeo just in time to watch the couple leave. He saw the man brushing the dust from the rear of his wife's jeans.

Damn. Look at him. He's takin' his danged time running his hand over her ass. I'd do more 'n that if I ever had her alone, but I think I'd rather have that detective, damn, she's forevermore one good lookin' woman.

The couple walked up the incline toward town clinging to each other like they were teenagers in heat. Barton hung in the shadows and followed them. When they reached the main street, they stopped within twenty feet from him and kissed each other. The man fondled the woman and tried to drag her into the shadow where Barton was hiding, but she protested. "Just wait until we get to the RV," she whispered and then nipped him on the ear with her teeth to tease him even more. She then sucked his ear lobe in her mouth. "You like that?" she asked.

"You big tease," he said. "Just wait 'til I get you on that king sized bed."

She grabbed her husband playfully by the arm and continued toward to the campground. They were completely oblivious of anyone around them. Their desire to please each other was all they cared about.

Barton followed them at a distance in the shadows of the overhanging roof that covered the plank sidewalk. They continued their banter through the main part of town and then turned left into the campground. Barton had to speed up when they entered the campground to see which campsite was theirs.

When they stopped in front of their luxurious motorhome, Chip tried to reach into his pocket for the door keys, but Tiffany's hand was there first. She played with him through his pocket before withdrawing the keys and dangling them before his eyes. "These are the keys to happiness," she teased, "and it awaits your highness beyond the portal." Chip laughed heartily at Tiffany's jesting and took the keys from her and unlocked the door.

Barton knew that women often scream when something unexpected frightens them, so he decided to take care of her first. He walked unsteadily toward them to give the impression he was drunk and weaved his way up to where they stood. He mumbled some unintelligible words as he drew near.

"Whatdaya want?" Chip snapped at Barton for the interruption.

Without a single word, Barton swung the tire iron he had hidden behind him and crushed the side of Tiffany Davenport's skull so hard that blood and brain matter splattered into her husband's face. Chip Davenport was too astonished to utter a sound, but tried to catch his falling wife before she crumpled to the gravel drive.

Barton struck the man in the back of the head as he bent over to catch his wife. The entire double murder took less than ten seconds. The murderer opened the door to the motorhome and dragged the two bodies inside. He peered out the door to make sure no one had witnessed the crime and shut and locked the door and turned on the lights.

Breathing heavily after having to drag the bodies inside the motorhome, Barton sat on the leather couch and surveyed his surroundings. The opulence impressed him immediately. "Damn!" he said aloud. "Just look at this place. They must be loaded." He chuckled and then said, "They used to be loaded. Now they ain't got jack."

He sat there for a minute catching his breath. This was not the time for mistakes. He rose from the couch and found a washcloth beside the sink and washed the blood off his hands and face and then opened the door and looked outside. A small amount of blood had spattered onto the side of the motorhome. Barton rinsed out the cloth and quickly wiped the blood off the exterior surface of the RV.

Back inside, he began searching for cash and jewelry or anything of value that he could carry back to the cabin without raising suspicion. The master bedroom was at the rear, so he started there. He opened the nightstand drawer and found a Smith and Wesson .357 revolver, which he held up to the light and admired. *Well, what have we here?* He stuck the pistol into the waist of his jeans and continued his search. He found a lady's jewelry box on the shelf in the closet. He crammed the contents into his pockets, quite satisfied with his discovery. *Boy, people just don't have a clue. They think just because they stick stuff up on a shelf, no one will ever find it. How dumb can you be?*

Barton went back to the kitchen and den area where the bodies lay in a heap and began rifling through the victim's pockets. He withdrew the man's wallet and found nine hundred and thirty-five dollars in cash and an assortment of credit cards. He stuffed the cards and cash into his pockets and began looking through the kitchen cabinets.

There wasn't much food in the pantry, just some canned vegetables and the like. He was moving the cans around looking for cash when he discovered a can of Campbell Soup that was not as heavy as the others. His hands shook with anticipation as he lifted the lid. Inside the can was a huge roll of cash. *Man, these people must have been selling drugs to have this kind of cash,* he thought. Barton thrust the can into his jacket pocket and looked around to see if he had missed anything—then he saw the ring sparkling on Tiffany's hand. He pulled it from her finger and added it to his spoils.

The thief then turned off the lights. "No sense in burning electricity when there ain't nobody home to enjoy it," he said aloud and then laughed.

Barton slowly opened the door and looked both ways. The campground was dark except for the occasional security light. He saw no one, so he stepped down from the RV, pulled the door closed, and smiled when he heard the lock catch. For the first time, Barton noticed the shiny, black Hummer H2 SUV parked in the corresponding parking place. *Damn! Where do these young people get all their money?* Shaking his head, he clung to the shadows as he made his way back out of the campground. The only sign of life the thief saw was an old man walking a dog near the end of the road, so he took a circuitous route toward town and then through the woods to his cabin.

As he reached the door to his ramshackle abode, another mournful howl arose from somewhere deep in the woods. Just hearing it sent shivers down Barton's spine. He could not help but wonder if it could have been his uncle's dog sending him a message. In a barely audible whisper Jerome Barton spoke, "Leave me alone, Uncle Bud; and take your damn dog with you." With that, he hurried inside the cabin and closed the door behind him.

CHAPTER 79

THE RODEO ENDED and the crowd filed out of the arena. Some of the spectators went to their trucks and cars parked nearby while others trekked up the hill in single file toward town. Small children, with their heads collapsed on their parent's shoulders, slept soundly as they were carried to their awaiting car seats. Some of the older folks often stepped to the side and let the younger, faster crowd hurry by. One older gentleman was heard saying, "Why did God waste all that energy on young people, we're the ones that need it." He laughed and stopped to catch his breath as if just quoting the old adage took all the energy he had left.

The Mooresville Bunch stood and stretched their muscles. "Dang, that was fun," Joanie exclaimed and then leaned toward Jake and added, "see there, I didn't say damn one time, ain't you proud of me?"

Jake laughed, "Joanie, you'll never change, I don't even

know why I try."

"It really ain't much use, Jake. I can't help it. It's just the way I am."

"I know," Jake said. "Do me a favor and just be Joanie and don't worry about it anymore."

"Hot dang," Joanie agreed, "I can do that."

"Did you like the rodeo, Carson?" Debbie asked.

"I certainly did. I can't remember when I've had so much fun. Just being a part of the Mooresville Bunch is fun in itself."

"We all get a little crazy when we get together," Gail said, "even James lets his hair down once in a while."

Jake, carrying his daughter up the hill to town, noticed that Marci had not joined them. He turned and saw her still standing near their seats, looking down at the arena. He called out to her and Marci waved back and then began walking up the hill to join them. Jake was waiting for her when she reached the top of the hill.

The excitement in Marci's voice was unmistakable when she reached Jake. "It's him," Marci said. "I know it's him and he's been here all along."

"Who's him? What're you talking about?"

"Jerome Barton. He's still here in Love Valley. He's the one that looks like Dewayne Allison. He's been watching me, too, sizing me up, seeing what he's dealing with."

"God, Marci. Are you sure?"

"I'd stake my career on it," Marci said.

"You've got to be careful, darling. Do you think he'll hit again?" Jake asked.

"I surely do and I don't think it'll be much longer before he does. He's staging now. I don't think he does it just for the money any longer. I think he enjoys the moment. The death blow, the sense of power he has over his victims gives him a rush."

"Do you know this for sure or are you just guessing?" Jake

asked.

"Call it a gut feeling if you will, but that SOB is here and I'm going to get his ass. Now let's go home," she said emphatically.

Jake and Marci caught up with the rest of the group and Joanie asked, "What were you guys doing back there, makin' plans for later tonight?"

"You're absolutely right, Joanie," Marci said and put her arm around Jake.

They all talked about the rodeo and Charlie Nance's antics during the intermission.

"It almost scared the shit out of me when that bull hit the barrel Charlie was hidin' in!" Joanie said. They all laughed as usual at Joanie and continued trekking up the hill to their respective vehicles.

Everyone had gone, but Marci, Jake, and Meredith. Jake buckled Meredith into her car seat and closed the door. He and Marci leaned against the car for a minute and talked further about the murders until Jake finally said, "Come on, darling, let's go home and have a perfect ending to a wonderful day."

"Okay," Marci said, "but by God I'm coming back and I'm gonna find that son of a bitch!"

"It's a good thing Meredith's asleep or she would've heard her mama cuss like Joanie," Jake said laughing.

"What'd I say?"

"Nothing, honey, you're just keyed up. It doesn't matter anyway. You'll get your man. But right now, what're you gonna do with the one you already have?" Jake teased.

"You're right, let's go home. I am keyed up and I think you should take advantage of the adrenalin rush before I lose it," Marci said with eagerness. "It's just like Scarlett O'Hara said, 'Tomorrow's another day!'"

CHAPTER 80

Barton REMOVED the Davenports' pistol from his jeans and laid it on the table. *That might come in handy some day,* he thought. *But, so far, the tire iron has worked just fine.* Barton liked the feel of it in his hand—the sense of power it gave him. He liked the rush he got when he felt the victim's skull give way from the force of his blow. *Why use a noisy gun when a tire iron gets the job done. I might need the guns at some point, but right now, I'm doin' fine.*

He knelt and removed the board from the floor of the cabin and retrieved the pillowcase filled with stolen cash and placed it on the table. Barton sat down at the table and fished the fake Campbell Soup can out of his jacket pocket, unscrewed the lid, and pulled out a huge wad of hundred dollar bills.

"Damn, look at the cash those dudes had," he said aloud as he unrolled the bills and began straightening them out on the table. "Man, look at that pile of C-notes," he said. Jerome divided the cash into neat stacks of $10,000 each and figured that he was nearing a hundred thousand dollars in cash. *By God, I can leave Love Valley just about anytime I want to now,* he thought. *But there's just one more thing I'd like to do first.*

His thoughts returned to the beautiful detective with the red hair and hot body.

CHAPTER 81

"SHE'S SOUND ASLEEP," Marci said as she quietly closed the door to Meredith's bedroom. "She's had an eventful day to say the least."

"That is one happy little girl," Jake said. "I'll never forget the look on her face when she realized that Freckles really belonged to her."

"I still can't believe you bought a horse, Jake McLeod," Marci said as he opened their bedroom door for her.

"Nothing is too good for the women in my life," he said as he pulled Marci's warm body next to his.

She pushed the door closed and looped her arms around his neck and kissed him hard, "You're something special, Jake McLeod; did you know that?"

"And so are you."

Marci broke from his embrace and began removing her clothes very slowly. As each piece fell to the floor, Jake grew more and more aroused. "You see what you're doing to me, don't you?"

"That's the plan," Marci teased, "and I see that it's working."

By the time her bra had joined the pile of clothing at her feet, Jake was already undressed and caressing her body. He wrapped her in his arms and they stood naked beside the bed kissing each other hard. Jake began kissing Marci's body all over, sending shivers up and down her spine. She took his head in her hands and guided his mouth to her breasts. A gasp emitted from her lips when he began kissing her hardening nipples.

"Jake McLeod," she whispered softly, "I remember now why I married you."

He gave a muffled laugh and then with slow deliberation began lightly swirling his tongue over the end of each nipple. Marci ran her fingers through his hair and closed her eyes as she relished the touch of his mouth against her breasts. "Don't you ever forget how to do that," she said breathing heavily. "That feels so good," she whimpered. "I'll give you twenty minutes to stop doing that."

"I don't think you can last that long," Jake said as he looked up into her eyes.

"I don't either," Marci agreed and took Jake's hand. "Let's lie down between the sheets, Mr. McLeod, and see what comes up."

Morning came early the next day. Marci had risen and made coffee before Jake stumbled into the kitchen.

He greeted her with a kiss, "Hi, beautiful."

"Hi, yourself," Marci said with a smile. "How're you doin'?"

"I'm doing okay for an old man. One of these days you're gonna kill me. I don't know how many more nights I can take like that one last night."

Marci hugged him, "What's the matter, Big Boy? Can't you

take it anymore?"

"Oh, I can take it alright, but I'll be damned if I can give it like I used to do," Jake said and laughed.

"Poor boy, do you want me to put on some help?"

Jake slapped her fanny with his hand, "Not yet. Not as long as I'm still breathing."

"Let me tell you something, Jake McLeod," Marci said seriously, "there is not a thing wrong with you!"

Jake laughed, "You mean, I'm still doing alright?"

"Alright, you're the one that's gonna kill me."

A surprised look came on Jake's face. He broke into a wide grin. "Well, I'll be damned. I've still got it going on, huh?"

"I love you, Jake McLeod. Don't ever change. You're a wonderful man even though you do some foolish things now and then."

"Like what?"

"Like buying a damn horse, for one thing," she said pouring him a cup of coffee. "Here, you look like you need this," and handed him the steaming cup.

"Thank you," Jake said, taking the coffee. He blew on it and took a sip. "You know as well as I do that Freckles is going to bring much happiness into that little girl's life."

"I'm just kidding, honey. I know it will. Shut up and kiss me, I gotta go to work. We have some unsolved murders, you know."

"How well I know," Jake said, "Do you think that new equipment the department got will help you?"

"We haven't had a chance to try it out yet. We just got it this week."

"Tell me again how it works?"

"The DeltaSphere 3000 3D Scene Vision program produces a 360 degree view of any scene. It has a camera that will feed images right into our laptop in high resolution."

"How will that help you?"

"It will give us something much better to show jurors when we get to court. It will be much better than just a video tape or still photographs."

"Technology gets better each day," Jake said.

"It really does," Marci agreed. "But even with the advanced technology, it's hard to stay a step ahead of the criminals."

"That's so true," Jake said.

CHAPTER 82

BARTON HUNG AROUND the cabin for three days thinking about what he was going to do next. The image of the beautiful detective with red hair kept haunting him. She was all that was on his mind. Even though he now had enough money to leave Love Valley, he could not make himself do it. He had to get a closer look at the detective and that meant going back to town. He knew she was tenacious and that she would not give up until the murders were solved, so he figured she would be in back in Love Valley soon. He would just have to enter the town, stay in the shadows, and wait for her. He ached to see her again. He grew more restless each day. *I want just one chance to be alone with her and then I'll hightail it out of the country.*

Barton hiked through the woods to his battered truck and removed the limbs he had used to camouflage it. He threw the last limb from the hood and climbed inside. Everything looked the same. He placed the key into the ignition and turned it.

Nothing happened. Zilch! He turned it again. Same results! "Damn," he swore. "I don't need this!"

Barton climbed out of the truck and threw open the hood and peered inside. It looked as if animals had been chewing on the wiring. "It ain't no wonder the damn thing won't start," he complained loudly. He then closed the hood with a bang and threw his new hat to the ground and swore. "Why does all this shit happen to me?" Barton kicked the dirt with the toe of his boot and hit a root hidden beneath the surface. "Ouch, dammit," he hollered as he hopped around on the other foot.

The door of the truck was standing ajar and Barton pulled himself back inside and sat there gathering his thoughts. He realized that he was stuck in Love Valley until he could boost a vehicle and that made him even madder. Getting the truck fixed was out of the question. There was no way he could bring a mechanic up there in the woods. It was definitely an unexpected glitch in his plans.

Barton climbed out of the truck, walked around to the front, and kicked the tire with a vengeance. "Damn, damn, double damn," he hollered when he realized he'd used the same foot to kick the root.

"Think, dammit, think," he said aloud. "What the hell am I gonna do now with no wheels?"

Stealing a vehicle while still in Love Valley had definitely not been the idea. He had planned on driving this old truck to South Carolina and stealing a truck there. Then he would head on to Florida where he could catch a boat out of the country. Barton knew that cruise ships left Miami regularly. He'd take a cruise to somewhere in Mexico and just not get back on board the ship when it was leaving to come back to the States. Now everything had changed.

It's just a setback. It's not the end of the world. Hell there are so many trucks up here, I should have no problem.

A light went off in his criminal brain. He remembered the Davenport's Hummer.

I'll go over there tonight and boost that thing. Hell, probably nobody even knows they're dead yet, so nobody will even know their Hummer is missin'.

It seemed as if the sun would never set. Barton wandered around the cabin restlessly after covering the truck with limbs again. He favored his right foot. It still hurt from the kicking incidences.

The darkness provided good cover as he hobbled back to town on his sore foot. He stayed within the shadows as he made his way to the campground where he found the Davenport's Hummer still parked where he had seen it on the night of the murder.

The campground was quiet. He saw no one stirring as he approached the door to the motorhome. Barton began picking the lock. *Why in hell didn't I get their damn keys?*

The lock soon gave and Jerome looked each way to see if anyone was coming. Seeing no one, he pulled the door open and almost vomited when the stench of decaying flesh hit him full in the face.

"Damn," he cursed and almost fell from the step. He took his handkerchief from his pocket and held it against his nose, stepped inside, and closed the door behind him. It didn't bother Barton in the least that he had killed the young couple, but the smell of death was too much for him. He gagged as he knelt to search the pockets of Chip Davenport's jeans for the keys. They were not there. He almost panicked when he searched the floor where he had dragged the bodies and still could not find the keys.

Then Barton remembered he had struck the couple just as they had unlocked the door. He turned off the lights and quietly went down the two steps that led to the ground. He looked around for a moment in the soft glow of the moonlight and saw a shiny object amid the loose gravel beside the bottom step. He breathed a sigh of relief, picked up the keys, and stuck them in his jacket.

Barton looked down through the rows of campsites, most unoccupied, and saw no one. He reached up and quietly closed the door of the RV, hurried to the Hummer, and unlocked it with the automatic opener. He climbed in gasping for breath and sat there in the quiet night for a moment, breathing deeply before driving away in his new set of wheels. Now to get the Hummer back to his cabin in the woods without being seen was going to be a problem. *I'll have to park this damn thing where nobody will find it,* he thought.

He drove up Fox Mountain Road and hunted for a place to hide the Hummer.

CHAPTER 83

"IREDELL COUNTY Sheriff's Department, Chief Deputy Ingle. How can I help you?"

The voice on the other end of the line sounded worried. "My name is Theodore Williams."

"Yes sir, Mr. Williams…"

"I have a little problem up here in Love Valley."

"What kind of problem, sir?"

"Well, you see, I run this little campground for folks to come up and park their trailers and motorhomes on the weekends for rodeos and the like."

"I see…"

"Like I was saying," Williams went on, "I have this one motorhome still here and there ain't nobody been seen around it for a week or more. Their Hummer was parked there for a few days and now it's gone. They paid their rent for just the weekend of the rodeo, but that was days ago."

The deputy listened patiently as the campground manager further explained his situation.

"You understand, I don't want any problems or to make a customer mad or anything like that, but they do owe us some more money."

"Have you tried to contact them, Mr. Williams?"

"Of course, I went over there several times and knocked on their door, but no one was there. You don't reckon there's something wrong, do you?"

"I'll send someone up there right away, Mr. Williams, and we'll check on it for you."

"Okay, thanks a lot. Andy said you guys would jump right on it."

"Mayor Barker's right. We'll get right on it."

Williams thanked him and Ingle immediately made a phone call.

"Detective McLeod here."

"You sound rather chipper this morning, Detective."

"Yeah, I guess so. What can I do for you this morning, Leroy?"

"Well, I just got a call from a man in Love Valley. I know you're working the murders up there, so I thought you might want to check this out."

"What do you have, Leroy?"

Ingle filled her in on the conservation he'd had with the campground owner. "You may have something there, Leroy, thanks a lot. Have you seen Jamie this morning?"

"Yes, ma'am, he just went into his office."

Marci said, "Call and tell him not to go anywhere. I'm leaving Mooresville right now."

"Will do," the deputy said and rang off.

Marci kissed Jake goodbye and hurried out the door. "I'll call you from the car," she said.

When Marci was on the road to Statesville, she called Jake and repeated the message from Deputy Ingle. "I don't know when I'll be home. I have a gut feeling about this and it's not good."

Jamie Campbell was waiting for her when she got to head-quarters. He jumped into the Charger almost before it came to a complete stop. "Morning," he said as he buckled up. "Do you think we're going up there just for a rent skip?"

"The truth is, I just don't know about that," she answered, "but I think I do know who's responsible for these murders!"

"Who?"

"Think about it Jamie. We've interviewed everybody within miles of Love Valley and not one person sticks out as a suspect. But there is a stranger in town we have not interviewed and he looks like Dewayne Allison. Remember how Mrs. Vanderhoot described her neighbor, Jerome Barton? She said he had a strag-gly beard and dressed like a cowboy."

"That's right," Jamie agreed.

Marci continued, "Dewayne had a beard and then shaved it off; so did the stranger."

"Go on," Jamie said.

"Well, I think Barton came to Love Valley after he killed his mother and thought he could fit in there, since it's known as the Cowboy Town. Maybe after killing his mother and uncle, he fig-ured he had nothing to lose and a lot to gain by robbing the victims. I don't know why he started the killing spree, but I know he's our man!"

"I'll be damned," Jamie said. "The son of a bitch has been in Love Valley all along right under our noses and using his looks to get away with murder."

"That's what I think," Marci said.

"So, do you think this rent skip has anything to do with Barton?"

"I guess we'll find out more when we get there," Marci said and sped the cruiser up Highway 115 toward Love Valley.

CHAPTER 84

THEODORE WILLIAMS was waiting for Marci and Jamie when they pulled into the driveway of the campground.

"Howdy. This is pretty darn quick service," he said grinning.

"Mr. Williams, I presume," Marci said extending her hand. "I'm Detective Marci McLeod and this is Detective Jamie Campbell. How can we help you?"

"The RV is right up here," he said, "just follow me." He led the way until they came to a brand new, Fleetwood Pace Arrow.

"Wow," Jamie said, "that thing must've cost a couple hundred thousand."

"It did, and a little more," Williams said. "They had a Hummer, too. His wife drove that up Saturday. Mr. Davenport brought the RV in on Friday morning and got it all set up for the weekend. The Hummer sat here for a few days and then one morning it was gone. Why would they drive off and leave an expensive RV like that and not tell anybody?"

"That's why we're here, Mr. Williams. You don't happen to have a key do you?"

"Me, heck no, people don't give me their keys and I don't want the responsibility anyway."

Jamie and Marci walked up to the RV and Marci gave Jamie a look as soon as she saw the door had been jimmied. "Mr. Williams, have you seen anyone suspicious around the campground lately?"

"No. I can't say that I have."

"How about anybody who wasn't camping here?" Jamie asked.

"Well, I did see Dewayne Allison the other night when I was walking my dog, but he didn't see me."

"When was that" Marci asked and glanced at Campbell.

Campbell raised an eyebrow; he understood the implication.

Williams continued, "Oh, that must have been the night of the rodeo. It was probably close to midnight, maybe even later. I remember Butch, he's my wife's little dog, scratching the door wantin' out and when he wants out, you'd better take him then," Williams chuckled.

"Jamie," Marcie said, "I think we need to enter the premises and do a protective sweep to be sure there's no one hurt inside the RV."

"I agree," Jamie said. "Let's see if I can get us in there." He pulled hard on the handle several times. The jimmied lock gave and the door popped open. The odor practically knocked them down.

Theodore Williams ran and vomited in the grass nearby. "What in the hell is in there?" he asked, wiping his face with his handkerchief.

"Mr. Williams, we'll have to ask you to keep back. Stand over there, please," Marci said, pointing toward the other side of the street. Williams obeyed and sat down in the grass mopping his brow.

Marci reached into her jacket pocket and brought out the Vicks VapoRub and handed the jar to Jamie. They both applied a dollop under their noses. "Okay, let's do it," she said and led the way into the motorhome.

The Davenports were lying on the kitchen floor. It was obvious that the skulls of both victims had been fractured. They quickly searched for offenders and then backed out of the motorhome, closed the door, and secured the scene.

"Jamie, call detective Warren at headquarters and tell him what we have here. Have him write up a search warrant for evidence in an obvious double homicide. Tell him to get it to a Superior Court Judge. We don't want any problems with this. Tell him to get it up here asap."

"Will do," Jamie said and left to order the warrant and Marci stayed at the scene. Theodore Williams stayed where he was and looked as if he was going to throw up again.

"Mr. Williams," Marci called out to him, "why don't you go back to your office. We'll come down there to get your statement."

"Thank you," Williams said with sincere gratitude.

Marci called her husband. "I'm going to be late tonight," she said. "Kiss Meredith for me."

"I love you," Jake said. "Please be careful."

"I will and I love you, too, Jake McLeod," Marci said.

CHAPTER 85

BARTON DROVE HALFWAY up Fox Mountain Road thinking about where he could hide the Hummer and how he could drive it around Love Valley. Stealing the Hummer might not have been such a good idea. *After they find them preppies, they're gonna be lookin' everywhere for this damn car!*

While slowly winding his way up the tree-lined road, he thought about his options. *I know what I'll do. I'll drive it down to Statesville, switch plates with an old truck and then steal the damn thing. Hell, just about everybody up here has an old truck.*

He grinned and felt much better after thinking through his problem. He turned the Hummer around before he had driven halfway up the mountain.

The temptation to test the power of the Hummer was too much for Barton. He reached a straightaway and pressed down on the accelerator. His heart raced when the vehicle's tires spun on the gravel road.

"Damn!" he said aloud. "This thing's somethin'!" He was driving faster than normal and loved the feel of the powerful engine. Barton rounded a sharp curve when he spotted a deer standing in the middle of the road. He slammed on the brakes to avoid a collision. The Hummer went into a skid that almost sent him tumbling down a steep embankment. When the vehicle finally stopped, he found himself gripping the steering wheel and breathing heavily. He sat there for a moment catching his breath, but the deer had already disappeared into the dark woods.

Damn, I gotta get hold of myself. I've come too far to mess up now.

He backed up and then headed down the road again, this time driving more sensibly. He didn't even stop at Bacon Road but made the turn up the hill toward Love Valley. He didn't see anything going on when he passed the road to the campground, so he drove on to Mountain View Road.

Barton pulled into the Walmart parking lot in Statesville and cruised around searching for the right kind of truck. *Something old and a little beat up*, he thought.

It was past midnight and the usually crowded parking lot was almost empty. He spotted an older Chevrolet pickup parked near the Tractor Supply Company that had a few dents and a little rust on the fenders. *Perfect! It looks like half the trucks in Love Valley!*

He drove slowly past the truck all the while watching to see if anyone was paying attention to him. No one was, so he parked the Hummer, got out, and walked over to the driver's door of the truck and opened it. "The damn thing's not even locked!" he said aloud. Barton slipped inside the truck and felt under the seat for a hidden key, but found none. On a hunch, he climbed out of the truck, walked to the left front fender, reached under it, felt around, and then broke into a wide grin. *I don't believe it. How dumb can people be?*

A little magnetic, metal box was fastened to the inside of the wheel well. He retrieved it, shook the box, and heard the wonderful sound of a key clinking inside. Barton hobbled back to the truck door on his sore foot and once again climbed inside the truck.

He opened the hidden box, removed the key, and inserted it into the ignition. The truck roared to life with the first turn. *I wonder why they left the truck here. Maybe they met some good old boys and are out drinkin'. Hell, I'm gonna leave them a damn Hummer with the keys in it, so why should they care?*

Barton quickly got out of the truck and ran back to the Hummer and wiped it down. *Hell,* he thought, *no sense making it too easy for 'em.* He took his knife and removed the Hummer's license plate and then did the same to the old truck. He swapped the two plates and then screwed them back on. He jumped into the pickup and drove slowly out of the parking lot, thinking, *ain't that ol' boy gonna be surprised?*

Driving the old battered truck reminded him of his own truck that wouldn't start. He'd just have to park this one in the woods near the other one so he could use some of the same limbs to cover it up. He'd probably have to scrounge around to find enough extra limbs lying around to cover them both. He couldn't afford to have anyone finding his hiding place. Fox Mountain Road loomed ahead and was void of any vehicle by the time he arrived back. It was nearly one o'clock when he drove up and parked the pickup.

The task of covering the newly stolen truck with limbs took him another thirty minutes, but he was satisfied with the job. Barton walked through the moonlit woods to his cabin and collapsed in his worn bed. Being dishonest had proven to be hard work—almost too hard to suit Jerome Barton.

CHAPTER 86

Detective Warren arrived at the scene and handed Marci a warrant that allowed them to search the premises for evidence in the double homicide. Armed with her warrant, she quickly entered the Pace Arrow followed by the crime scene techs. One of the techs was carrying the newest addition to the sheriff's department's crime-fighting arsenal—the DeltaSphere 3000.

The young technician, Steve Dalton, carefully went about his business, setting up a tripod mounted with the 3D Scanner and laptop computer. With the new technology, the sheriff's department was now able to view, measure, diagram, and reconstruct the crime scene in a matter of minutes and then present to the courts their findings from the initial investigation. Months or even years after a crime scene had been disturbed; the technology would allow them to make additional measurements as needed. In high-resolution, the DeltaSphere took only twelve minutes to make over nine million measurements.

Marci was hopeful that this new technology would help catch this out-of-control killer. Even though the technician was a professional, Marci could not help but give advice. "Photograph everything, Steve," Marci said. "Get close-ups of the victims' skulls. Capture any blood spatter you see. Maybe the lab boys will find some usable prints this time."

"Yes, ma'am. Maybe this new DeltaSphere will help catch the perp," said Dalton

Little did they know that the murderer was only a mile away, hidden in the woods.

A short time later, Dalton had what he needed in the kitchen and den and moved on to the bedroom. After he had cleared the den and kitchen, Marci knelt beside the woman and examined the fracture in her skull and then moved on to the male victim. 'He's covered with blood and brain tissue that probably came from his wife's wound," she said to one of the crime scene techs.

"Yeah, we figured that," Roscoe Golden, a skinny man in his fifties, agreed. He was one of the best techs in the Crime Scene Investigation Unit and she was glad he concurred with her findings.

"It looks like they were killed outside and dragged in here," he said looking up from the male victim. "There's some blood in the gravel in front of the door."

"Do you think it's the same perp, Roscoe?"

"Yep, I sure do; in fact, these wounds are just like all the rest. This guy sure likes his weapon."

"Roscoe, I think I know who the perp is," Marci said.

The tech looked up in surprise. "You do?"

"Yes," Marci said. "It's Mr. Beckett's nephew, Jerome Barton."

"You think so?"

"I know so," Marci said with conviction and shared what she knew with him. "I just need concrete evidence to tie him to the murders."

"Alright then," Golden said, "let's find something here that will help us nail the bastard."

While they were talking, a tech called out from the door of the kitchen. "There's a bloody washcloth wadded up in the trash can. The killer must have tried to wipe off some of the spatter from the side of the RV with it. There are still some visible traces of blood near the door. He didn't get it all."

"Anything in the kitchen?" Marci asked.

"It looks like we have some good prints here, Detective. Evidently he rifled through the cabinets. By the looks of this RV, I'd guess these people were pretty well off."

"They had a Hummer and it's missing, too," Marci said. "The campground manager said the address they gave him was Winston-Salem, but he didn't know what they did for a living. We're trying to find out something about them now. We need to notify the next of kin."

"These big motorhomes don't come cheap," Detective Warren called out.

"You're right about that," Jamie Campbell joined in. "Where do people this young get so much money?"

"Maybe we're looking at what drug money can buy," Marci said.

Campbell shook his head. "Maybe so."

"Alright," Marci said to Jamie, "while the guys are finishing up in here, you and Warren hit the street and see if anyone saw or heard anything. I'll walk down to the campground office and get Mr. Williams' statement."

"It was like I was telling you earlier," Williams said. "I was out walking Butch, that's my wife Mildred's dog, and I thought I saw old Dewayne Allison coming down the hill from the direction of the Davenport's RV. I remember thinking at the time, what in the world would ol' Dewayne have in common with people like that."

Marci winced at the thought of anyone suspecting Allison of the murders. She knew now that it was definitely Barton that killed the Davenports.

"What were they like," Marci asked, "the Davenports?"

"They were okay I guess. Personally I thought they were kind of snooty. They acted like they were a little better 'n anybody else, if you know what I mean."

"I could see by their RV that they must have been well off," Marci said.

"I don't know nothin' about that," Williams said. "But that man sure flashed a lot of money around like he was proud of it."

"Did he use a credit or debit card when he paid for his site?"

"Him? Hell no. He insisted on paying cash for everything. Like I said, he liked for people to know he had money."

"Tell me about their Hummer," Marci said. "You said it was parked at the campsite for several days after the rodeo, but then disappeared."

"That's right. One morning it was just gone. That made me a little suspicious right there!"

Marci asked him a few more questions, got the license plate number for the Hummer, took his statement, then thanked him for his help and walked back up the street to the motorhome.

The coroner was loading the body bags into the van when she got there. "Well, Detective," he said, "we'll rush the autopsies on these two and get back to you as soon as we can."

"That'll be a big help, thanks," Marci said. She couldn't help noticing the coroner's white hair blowing in the Brushy Mountain breeze. *Damn, we're all getting old,* she thought. Marci watched as he climbed into the van and drove away.

The murder cases were taking their toll on Marci and she herself suddenly felt older. *I don't know how much longer I can do this, but one damn thing's for sure, I'm gonna nail Jerome Barton's hide to the wall before I quit.*

Marci looked up at the sky and took note that the sun was shining. The trill of a mockingbird from its perch in a nearby pear tree caught her attention. *He must be calling out to his mate,* she thought. These were just simple things, but they were enough to buoy her spirits. *God still cares,* she thought, *and that will have to be enough for me right now. Even amid these horrible deaths, the beauty and wonder of life endures.*

CHAPTER 87

MARCI DROVE TO Dewayne Allison's trailer and knocked on the door but got no answer. *Maybe he's working somewhere,* she thought. She sat down on the steps in the warm sunshine to rest for a few minutes before she heard footsteps on the graveled path.

"Whatcha doin' here, Detective?" Allison asked as he walked up.

"Just resting and thinking, Dewayne," Marci said.

"Thinking about what?" he asked.

"You, Dewayne. Sit down and let's talk a little bit."

"What's goin' on?"

"Where were you the night of the rodeo?"

"I was at the rodeo. You saw me there."

"I mean after the rodeo, about midnight or a little after."

"I guess I was home in bed. Since I don't drink anymore, I just come on home and watch TV a little bit and go to bed after the news."

"Were you here by yourself?" Marci asked.

"Why yeah? What's this all about?"

Marci waited for a moment before continuing, "Dewayne, I believe you," she said.

Allison repeated his question, "What's this all about? You got me worried!"

"There was a double murder after the rodeo, sometime after midnight."

"Oh, no! Where?" Dewayne asked even more perplexed.

"In the campground," she answered.

"Who were they?"

"A young wealthy couple from Winston-Salem."

"I'm real sorry to hear that," Dewayne said, "but I was right here in bed."

"I told you I believe you, but a witness saw you in the campground around that time."

Dewayne sat down on the step beside her and said, "You gotta believe me, I was here all the time. It must be that other guy that looks like me."

Marci fixed her gaze on Allison. "Listen, Dewayne," Marci said making sure he was paying attention. "I'm convinced he's the one responsible for all these murders, but he wants us to believe it's you. Trust me; we're doing our best to catch this man."

"What should I do? Should I just leave Love Valley until he's caught?"

"No, just sit tight. I just wanted you to know that I do not consider you a suspect."

"Thank you," Dewayne said, "that means a lot to me. Nobody's ever believed in me before. You're the first person that ever thought I was worth somethin'."

"I believe there's good in everybody, Dewayne. We just had to find that good in you," Marci said as she gave his shoulder a hug.

Marci heard him sniffle and saw him wipe his eyes with his sleeve. She got up, brushed off the seat of her pants, and extended her hand to Dewayne who was still sitting on the steps. "Come on, Dewayne," she said and helped him up. "We have lots of work to do."

"What can I do?"

"You're going to tell me everywhere you go from now on. When a witness says they saw you here or there, we'll know whether it was you or the imposter. Then we'll know where he's been. That doesn't sound like much, but right now, we need all the help we can get."

"Okay, I'll do just about anything to get this monkey off my back," he said. "I'll let you know every step I take. I'm tired of people thinking I'm somebody else."

CHAPTER 88

THE CRIME SCENE Investigation Unit was finishing their work at the RV as Marci retuned from talking to Dewayne Allison.

"How's it going?" she asked one of the men packing up his gear.

"I think we have about all we can gather from the scene," he said. "Good luck catching the bastard who did this," he added.

Marci stepped outside and looked at the sun shining overhead and thought, *How can anybody do this, just kill people in cold blood? For what? Money? The thrill of it? What motivates people like Jerome Barton?*

Having no answer to her question, she found Jamie Campbell and motioned for him to join her and they climbed into their cruiser. She was in the process of telling Jamie about her visit with Dewayne when her cell phone buzzed. She nodded a few times and said, "We'll be there in twenty minutes."

"What's up?" Jamie asked.

"The Statesville Police found the Hummer."

"No kiddin', where?"

"In front of the Tractor Supply Company in Statesville," Marci said. "The plates have been switched. They're going over the vehicle now for prints and I betcha the prints on the Hummer will match the ones in the motorhome."

"And I'll bet they're Barton's." Jamie said. "He probably ditched the SUV because it was so recognizable and would tie him back to the Davenport murder scene."

Twenty minutes later, Marci and Jamie pulled up to the stolen Hummer and got out of the Charger. A uniformed police officer and a deputy were questioning a man dressed in a checked shirt and blue jeans. The man was waving his arms wildly and nearly yelling at them. "I don't care about this damn Hummer; I want to know where my pickup is."

"What's the problem?" Marci said as they walked up in time to hear the end of the conversation.

"This gentleman says somebody stole his pickup truck last night. He'd left it parked here and rode home with a designated driver. He's had one DUI and didn't want to take a chance on another."

"We're sorry your truck was stolen and we'll do everything we can to get it back for you," Marci said trying to assuage his anger. "What make, model, and year was your truck, sir?" she asked.

The man calmed down considerably as a result of Marci's intervention. "It's a 1981 Chevrolet C-10 Fleetside. I bought the thing new. It's a great truck."

"What color is your truck, sir?"

"Well, it's hard to tell. It was red at one time, but now, it's beat all to hell and mostly covered with rust."

Marci could see Jamie grinning as she patiently listened to the disgruntled man describe his truck.

"And that ain't all," he continued, "that's my tag over there on that Hummer."

"I see," Marci said. "By the way, how did you get here this morning?"

"My son brought me," the man said, "but he was late for work, so I told him to go on."

"Well, let me talk to the officers here for a moment," Marci said.

"Okay," the man agreed and walked off a short distance and lit a cigarette.

Marci talked to the officers briefly and then told the owner of the stolen truck, "Thank you for understanding. We'll do our best. And, sir, that was a wise choice taking advantage of a designated driver. I wish more people would do that and not drink and drive. An officer will drive you home."

Marci and Jamie climbed back into the Charger and headed to headquarters to sort out the latest events and get them written up. On the way downtown Marci said, "At least we know what Barton is driving now. That's more than we had this morning."

Jamie agreed, "Every little bit helps. But what I don't understand is why he's still hanging around Love Valley."

"When we catch the bastard, I'll ask him," Marci said with conviction.

CHAPTER 89

RIDING TOWARD THE arena around noon, Wish Phillips called out, "Hey, Dewayne," when he saw a familiar looking figure walk out from behind the Presbyterian Church. Wish received only a brief wave in response.

Man, looking like this Dewayne guy might end up being a good thing for me, Barton thought as he turned and walked up Mitchell Trail instead of heading toward town. He didn't want to face the friendly cowboy and let him discover that he was not Dewayne Allison, but an imposter. The waitress at the Silver Spur, the girl in the gift shop, and that female detective knew there was someone in town who looked like Allison; and that was three too many. He had to decide what to do about them. He knew what he wanted to do with the detective. He'd just have to find a way to make that happen.

Wish watched the man scurry up the road and disappear into the woods and wondered what Dewayne was doing up there in the woods. He turned his horse and was heading up Mitchell Trail to see where Allison was going when he heard his name.

"Wish! Where are you headin'?" Charlie Nance called out as he ambled down the rock steps toward the arena. "I saw you riding around down here and I thought I'd come out and say howdy."

"I was just getting in a little riding when I saw Dewayne Allison come out from behind the church," Wish explained. "I hollered at him, he waved, and then just turned up the road like I hardly even existed. The son of a gun went into the woods, Charlie. It was kind of like he didn't want to see me."

"What'd he do that for?" Nance asked and rubbed his mustache with his hand.

"I don't know. I was heading up that way to find out when you called my name. You want to ride with me and see what he's up to?"

"Sure, why not. Let me saddle up, it'll only take a minute." Wish followed Nance to his stables and dismounted while he saddled his sorrel. "Dewayne's been saying there's somebody around town that looks just like him and it's got him spooked," Charlie said. "Maybe that's who you saw. It might not even be Dewayne."

"You know, I didn't think about that, you may be right."

Nance finished tightening the cinch and swung up onto his horse and said, "Okay, Podna, let's go see what's goin' on with this dude."

The two men turned up Mitchell Trail and rode for a piece before Wish stopped. "I think this is about where he left the road and headed into the woods."

They dismounted and Nance knelt to look at some freshly disturbed leaves. "Yeah, it looks like he took off through here," he said pointing through the trees.

Wish said, "Why don't we ride down to Dewayne's trailer, first and see if he's home. If he is, then we'll know for sure that it was the imposter."

"Good plan."

They quickly mounted and headed down Mitchell Trail to Dewayne Allison's trailer.

Allison was sitting on his steps drinking a cup of coffee when the two cowboys rode up. "Wassup?" he asked as the two men swung down from their saddles.

"How long you been sittin' here?" Nance asked.

"Why?"

"Well, Wish here thought he saw you near the church twenty minutes ago."

"Dadgum!" Allison said as he threw out the rest of the coffee and rose from his seat. That wasn't me. I gotta call Detective McLeod. She told me to let her know if that cowboy ever showed his face again. She thinks he's the murderer. We gotta get her up here and I mean *quick*."

Nance handed Allison his phone, "Here, call her now if you can get a signal, I got her on speed dial."

Allison punched in the number and Marci said, "Hey, Charlie. What can I do for you?"

"Hey, Detective, it's me, Dewayne. Dewayne Allison. I'm using Charlie's phone. I can barely hear you with all that static. Can you hear me alright?"

"Yes, I can hear you, Dewayne. How can I help you?"

"You told me to call you when somebody thinks they saw me and they just did!"

"Tell me exactly where this happened, Dewayne."

Allison explained the situation. He listened intently for a minute and said, "Okay, we'll wait right here for you. And thank you, ma'am."

"What'd she say?" Nance asked.

"She said for us to wait on her and Detective Campbell because this guy is really dangerous."

"How dangerous can one cowboy be?" Wish said.

"Dangerous enough to kill six people in Love Valley," Nance said.

Wish thought a moment and added, "Well, at least he don't have a gun."

"Maybe he does," Dewayne said, "Bud Beckett's is missing.

CHAPTER 90

"WHAT WAS THAT all about?" Campbell asked when Marci got off the phone.

"That was Dewayne Allison. He said Wish Phillips just saw his lookalike enter the woods behind the church at Love Valley."

"What!" Jamie said. "He actually saw him?"

"That's what he said. We better get up there. Let's have some deputies meet us there and the K-9 unit, too," Marci said.

Jamie and Marci set out once again for Love Valley and discussed the latest development in the case on their way up Highway 115.

"How reliable do you think this information is that Dewayne just gave you?" Jamie asked.

"Very. I trust Wish and Charlie Nance," Marci said. "I told Dewayne to let me know when there was a sighting of his lookalike and to tell me where he was at the same time."

"Where was Allison when they supposedly saw Barton?"

"Dewayne was sitting on his steps drinking coffee when Wish Phillips saw the man enter the woods. It just verifies what Dewayne and I have both witnessed. This may be the break we've been waiting for."

"I sure hope so."

"We gotta find Barton soon. I'm getting too old for this."

"I haven't wanted to say anything, Marci, but you don't seem like yourself lately. I've never seen a case get to you like this one."

Marci turned her eyes toward him as she steered the Charger northward and leveled him with her gaze. "What do you mean, Jamie?"

"Well, it's just that you seem more agitated than normal and maybe a little short tempered, too. You've even shed some tears over this case."

Marci was silent for a moment and then turned to Jamie. "I've noticed it myself and even Jake has said something about it. Maybe it's about time I hang up my shield and call it quits."

"Don't talk like that, Marci. You're the best detective we have on the force. I know this one has been dragging on for weeks, but we're getting closer every day."

"I haven't been feeling really well lately either. Maybe I just need to go for a checkup when this is all over," Marci said. "I'm sorry I haven't been myself and thanks for putting up with me and all my moods."

"Heck, Marci, I'd rather work with you than any detective in the whole department," Campbell said.

She reached over and put her hand on his and said, "Thanks, partner, I needed that."

The move of affection took Campbell by surprise. "No problem, I meant what I said."

"Okay," Marci answered, "now let's go get this son of a bitch before he strikes again."

CHAPTER 91

J AKE WAS WORKING on a watercolor, painstakingly painting the wood grain on the boards of an old deserted house. He added some colorful, yellow daffodils poking up through a bed of dried leaves. The contrast between the browns and grays of the old weathered house and the yellow flowers was stunning. Jake was so engrossed in his painting, he didn't hear the door chime.

"Somebody's here, Daddy," Meredith told him.

"Thank you, Meredith, I didn't even notice." Jake swirled his Winsor & Newton brush around in the jar of water on his drawing desk.

"Anybody home?" Joanie Mitchell called out.

"Back here," Jake hollered as he removed the brush from the water, put the point into his mouth, and gave it a twirl. Jake always did that to help keep a fine point on his brushes.

"Well, looky here," Joanie said as she entered the studio.

"Who's this pretty little girl, Jake?"

"Oh just some kid that wandered in off the street," Jake teased, enjoying the expression on Meredith's face.

"I did not," Meredith said, "I've been here all mornin'."

"We're just teasing you," Jake told her. "Right, Joanie?"

"Hey, sweets," Joanie said and winked at Meredith.

"Hey, Joanie," Meredith said and tried to wink back. "Y'all are always pickin' on me."

"That's because we love you and because you're so doggone cute," Joanie said.

"Okay," Meredith said and returned to her coloring book.

"What's up, Joanie?" Jake asked.

Never one to beat around the bush, Joanie waded right in, "Is Marci feelin' alright?"

"As far as I know," Jake said, a little perplexed at the question.

"She seems a little agitated lately to me," Joanie said matter-of-factly.

"Well, I do think the case is beginning to get to her."

"I think so, too," Joanie agreed. "Did you see the way she just took off during the rodeo and never came back until the damn thing, excuse me, the doggoned thing was about over?" Joanie stole a glance toward Meredith and wondered if she had heard the bad word.

"We don't say damn no more," Meredith said without looking up.

Joanie and Jake laughed out loud at the precocious little girl who continued to color as if nothing out of the ordinary had happened.

Trying his best to refocus on Joanie's question, Jake finally said, "Yes, I have noticed that she hasn't been herself lately. I don't know what to do, other than let her ride it out."

"Well, I don't mean to butt in or anything. I just wanted to let you know I'm nearby if you ever need to talk. Women can be pretty difficult to figure out sometime."

"You're telling me," Jake said and laughed. "Joanie, you can always make me laugh when I need it the most. Thanks for your concern, too. That means a lot."

"Why, hell, what're friends for," Joanie said.

From the other side of the room a small voice was heard. "We don't say hell no more, either."

Laughter erupted and Meredith laid down her crayons and came over to Joanie and asked, "What's so funny?"

"Little girl, you're somethin' else, did you know that?" Joanie said and picked Meredith up and hugged her.

"I know, Daddy says I am."

Joanie hugged her fiercely, sat her down, and then ran her fingers through Meredith's beautiful red curls. "Just remember what I said, Jake McLeod. I'm always available to listen or shop sit or anything. Just let me know."

"Thanks for offering, Joanie. I don't know what in the world I would do without you women in the Wednesday Night Club."

"Aw hell, Jake, that's what friends are for."

Meredith looked up and pointed her little finger at Joanie and said, "'Member, we don't say hell no more."

"I gotta go before I say anything else I shouldn't." Joanie's laughter could still be heard as the front door closed behind her.

CHAPTER 92

JEROME BARTON HAD watched Wish Phillips and Charlie Nance ride up Mitchell Trail. He'd seen that they'd stopped right where he had entered the woods. *What the hell are they doing?* The undergrowth allowed him to observe the cowboys as they dismounted and examined the entrance to the path he had made. *I covered my tracks. Why don't them nosy sonsabitches mind their own business? I ain't bothered them!*

One of them pointed in his direction. *What the hell am I gonna do if they come up here? The pistols are back in the cabin.*

Barton didn't move a muscle, or hardly even breathe, for what seemed like several minutes. Finally, the two men mounted their horses and rode down the hill toward town. In the back of his mind, he worried they might have seen the path that led to his hidden trucks.

As soon as the two cowboys were out of sight, Barton headed deeper into the woods to his stolen truck. His mind raced as he made his way up the tree-covered hillside. *Maybe it's time I get outta here. But dammit, I still want that pretty detective.* Barton had very mixed emotions about leaving Love Valley.

The trucks were still covered with branches, just as he had left them. Barton, dressed in his new overalls, uncovered the C-10 Fleetside he had stolen, climbed inside the cab, and sat there for a minute thinking about Marci McLeod. Closing his eyes, he pictured her the way she looked the night of the rodeo—tight jeans and checkered shirt. He discovered that he was becoming aroused. It had been a long time since he'd had a woman. He ached for Marci McLeod.

The truck started on the second try and Barton headed out of the woods a different way than he had driven in. This time he drove up the hill to Starbuck Trail, then down to Fox Mountain Road, over to Coolbrook Road, and then to Highway 115. He thought it would be smart to change his route.

Barton decided to head to Statesville while he was on Highway 115. It was only about fifteen miles to McDonald's and he was suddenly having a Big Mac attack.

That's just what I need—a big juicy hamburger and a large order of fries.

He sped along Highway 115 heading south thinking about all that money he had hidden back in his cabin—almost a hundred thousand dollars; but he was still not satisfied.

He wanted that female detective before he left North Carolina. He had plans for her. If he could just see her right now, he would be happy. Just a glimpse of her would make his day.

CHAPTER 93

Detectives MCLEOD and Campbell had just left Statesville and were driving north on Highway 115 as Barton was heading south in the stolen Chevrolet pickup truck. A few miles north of the city limits, Barton cringed when he saw a sheriff's car coming toward him in the other lane. As it sped past him, he saw Marci McLeod at the wheel.

"Damn! That was her," Barton said. He checked the rearview mirror. *I wonder where she's goin'?*

Barton decided to see where the detectives were heading in such a hurry and pulled into the nearest driveway, turned around, and headed back north. He sped up to get the cruiser in sight and followed it at a safe distance and watched it as it turned left onto Mountain View Road. *Damn! Why are they in such a hurry to get to Love Valley?* He pulled into the parking lot at Phil's Food Mart and backed the truck into an out-of-the-way space. *I think I'll just sit here awhile and see what the hell is goin' on!*

CHAPTER 94

CHARLIE NANCE, Wish Phillips, and Dewayne Allison were waiting anxiously by the arena. Marci pulled the cruiser up beside them.

"Good morning," Marci said as she got out of the car and then looked at her watch and added, "or should I say good afternoon." It was then she realized that neither she nor Jamie had eaten lunch.

Wish jumped in before she had a chance to say anything else. "Dewayne said you think that this imposter may be the murderer?"

"Yes I do. Jerome Barton is Bud Beckett's nephew and I think that's why he ended up here in Love Valley. We also think he killed his mother in Galax, Virginia before coming here," Marci admitted. "Now, tell us what you saw, Wish."

"The man, who I thought was Dewayne, came out from behind the church and I hollered at him."

"Then what happened?" Marci asked.

"That's when he took off up the road and went into the woods. He acted like he didn't want to talk to me. Well, that made me a little suspicious; I ain't never seen Dewayne when he wouldn't talk to me."

"Can we go on up there and find this dude?" Dewayne said. "I'm tired of people thinking I did something I didn't. Some people think I'm even stuck up now because of him. Well, doggone it, I'm still the same old Dewayne, I'm just sober now."

They all gave an uneasy laugh and Jamie asked Wish, "Can you show us exactly where he went into the woods?"

"You bet. Me and Charlie rode up there and found the exact spot. It looked like he'd tried to cover his tracks some, but he didn't fool Charlie."

Nance said, "He'd scattered leaves over his trail hoping that would fool somebody. If you ask me, he thinks he's a whole lot smarter than he really is."

"You're probably right," Marci agreed. "Let's go have a look."

Wish and Nance led the way on their horses while Allison rode with the detectives in the cruiser. Marci pulled over to the side of the road behind the church.

The cowboys dismounted and tied their reins to some small bushes near the road. The detectives and Allison followed them to the edge of the woods. "This is where he went in," Nance said pointing to leaves that Barton had scattered over the entrance to his path.

The cowboys stood aside as Jamie and Marci knelt and examined the floor of the forest. "Looks like they're right," Jamie said as he helped Marci stand. The two detectives brushed dirt and leaves from their knees and walked over to the trio of cowboys.

"He definitely tried to cover his tracks," Marci said. "You

guys did a good job. This just might be the lead we've been look-ing for and we appreciate you calling us before you went off traipsing through the woods after him."

"We might look it," Nance said with a grin, "but we ain't that stupid."

Marci couldn't help but laugh. Charlie Nance always added a little levity to the most serious of occasions. "I never thought you boys were stupid, Charlie—maybe sometimes just a little impetuous."

"I ain't sure what that means exactly," Allison said, "but it sounds pretty good to me."

Marci grinned.

Not waiting for a definition of the word, Wish asked, "Well, are we gonna follow his trail or not?"

"Jamie called in the latest developments and requested backup and the K-9 unit while we were on the way here. We'll just wait for them to arrive before we go any further."

Marci and Jamie waited beside the road with the three cowboys and talked about how Love Valley had changed since the murders. Charlie and Beth Nance had been trying to make Love Valley a family-friendly destination. All the news on televi-sion about the murders in Love Valley had had an adverse effect on the fragile economy of the small town. There was even talk of cancelling one of the upcoming rodeos.

While they were waiting, Marci's stomach complained nois-ily from the lack of food. "It sounds like we all could use a bite to eat," Nance said. "Let me go up to The General Store and get us some burgers."

"You must have heard my stomach talking," Marci laughed. "That'd be great, I could eat a horse."

Nance looked at his sorrel. "Maybe I'd better hurry, then," he joked.

He returned shortly with burgers, fries, and Pepsis and they all ate hungrily. They had just disposed of the wrappers and cans when the K-9 unit arrived in a Chevy Blazer. Four deputies also pulled up in two separate vehicles.

Marci introduced the K-9 officer, Blaine Oliver, to the three Love Valley cowboys and then gave him the latest updates on the case.

"Sounds like we're finally on to something," Oliver said.

Marci and Jamie showed the K-9 officer where Barton had entered the woods.

"Sure looks like this is where somebody went in. Let me get my dog and we'll see if we can find him."

CHAPTER 95

BARTON MADE A quick trip into the store to get something to eat and hurried back to his truck. He had just finished his sandwich and beer when he noticed two sheriff's cars slow down and turn onto Mountain View Road.

As he was wadding up the paper bag that had held his lunch, he saw a Chevy Blazer with the Iredell County Sheriff's Department logo on its doors follow the cruisers down Mountain View Road. *That's a damn K-9 unit. I'd better check this out.*

Barton pulled out of the lot, drove by the intersection, and then turned left on Brookhaven Road. He drove a short distance and pulled off the pavement. *I'll bet that damn cowboy that waved at me this mornin' has something to do with this. Hell, they've probably found my old truck by now!*

Barton decided to drive a little closer to Love Valley to see if he could sneak back to his cabin and get his money. He hoped he had not waited too long to make his getaway. Barton was shaken now and sweat dampened the band of his new Justin hat. He pulled back onto the road and drove to the next intersection. He stopped and waited for a moment to be sure no more sheriff's cars were coming by before taking a right onto Mountain View Road. He drove past Love Valley Road, turned right onto Bacon Road, and then angled back to Fox Mountain Road where he turned left and sped up the mountain.

Soon, Barton saw the green county road sign that read Starbuck Trail ahead on his right. He drove slowly past the sign and up to the crest of the hill where the gravel section of Fox Mountain Road gave way to pavement at the Alexander County line. He turned right on the paved road and headed down the mountain, but after only a few hundred yards the pavement ended abruptly. Barton slowed down when he hit the bumpy unpaved section and swore under his breath, but continued the descent toward Fox Mountain Lake. He realized he had to find a place soon to park the truck, but yet not too far from the cabin where he could gather his belongings and, more importantly, the money. He saw a narrow lane that turned to the left near the lake and disappeared into the woods. *Perfect*, he thought.

Barton swung the truck up the lane and bounced along for several hundred yards before coming to a stop. He figured that his cabin would be about a quarter of a mile back up the hill and to his left. He stopped the truck, climbed out, and raced through the woods toward his cabin.

They can't catch me now; I'm leaving. It's not fair, he thought. *I haven't even got a hold of that female detective yet.*

Barton's thoughts raced as he stumbled through the unfamiliar woods. He had not been on this part of Fox Mountain before. He was now just running on instinct toward his cabin. Briars tore his western shirt and his new white hat was covered in dust and dirt as he fought his way through the trees and undergrowth.

The ramshackle cabin suddenly appeared out of nowhere. He'd been right all along. He threw open the door, raced inside, and immediately fell on his knees before his hiding place. He got the knife out of his pocket and began removing the board he had removed so many times before. After the Cameron robbery, Barton had emptied the money from the small sack he had been using into the larger pillowcase to make it easier to handle. He gave a sigh of relief and quickly retrieved it. Barton found the stolen pistols near his bed and crammed them into his overalls. He left everything else and tore out the door and raced back down the hill and through the woods toward the truck he'd parked near Fox Mountain Lake.

I'll just have to get up with that detective some other time, he thought as his truck came into view.

Barton's thoughts of Marci McLeod were interrupted when he suddenly heard that mournful howl he had heard before. The pitiful sound rose up from near his cabin and the warm mountain breeze did little to dispel the chill that ran down Barton's spine.

CHAPTER 96

IT DIDN'T TAKE long for the Iredell County K-9 Unit to get down to business. The officer opened the door to the Blazer and brought out a lean Bloodhound that was raring to go. The dog was trained not to bark while following a scent. The hound steadily pulled the K-9 officer along with Marci, Jamie, and the deputies not far behind. The three cowboys brought up the rear of the chase as they had been instructed.

Dewayne felt that catching the imposter would surely simplify his life. "You reckon we'll find him?" Dewayne asked, hoping that the thief who had stolen his identity was about to be apprehended.

"We can hope," Charlie said.

"I hope we get him for your sake," Wish said. Wish had, as most of the people of Love Valley, taken a liking to Allison now that he had turned his life around. The man now had a steady job and, as far as anyone knew, neither he nor Shorty Parsons had

had another drink.

They had only been on the trail for a few minutes when Oliver motioned for them to stop. Without speaking, he turned to Marci and pointed toward an old Chevrolet pickup truck partially covered by limbs. The truck had a large patch of rust on the driver's door and several spots on the fenders.

Marci motioned for the others to wait where they were while she and Campbell followed the K-9 officer to the truck. The detectives had their Glocks drawn in readiness hoping to find the perpetrator hiding in the vehicle. Jamie quietly made his way around to the other side of the truck while Marci approached the driver's door. She grabbed the handle with her left hand and jerked it open in one quick motion.

"Out with your hands up, Barton!" she ordered. The cab was empty. "Damn," she said. "The bastard's not here!"

"Look over here, Detective," Oliver said pointing to numerous limbs that had been strewn across the ground nearby. He knelt and examined the scene. "There's been another vehicle here at one time."

Jamie spoke, "I wonder why he had two vehicles up here?"

Marci signaled for the three cowboys to join them.

"It don't look like this piece of crap would make it very far anyway," Nance said after seeing the condition of the truck.

"No, it doesn't," Marci agreed. She slipped on her latex gloves and opened the hood and peered in. "It's no wonder he left it here," she said. "Look at this."

They all joined Marci and stared at the freshly chewed wiring.

"Boy, I'll bet that pissed him off," Charlie said.

Marci grinned, "I imagine so."

"This is why Barton had to steal that truck in Statesville," Campbell said. "He figured out the Hummer would be too easily recognized and he still had to have wheels."

"He's pretty damn smart to be so dumb," Charlie said. "He oughta know he ain't gettin' away from here."

"I've never met a crook yet who didn't think they could out-smart the police," Marci said.

"But six murders in a town this size," Charlie said. "What was he thinkin'?"

"He's been staging," Marci said. "He actually thinks he's invincible. Barton's probably been watching us for weeks and getting his kicks from laughing at us. But not to worry, we're really close to nabbing his ass."

"What do you want to do first?" Oliver asked Marci. "There are tire tracks here that don't match the tires on that old truck," Oliver said. "We can follow the tire tracks or we can let the dog stay with the scent that takes off that way," the K-9 officer said as the bloodhound pulled him toward Fox Mountain,

Jamie looked to Marci for guidance. "What do you think, Marci? It's your call."

"I think he's probably rabbiting. He's more than likely taken the other truck and is getting ready to leave the area; otherwise he would've walked to where he was going if he was still confident we weren't on to him."

"What do you want to do?" Jamie asked.

"Let's follow the tire tracks. Maybe we'll find out where he's been holed up for the past several weeks. That's probably where he's heading. If he's going to load up and leave, we'd better hurry if we're gonna catch him." She ordered one of the deputies to stay and secure the scene and then radioed for the crime scene unit.

Leaving the deputy behind, they set out following the tire tracks. They were easy to follow. It was evident that Barton had spun the wheels of the truck in several places for traction.

"He drove the truck up the hill through the woods," Oliver said. "I guess he knew where he was going, but I sure as hell don't."

Charlie Nance spoke up, "It looks like he's headin' toward Starbuck Trail."

"Where will that take us?" Marci asked.

"It just winds around and eventually leads to the top of a mountain."

They followed the tracks and just like Nance said, they came out on Starbuck Trail. "Damn," Marci said exasperated, "now which way?"

"I can't see him going up a dead end road. That'd be real dumb," Nance offered his opinion.

"Nobody ever said he was smart, but I do agree with you," Marci said.

Respecting Nance's instincts, Marci asked, "Knowing the country up here, Charlie, which way do you think he would have gone?"

"If I was him, I would've turned left and headed over to Fox Mountain Road. That'll take him back down toward Love Valley or across the mountain to Coolbrook Road."

"Where will that take him?" Marci asked.

"If he turned right, he'd go to Highway 115 or if he turned left, he'd end up on Linney's Mill Road."

"In other words, from there, he could go anywhere," Marci said. "How far to Fox Mountain Road?" she asked Charlie.

"It's not far. Starbuck's not that long."

"Okay then, let's go," Marci said. "Lead the way, Blaine, we're right behind you."

CHAPTER 97

WHERE STARBUCK TRAIL ended at Fox Mountain Road, the K-9 officer knelt and gave the dog a deserved drink of water. Oliver looked up at Marci for directions. "What now?"

Marci, out of her element in the Brushy Mountains, knew she was dependent on the cowboys' help. "Okay, guys, where would you go around here if you wanted to hole up?" she asked.

Wish grew quiet momentarily before offering his opinion. "Well, I've lived up here just about all my life and I can't think of but one place he might've holed up."

Anxious for any lead, Marci asked, "Where, Wish? We have nothing to lose if it doesn't work out."

"Well, there's the old Wilcox cabin down the mountain a ways. That place might've fallen down by now. There ain't nobody lived in it for years."

"Can you take us to it?"

"Yeah, I reckon so."

"Anybody else want to add something; speak up now," Marci said. After waiting a moment with no other forthcoming ideas, she forged on. "Okay, Wish, lead the way."

They turned right on the graveled county road and headed up to the top of the hill. "Sure hope you're right, Wish," Jamie said, panting from all the exertion. As they rounded a curve they heard a vehicle on the road and then saw a cloud of dust down the hill from them.

"Where'd that dust come from?" Jamie asked. "Nobody passed by us."

"Is there another road down this way?" Marci asked.

"There's a driveway that goes up and around the lake," Wish said. "Somebody could've come outta there and kicked it up."

"That's right," Allison agreed. "There's a lake down there. It ain't too far from here."

"The cabin ain't too far from the lake either," Wish added.

They hurried and found the small lane that ran beside the lake just as the two cowboys had said.

"Hey, look here!" Nance said, pointing to fresh tire tracks.

Oliver knelt and examined the tracks and then the bloodhound tugged at the leash. He rose, followed the dog's lead, and then said with excitement, "Barton's been here. Look at this." He pointed at several boot prints in the loose dirt.

"Let's see where the dog leads us," Marci said, growing more excited by the minute.

After going several hundred feet through the woods, Wish said, "Hey, we're headin' toward that old cabin I was tellin' y'all about. It can't be more than a quarter of a mile to it."

They followed the dog as he wound up and down a few hills through the woods. "Look," Dewayne said pointing ahead. The deserted Wilcox cabin appeared among a copse of trees.

"Good job, Oliver," Marci said. "Give that dog an extra treat."

"You don't think he stayed in that fallen-down thing, do you?" Dewayne asked.

"We'll find out in a minute," Marci said as they forged ahead.

The door to the cabin was closed. Marci motioned for the cowboys to stay back. She, Jamie, and the three deputies split up and approached the cabin from two different directions. Marci edged up beside the door with pistol drawn. "Come out, Barton, if you're in there. I'm only going to count to three. By then, we'd better see your sorry ass out here with your hands up."

"One," Marci began, "two," still no sound from within. "Three." Marci pivoted and with a two-hand grip on her Glock was ready when Jamie kicked in the door.

The door flew off its hinges from the force of Campbell's kick and crashed to the floor of the cabin.

Then there was silence.

After peering inside the empty cabin, Marci lowered her gun. "He's gone," she said breathing heavily from the adrenalin rush. "The bastard's gone."

"The dog followed his tracks all the way here, so we know it's him," Oliver offered.

"Oh, it's him alright," Jamie said. The detectives stepped inside the gloomy interior and began a thorough search hoping to find any lead. Campbell made his way around the table and almost stepped into the hole in the floor. "This must have been where he hid his loot."

Marci walked around the table and peered over Jamie's shoulder as he knelt to look inside the opening in the floor. "Anything in there?"

Campbell reached into the hole with his latex-gloved hand and withdrew a knife. "Looky here," he said showing her where the blade point had been broken off. "You want me to get the crime scene techs up here, too?" he asked.

"Yeah, we're gonna have to. Tell them to drive up Fox Mountain Road. It'll be easier."

"We need to alert the highway patrol to be on the lookout for Barton," Marci said. "The son of a bitch could be headed anywhere."

"We were so close," Jamie said with frustration. "So close."

After a quick search of the cabin, nothing was found that even gave them a hint as to where Barton was headed. Marci sent a deputy out to the edge of the woods to show the CSI Unit where to enter the woods to get to the cabin.

Dejected, Marci walked back outside the cabin and faced the cowboys. Charlie could see the disappointed look on her face and was the first to speak. "That was so close, Marci. You put him on the run."

"I didn't want him on the run. I wanted him in cuffs," she said with a frustrated groan.

"It must have been him that pulled out of the lane down by the lake," Charlie said. "If it was and he got to the end of Fox Mountain Road, he could turn left on Coolbrook and head for Linney's Mill Road."

Marci paused for a moment and then added, "Or like you said earlier, he could turn right and be headed toward Union Grove to pick up I-77."

Dewayne Allison joined in the speculation. "Or, he could just head down 115 toward Statesville and pick up I-40 and then go anywhere."

"There's no telling where he's gone," Marci said. "He's probably got money, so he may even try to make it to Mexico if he had enough sense to get a passport."

Everybody laughed and then Charlie said, "Anybody can get into the United States, but they might not let him into Mexico."

"Why not?" Marci asked.

"Would you let anybody that looked like Dewayne Allison into your country?" Nance said.

Even Dewayne Allison couldn't keep from laughing. The mood lightened momentarily until Marci said, "Alright boys; fun time's over. We've still got a killer on the loose."

CHAPTER 98

Barton SPED down Fox Mountain in a cloud of dust heading toward Coolbrook Road. *Maybe I'll make it out of here yet.*

He took the three stolen revolvers: Beckett's .45, the .357 from the motorhome, and the .38 he had picked up at the Cameron's and hid them under the seat of the truck—they were close enough if he needed them.

The stop sign at the end of Coolbrook Road stared back at him as if asking, "Which way you goin' Buster?"

He had no idea.

What he really wanted was that female detective. He willed himself to quit thinking of her. He had to make some decisions. He sat at the intersection until he saw a car drive by on Coolbrook Road heading northwest. For the lack of a better idea, he pulled out and followed the automobile. His mind was made up, at least for awhile.

At the next intersection, the car turned right onto Linney's

Mill Road and Barton turned left. He soon approached pictur-esque Linney's Mill situated on Rocky Creek. He noticed a swinging bridge that spanned the stream behind the mill. Two children were running across the bridge making it sway back and forth. Several men clad in jeans and flannel shirts were loading sacks of feed into trucks that were backed up to the loading dock.

After a mile or more, a narrow bridge loomed ahead of Barton and he was forced to make another decision. Immedi-ately after the bridge, a road branched off to the right and headed up a mountain. He read the name on the sign, Brushy Mountain Road.

While stopped at the intersection, he heard an approaching vehicle, so he took a quick look into his rearview mirror. A red, Ford pickup truck was barreling down the hill toward him. He had to make up his mind quickly. He decided to stay on Linney's Mill Road and see where it would take him.

His mind raced. He thought of the cowboy that had seen him behind the church. He was sure he was the one who had brought all those sheriff's cars and the K-9 unit to Love Valley. He thought of the detective again and really regretted he had not had his time alone with her.

After a few miles, the road swung left. A road sign now read: Sulphur Springs Road. *What happened to Linney's Mill Road,* he thought. *Damn, I'd better pay attention to where I'm goin'.*

He continued driving and thinking…thinking and driving. Thoughts of the detective began to haunt Barton. Next he turned left on Jim Millsaps Road. He was wandering aimlessly now and that road soon came to a dead end at Cheatham Ford Road. Without hesitation he turned to the right and continued driving.

Another intersection soon appeared and he was faced with yet another decision. Barton began to panic. He had no idea where he was, so he just made a left onto Sharpe's Mill Road. He slowed down and tried to think. The road crossed back into Iredell County and was now Damascus Church Road. *I've heard of this road,* he thought. *Where do I know it from?* He became more agitated when he couldn't recall where he had heard the name of the road. *I gotta quit thinkin' of that damn woman and get my mind on what I'm doin'.* He decided to just stay on Damascus Church Road and not make any more turns.

He had to find out where he was because he was completely turned around now. Suddenly a Dodge pickup truck appeared out of nowhere and he almost hit it head-on. Barton swerved, just missing the truck; he ran onto the shoulder of the road, throwing dirt high into the air.

After the near accident, Barton steered the truck back onto the pavement. He tried to get his thoughts under control and get his nerves calmed down. His breath came in short, ragged gasps. Just then a stop sign loomed ahead that marked the end of the road.

The road ended on Highway 115 at Phil's Food Mart. "Damn!" he shouted aloud and hit the steering wheel with the heel of his hand so hard it made him wince. "Damn, damn, damn," he repeated. "I ain't three miles from Love Valley. I've been going around in one big damn circle."

Sitting in the truck, staring in disbelief at where he had ended up, he saw another car from the sheriff's department race by and turn onto Mountain View Road.

"What the hell," he said as he turned left on Highway 115 and then onto Mountain View Road. He made sure he stayed well behind the sheriff's car and kept a steady pace.

By God, he thought, *I'm gonna find out what's goin' on up there. Maybe I'm overreactin'. And besides that, there's that female detective. Maybe I can get another look at 'er before I head out for good.*

CHAPTER 99

THE CRIME SCENE UNIT drove up Fox Mountain Road and pulled over when they saw the deputy waiting for them. He helped them unload their equipment and carry it to the cabin. Marci was standing beside the open doorway talking to Jamie and the K-9 officer when they arrived. "Okay, men, it's all yours."

"Well what do you think, Marci?" Jamie asked after his partner left the cabin. "Has Barton left the area or is he still hanging around?"

"Let's run down to Phil's and we can talk about that on the way there. Maybe we'll hear something from the highway patrol. I need a bathroom break any way."

"Me, too," Jamie said.

"I can't explain it, but I think he's still here," Marci said on the ride down the mountain.

Jamie thought for a minute. "You know it's almost like he's just playing with us—teasing us."

"Those days are over," Marci said, "Barton's days are numbered and he should know that by now. Something seems to be keeping him here and that's what I don't understand."

"We'll have to ask him when we catch him," Jamie said.

As the detectives were pulling into the parking lot of Phil's Food Mart and Restaurant, a man ran up to them waving his arms.

"What's wrong, sir?" Marci asked the man who was clearly out of breath. He was wearing a pair of Pointer Brand overalls with the button on one side of the bib missing. The bib flapped wildly as the man gestured with his arms.

"I want to report a man driving an old, beat-up Chevy truck that just about ran me off the road"

"Did you see what color the truck was, sir?"

"Yeah, it looked like was red at on time, but it had so much rust on it, it was hard to tell," the man said and spit a stream of tobacco juice on the asphalt. "Excuse me, ma'am, I was about to drown. Nasty habit."

"That's okay," Marci said, but couldn't help but grin. "Go ahead and tell us what you saw."

"Well, I was driving up Damascus Church Road," he said pointing to the road that ended near the store on Highway 115, "when this old pickup came toward me in my lane. I don't think he had his mind on what he was doin' by the way he was drivin'."

"Can you describe him?" Jamie asked.

The man took off his hat, wiped his brow, and put it back on before answering. "I sure can," he said with assurance. "I can even do better than that. I can tell you who it was. It was that Dewayne Allison."

"Dewayne Allison!" Marci said.

"Yes, ma'am. I knowed Dewayne Allison all his life and to tell the truth, it kinda shook me up seeing him driving like that. I heard he'd quit drinkin', but he was drivin' like he was drunk, if you ask me. I don't wanna git ol' Dewayne in any trouble or nothin', since he's tryin' to do better, but he coulda killed me."

"You won't get Dewayne in any trouble, I promise," Marci assured him. "Dewayne's up on Fox Mountain right this minute helping us track the driver of that pickup."

"You mean that wadn't Dewayne?"

"No, sir. Dewayne was definitely not the man driving that truck."

"Well I'll be hornswoggled," the old man said. "I really thought it was him. Hell, I turned around and to give him a piece of my mind."

Marci asked the old man, when he finished wiping some stray tobacco juice off his chin, "Did you see which way he turned when he came out on 115?"

"I sure did and I almost caught up with him, too. Just as I turned into the parking lot, I saw him turn left at the Love Valley sign up yonder," the old man said pointing toward Mountain View Road.

Jamie thanked the man and took his name in case he needed to get back in touch with him later.

"Glad to help," the old man said. He released one more stream of juice and then took the tobacco out of his mouth and threw it into the grass. "I gotta get me some more chewing tobacco," he said and went inside the store.

"Damn," Marci said. "That Barton is gonna drive me nuts. Get me a Diet Pepsi while I call the sheriff and then I gotta pee!"

Jamie ran into the store and was back with Diet Pepsis by the time Marci got off the phone with Sheriff Charlie Nichols.

She raced to the bathroom, came back, and climbed into the cruiser. "Okay, Tonto, let's ride," she said with a wide grin. "The sheriff's on his way with the posse."

CHAPTER 100

JEROME BARTON DROVE slowly up Mountain View Road staying well behind the sheriff's department cruiser. "What was I thinkin'?" Barton said under his breath. *This damn place is crawlin' with the law and here I am drivin' around hopin' to get another look at the woman that wants to put me in jail. I must be losin' it.*

Suddenly a Crown Victoria appeared in his rearview mirror and he gasped. Sweat ran down his shirt as he gripped the steering wheel tightly anticipating a showdown on Mountain View Road. He slowed the truck and the car sped up behind him, but quickly blew passed and continued toward Love Valley.

He noticed that the driver was an elderly woman. "Damn," he said. *I thought that was the law. What the hell was an old woman doin' drivin' one of them Crown Vics for anyway? They oughta give the old buzzard a ticket for speedin', too.*

Barton realized that he had just dodged a bullet. He thought, *Maybe they don't even know I stole this truck.* He relaxed a little, but turned left on Brookhaven Road just to play it safe. *No sense in actin' plumb crazy. But, damn, I'd like to see that woman up close and personal.*

Barton continued down the country road for a while having no idea where it would lead him except away from all the sheriff's cars. His thoughts were running wild now. One minute, he thought he was safe and the very next minute he thought he was going to be caught. He slowed the truck and turned left on Shoemaker Farm Road. Little did he know that the road just made a loop and brought him right back to Brookhaven.

Jerome pulled over beside the road among some weeds near a barbed wire fence and tried to decide what to do. He checked to make sure the three stolen pistols were still under the seat. He picked them up and made sure they were loaded, laid them on the seat beside him, and gave each one a reassuring pat. He then doubled-checked the pillowcase containing the stolen cash, looked into his rearview mirror, and pulled back onto the road. "Well, let's see where this goes," he said.

Barton was surprised to see Brookhaven Road when he pulled up to the stop sign. "Damn, do all these dumbass roads up here go nowhere?" He turned left and drove for a short distance and then turned off to his right hoping that Clanton Road would lead him away from Love Valley.

Shortly the road ended at the Alexander County line. Without thinking, Barton turned right and saw the sign that read Mountain View Road. *Dammit, it looks like every one of these damn roads go to back Love Valley.* It was then he saw a Dodge Charger speeding toward him.

CHAPTER 101

T HE SHERIFF'S CAR sped by and Barton heaved a big sigh of relief. He glanced into the rearview mirror to see where the cruiser was heading when suddenly he saw the cruiser's brake lights come on. The car spun around in the middle of the road and headed back toward him.

A lone young deputy was driving the Charger and Barton could see him plainly in his mirror as he switched on the rack of blue lights. Barton pulled over onto the shoulder of the road and waited for the deputy to approach his truck. He noticed that the officer was reading his license plate and speaking into his shoulder mic. The young deputy then walked up to Barton's window.

"Can I see your license please," he said politely.

"Sure officer," Barton said, "let me get it for you." He acted as if he was retrieving his license and brought the .38 Smith & Wesson he had stolen from the Cameron house to the open window and shot the young deputy in the chest before the man could react. The surprised officer staggered back from the blast and then Barton fired again, this time hitting the officer underneath his left arm as he was falling to the ground. He landed in the middle of the road on his back. The sound almost deafened Barton inside the truck. He was still shaking when he saw the young deputy lying across the yellow line on the pavement.

He quickly put the truck in gear and spun the tires in the grass on the shoulder of the road before they gained traction and squealed onto the blacktopped surface of Mountain View Road.

"Come in, Sherrill," Marci called into her mic. "Come in," she repeated. When she got no answer, she said, "We've got a problem, Jamie. Sherrill just called in the tag that was stolen off the Davenport's Hummer. It's now on that stolen Chevrolet pickup." Marci's words caught in her throat. "Sherrill's not answering, Jamie. If that son of a bitch kills a deputy, he'll never make it out of Iredell County alive."

"Where was Sherrill when he called it in?" Jamie asked.

"On Mountain View Road, let's go."

They climbed into their vehicle. Marci drove and Jamie radioed for backup as they raced toward Mountain View Road. After driving several miles, Campbell exclaimed, "There's his car up ahead."

Marci screeched the cruiser to a halt when she saw the deputy lying in the middle of the road. "Call 911 for an ambulance," she said to Jamie as she leaped from the car and ran toward the fallen officer.

"Bryan, Bryan," she said as she knelt beside the deputy and grabbed hold of his hand. She felt a weak pulse and then cried loudly, "Don't you die on me!"

Blood was pouring from his side. Marci yelled for Campbell's handkerchief and pressed it on the wound to stop the flow of blood as much as possible. Marci pled to the unconscious man, "Can you hear me? Help's on the way."

It was as if an eternity had passed before she heard him speak in a voice so weak she could barely hear him. "What happened?" he asked and blinked his eyes several times and looked up at Marci.

"You got shot," she said through her tears. "Just lay still. Help's coming."

The deputy shook his head and tried to get up.

"Just lay there, don't move," Marci ordered with urgency.

The young man looked up at Marci again and closed his eyes. Deputy Sherrill's head tilted back on her lap as he lapsed into unconsciousness. Marci wiped away the tears on her sleeve and gazed upon the limp body she had cradled in her arms.

She could hear Jamie talking, but her thoughts and prayers were for the fallen deputy. She opened her eyes and Campbell was beside her. "The ambulance is on the way. How is he?"

"He losing a lot of blood, I hope they hurry! You'd better radio in and tell everybody what's going on. It looks like we just missed the bastard again. He must be heading to the interstate now unless he gets lost on these country roads."

"The whole department was listening in on the radio; they know what's going on and I requested help from the highway patrol."

"Thank you, Jamie. Pray for this poor boy."

"I have been." he said.

"It looks bad. He took one in the vest, but it looks like a second shot missed the vest and got him under the arm. That's where all the blood is coming from."

"Detective, you have blood all over you."

Marci didn't care

Soon, two more cruisers arrived and one of the deputies took over directing the traffic.

Marci and Jamie continued listening in on the radio correspondence as the Iredell County Sheriff's Department combed the surrounding roads in search of Jerome Barton.

After several minutes, more sirens were heard in the distance and flashing red lights soon appeared. The med-team arrived and took over the care of Bryan Sherrill. He was breathing, but his pulse was very weak.

Barton's lack of knowledge of northern Iredell County roads became more frustrating to him by the minute. He had turned left on Brookhaven Road after his encounter with the deputy and drove as fast as he could around the road's unfamiliar curves. A sign up ahead read Carderwoody Road and he swung the truck to the left onto it, barely slowing down. *I'm gonna lose them bastards,* he said to himself. The country connector road was short and ended on Highway 115. Not wanting to head back toward Statesville, he turned the wheel left and sped north until he saw the intersection of Prospect Road. It led to his right, so he immediately turned and sped east. *I gotta get off this main highway, but I need to get to I-77.*

He soon came to Meyer's Mill Road, but opted to continue on Prospect Road and still head east. Barton saw a sign indicating that he was now on Trumpet Branch Road and that was all he knew. He was completely lost. It was getting dark and Barton was tired.

I need somewhere to spend the night, he thought. *I gotta think some things through and find a way outta here.* It was then he spotted a small house with a FOR SALE sign in the yard. He pulled into the driveway of the modest home and sat there for a minute to catch his breath. No car was in the carport and it appeared that no one was home. He knew that people sometimes still lived in their houses while they're trying to sell them, so he had to play it safe. Barton sat in the truck for a minute sizing up the situation before making any rash decisions. The grass had grown up in the driveway and the house had a deserted look. Barton pulled the truck under the carport, got out, and walked to what appeared to be the kitchen door and knocked. No one came to answer his knock, so he used the butt of the .38 to break the glass in the door and reached in to unlock the door.

He stepped inside and called out, "Anybody home?" His voice echoed through the house. Barton walked from room to room finding no one there. The house was completely empty. Barton was thirsty, so he checked the kitchen faucet, but found it was not working. "Damn," he said as his voice echoed through the empty rooms.

He went back outside and decided to move the truck to a secluded spot behind the house. Barton rummaged through the truck and found a stale pack of cheese crackers and a half-empty bottle of water that he took with him back into the house. A hollow feeling overcame him and he plopped down wearily on the cold, linoleum floor. He greedily wolfed down the crackers and drained the remaining water from the bottle and angrily threw it across the room.

It's a good thing I got them pistols. I showed that damn deputy. They'll never find me here. There ain't even another house around. At least this place beats that old log cabin.

Barton curled up in a ball on the floor and drifted off to sleep thinking of Detective Marci McLeod.

CHAPTER 102

THE SUN HAD set on another day and Jerome Barton had once more eluded capture. Marci was tired beyond belief and wanted to go home. First, she stopped at headquarters, washed off, and changed into the extra clothes she kept there for emergencies. She didn't want Jake to see her covered in blood.

"Marci," Jake said as she fell into his arms. "Are you okay, honey?"

"I think I had one of the worst days of my career," she said with tears welling in her eyes.

"What in the world happened?" Jake asked as he enveloped her into his warm and assuring embrace.

Marci told him about the deputy getting shot and the frustration of losing their suspect again. She pressed her head into his shoulder and began to cry.

"Let me get you something to drink," Jake said, "a glass of Pinot Grigio might be just what you need. Whatdaya say?"

"No, I don't think so," Marci said. "I think I'll just go to bed, I am exhausted. They'll call me if anything changes."

"Are you sure you're okay?" Jake asked concerned.

"It's just that we were so damn close to catching the bastard and he slipped right through our fingers. It's like we're just a bunch of Keystone Cops. He's hanging around for something, just taunting us. God, I want this to be over," she said and then fell from his embrace and slumped to the floor.

"Marci," he screamed and swept her into his arms. "Marci," he repeated, but she had passed out and did not hear her name being called.

Jake carried his unconscious wife into the master bedroom and laid her gently on the bed and then ran to the bathroom for a wet cloth.

"Marci!" Jake said and repeated her name over and over as he wiped her brow gently with the cool soothing cloth.

She stirred and looked up at him through bleary eyes. "How'd I get here?" she asked.

"I carried you. You passed out on me. What's wrong, Marci? Are you sure you're okay?"

"I'm fine, honey, just a little tired, that's all. Please pray for Bryan. I feel so bad about him getting shot."

"Just lie still, don't move," Jake warned.

Marci didn't stir again until Jake returned from the kitchen. "Here try this," he said and handed her a steaming cup of herbal tea.

Marci sat up and took the cup with gratitude. "Thank you," she said, "this is just what I need," and took a sip of the warm liquid.

Jake checked on Meredith and found her sound asleep and returned to the master bedroom to find Marci lying on her back, snoring gently. The half-empty cup sat on the nightstand. Jake smiled as he gazed down at his beautiful wife and then fetched an afghan from the linen closet, covered her, and quietly left the room.

Slanting rays of sunshine highlighted the dust motes that floated through the air beneath the McLeod bedroom window. Marci sat up, rubbed her eyes with her knuckles, and called out, "Jake, where are you?"

He answered, "I'm in the kitchen; can I bring you some breakfast? You've been out since seven o'clock last night."

"What time is it?"

"It's ten after eight."

"What!" she cried out. "Why didn't you wake me?"

"Jamie called and said there was no change in the investigation and they still don't know where Barton is. He also said that Bryan Sherrill is in critical, but stable condition. Why don't you just lie there and I'll bring you breakfast in bed."

Instead of staying in bed, Marci got up and headed for the bathroom. "Will you fix me a couple of eggs, bacon, and coffee while I shower?" she asked. "I gotta get up there. And Jake," she said, "I love you."

"I love you, too, that's why I let you sleep. You were totally exhausted. You'll think much more clearly today after that good night's rest. I've already called the sheriff and told him you would be a little late."

"What'd the sheriff say?" she called out as she turned on the shower.

"He said he understood. He's worried about you putting in so many hours and said to remind you that there are other people on the force, too."

"That sounds like Charlie," Marci said laughing.

Jake had eggs, juice, bacon, toast, and coffee waiting for her when she came to the table dressed and ready for work. Her hair was still damp from the shower and Jake came over and kissed the top of her head while she was eating. "You smell so good right out of the shower," he said and kissed her neck.

"You better stop that right now," Marci said, "or I'll never get to work."

"Work will be there. Take your time."

"Where's Meredith?" Marci asked.

"Joanie came and took her to McDonald's and then they're going to open the gallery."

"What in the world would we do without our friends," Marci said rising from her chair and lacing her arms around Jake's neck.

"I honestly don't know. They're the best, that's for sure."

Marci tilted her head up and kissed Jake on the lips and said, "I really have to go now."

"I know. You go and catch the SOB that has turned our lives upside down. I'll be here."

"Thanks for understanding, darling, and Jake…"

"Yes?"

"Don't go back to Love Valley 'til this is over."

"Deal," he said and kissed her again. "Now get up there and do your thing."

With that, Marci was out the door and headed for head-quarters.

A few miles up the road her cell phone rang.

CHAPTER 103

BARTON SPENT a fitful night on the hard, cold floor of the deserted house and woke up with an excruciating headache. "Damn," he said grabbing both sides of his head in his hands. *What the hell else can go wrong? Why does everything have to happen to me,* he complained to himself.

Looking out the window, he was disappointed to see that low-hanging clouds had obliterated the sun and had removed any way for him to determine which direction he needed to go.

Cars were beginning to pass by the house now that daylight had come. *What if some nosy neighbor drives by and notices my truck in back of the house? Hell, I better get outta here while the gettin' is good.*

Barton went to the bathroom and relieved himself and then remembered there was no running water. *Hell,* he thought when zipping up his fly, *what difference does it make any way? They should-n't have turned the water off!*

The sound of another vehicle was heard in the distance and

Jerome raced to the window just in time to see an old man driving a GMC pickup. He watched as the driver slowed in front of the house before eventually going on down the road.

I better get goin' now. I didn't like the way that old man slowed down and looked at the house. Maybe he knows the folks that own this place.

Barton's throbbing headache made his morning even more miserable. *Damn this hurts. I got to get me something for my head. It hurts like a sonovabitch.*

He panicked when he got to his truck. Even though he'd parked it behind the house, it still could be seen from the road.

After a final look to see if someone was coming down the road, Barton opened the door and climbed in the pickup.

A grinding noise came from under the hood of the truck when he turned the key in the ignition. He tried again, still nothing. Once more he tried and this time the sound was weaker.

More curse words spewed from his mouth in torrents when he realized that the battery in the truck was dead. *Why in the hell can't nothin' go right? Of all the trucks I could steal, I had to get one with a damn no-good battery.*

Frustrated, Barton grabbed the pistols from the seat and threw them into the pillowcase full of money, climbed out of the truck, and slammed the door so hard the fenders rattled. Barton looked both ways down the road trying to decide which way to go when he heard another approaching vehicle.

Standing beside the empty carport, he watched as a lone woman, who appeared to be in her forties, slowed her Volvo and came to a stop in front of the house. An idea suddenly materialized in the murderer's brain. "Help me!" he yelled as he ran down the driveway. 'Please help me!"

With a puzzled look on her face, the woman lowered the passenger window and asked, "What's wrong? What happened?"

Without hesitation, Barton said as he peered into the Volvo,

"My truck won't start! Can you give me a lift?"

Before she gave him an answer, she asked him, "Are you going to buy the Webster's house?"

"Well, I have been looking for a smaller place and this one sure looked good to me so I thought I would check it out while I was in the area."

She noticed the sack he was carrying and said, "I'm just going to the store; will that help?"

"Yes, ma'am, it sure will," Barton said.

The woman was hesitant, but flipped the locks. Barton climbed into the automobile with the woman and promptly pulled the .45 out of the sack and pointed the weapon toward her. "Get out!" he ordered, "or I'll kill you where you're settin'."

Terrified, the woman pled, "What are you doing?"

"I'm takin' your damn car, that's what I'm doin'."

"Please don't hurt me," she begged. "I'll do anything you say, just don't hurt me. I have three children. They need their mother."

"Okay, just shut the hell up and get out of the car. Leave your purse and get outta here before I change my mind."

The woman fled from the car and ran up the driveway and disappeared behind the house.

Barton raced around the car, climbed into the driver's seat, and sped away. A mile down the road, he pulled over and stopped on the shoulder of the road and retrieved the woman's purse and rifled through it. He found her cell phone and several dollars stuffed among an assortment of grocery coupons.

Barton eased back onto the road, noticed the digital compass in the Volvo, and realized he was now heading west. He felt he should get off Trumpet Branch Road as soon as possible and turned left at the next intersection. He was now headed down Eupeptic Springs Road and had no idea where it would take him.

The owner of the Volvo had wasted no time in flagging

down the next automobile that had driven by the Webster house and had them to promptly dial 911 on their cell phone.

CHAPTER 104

"DETECTIVE MCLEOD," the deputy said when Marci answered her phone. "I think we've got a break. A Mrs. Harriet Costner just reported that her 2007 Volvo Wagon was carjacked less than five minutes ago. By the description she gave us, I'm sure it's Barton and he's heading west on Trumpet Branch Road."

"That's great news," Marci said. She quickly asked the deputy, "Trumpet Branch doesn't come out on 115, does it?"

"No, ma'am, it crosses over Eupeptic Springs and Myer's Mill Road. After Myer's Mill the road becomes Prospect Road and that will come out on 115."

"Thanks," Marci said. "Are there any other ways he can get out of there besides Prospect Road?"

"Yes, ma'am. He could take Eupeptic Springs and that would take him south toward Friendship Road. If he turns east from there, it's a straight shot to Jennings Road and I-77—that is if he knows to turn to the right when he gets to Tomlin Mill

Road."

"The perp's from Galax, Virginia. He probably doesn't have a clue where he's heading," Marci said.

"Detective," the deputy said. "The woman who owns the Volvo wagon also told us that her purse is still in the car and it has her cell phone in it."

"It gets better all the time," Marci said. "Has Detective Campbell come in yet?"

"Yes ma'am, he's right here."

"Tell him to stay put. I'm almost there."

Ten minutes later, Jamie Campbell met her at the door. "We're gonna get the bastard today," he said excitedly. "I've contacted the highway patrol and they already have two cruisers headed toward the intersection of Tomlin Mill Road and I-77."

"Good work," Marci said, "but let's not congratulate ourselves too early, he could turn and head the other way. He doesn't have a clue where he's going. Let's put a tracer on that cell phone and find out exactly where he is."

"That's already in place," Jamie said with pride.

"Good. Do you have that lady's cell phone number handy?" Marci asked.

"I sure do," Jamie replied. "Why do you want it?"

"Come on, let's get going and I'll show you on the way."

CHAPTER 105

W HILE DETECTIVE Campbell drove, Marci picked up her phone and dialed the Costner woman's cell phone.

Jamie mouthed the words, "What the hell are you doin'?"

Marci put her hand over the microphone and whispered, "We are going on the offensive. I am calling Mr. Barton."

"You're crazy, McLeod. Do you think he'll even answer?"

"I surely do. Just wait and see."

Marci could hear the phone ring on the other end. On the fifth ring, Barton answered with a tentative, "Hello."

"Hello, Jerome," Marci said sweetly. "This is your worst nightmare calling."

"Who the hell is this?" he barked.

"Why, Jerome, I'm disappointed that you don't recognize my voice."

"Who is this, dammit?" he demanded.

"Why, Jerome," Marci said, "you knew it would only be a

matter of time before we caught you!"

"Who is this?" he asked again.

"It's Detective Marci McLeod. Would you like to meet me personally so we can talk face to face? We're not very far from you now."

"You're just jerkin' my damn chain. You ain't nowhere near me. You don't have a clue where I am."

"Aren't you on Prospect Road, Jerome?" Marci asked, really shaking him up.

Barton saw the intersection ahead and quickly made a left turn almost throwing the Volvo into a skid. He headed south on Eupeptic Springs Road as fast as he could and still keep the Volvo under control.

Marci was guessing now, but asked, "How do you like Eupeptic Springs Road, Jerome? It's a pretty drive, isn't it? I'm not that far away, why don't you wait on me?"

Barton lowered the driver's window and threw the cell phone across the highway and into a weeded ditch. He screeched to a halt when he came to the stop sign at Friendship Road. He sped down the rural highway until he approached another stop sign. Without thinking he turned back left onto Jennings Road and soon saw where it turned into Tomlin Mill Road. He'd seen that road before and knew it would lead him to the interstate.

With renewed hope, he drove the short distance toward the interstate, but his hopes were dashed when he saw two North Carolina Highway Patrol cruisers waiting near the ramp. He panicked and swung left on Woodpecker Road. *Who in the hell named these roads up here,* he thought. He drove as fast as he dared on the unfamiliar road. A sharp curve loomed ahead and the Volvo skidded violently, but he kept the wagon under control. Suddenly, he heard the sound of sirens in the distance and he looked in the rearview mirror, but saw no one following him.

One of the troopers near the I-77 ramp saw the Volvo

swerve onto Woodpecker Road, so he sped north to where it would intersect with Jennings Road. Jerome was just entering the intersection when he saw the trooper fast approaching and pressed hard on the accelerator. He put the wagon into a sideways skid and barreled up Jennings Road with the trooper in hot pursuit.

"I am giving chase as we speak," the trooper said into his radio. I have the perp in sight heading north on Jennings Road."

Marci and Jamie had been patched through and were listening to the transmission as events unfolded. "Let's get up there as fast as we can, Jamie," Marci said.

She pressed the mic in their Dodge Charger and spoke to the trooper in pursuit. "Slow down but keep the bastard in sight. Let us know if he turns off anywhere."

"Will do," he said as he backed off slightly.

Marci and Jamie sped up Highway 115 with blue lights flashing. "We can be in the area by the time he gets there," she said.

"There are so many roads branching off Jennings, I just hope we'll find him," Jamie said.

"We'll find the bastard this time," Marci said with conviction. "You just keep driving."

Jamie couldn't help but smile at Marci's renewed fervor in finding the killer who had eluded them for so long. "Yes, ma'am," he said and kept the cruiser speeding north.

"We've lost him!" the trooper said on the radio.

"You what?' Marci barked into the microphone.

"I backed off just a little and when I rounded a curve, he was gone."

"Where are you now?" Marci asked.

"Just past Weisner Road. He must've taken it. I'm gonna swing around and hope that's where he went."

"Turn here on Prospect Road," Marci ordered Jamie.

"That'll take us close to him."

Jamie quickly swerved the cruiser onto Prospect Road. "Where to now?" he asked.

Seeing an intersection ahead, Marci suggested, "Turn right on Eupeptic Springs."

The trooper's voice came back on the line, "He's abandoned his vehicle on Clifford Road."

Seeing the sign, Marci yelled, "Stop!" Jamie hit the brakes and skidded to a halt.

Turn here on Clifford Road. That's where the bastard is," Marci said. "Call the K-9 unit again. He's abandoned the car and is on foot. We've got him now."

CHAPTER 106

BARTON PRESSED the accelerator hard and took a speedy right onto Clifford Road. He hoped the trooper hadn't seen him make the turn. He looked in the mirror and there was no sign of anybody following. Jerome knew that he could not keep outrunning them in the car, so he slid to a stop beside a barbed wire pasture fence. He grabbed the sack with the money and the pistols and hurriedly crossed over the fence and headed toward a distant patch of woods.

He was breathing hard when he reached the edge of the trees. The trooper pulled in behind the Volvo and immediately got on his radio. Barton saw him through the trees and turned and headed deeper into the woods. "Damn, what else can go wrong?" he said aloud. *I shoulda left when I had the chance. That woman is goin' to be the death of me.*

"There's his car, pull over," Marci said. She and Jamie bounded out of their Charger and ran to the trooper who was waiting beside the Volvo.

"Any sign of the perp?" Marci asked.

"No, ma'am, but he crossed the fence over there and headed for the woods."

Jamie asked the trooper to stay with the vehicle in case Barton returned to the Volvo and then he and Marci crossed the fence. "Look here," Jamie said pointing to footprints in the sparse pasture. "It looks like he went that way."

"Well, what are we waiting for?" Marci asked. "Let's go get the bastard."

"Don't you think we should wait for backup?"

"I've waited long enough. If we're not careful, we're gonna lose him again. I'm not waiting any longer."

Jamie radioed Sheriff Nichols that they were in pursuit on foot. Carefully following bent blades of grass and an occasional footprint, the pair made their way across the pasture.

"You haven't forgotten he's armed, have you?" Jamie asked.

"No," Marci said. "I haven't forgotten."

The woods were thick with pine, poplar, hickory, and oak. A few gum trees grew randomly between them. The forest floor was covered with a mixture of leaves and pine needles. "It looks like he's been through here," Jamie said as he knelt and examined the disturbed leaves and broken limbs left behind as a result of Barton's hasty retreat.

A hundred yards deeper into the woods, the trail seemed to disappear. "Dammit! Where did the bastard go?" Marci peered through the trees and saw nothing.

"Don't you think we should wait for backup?" Jamie asked again.

She was about to answer when a gunshot exploded from behind a tree.

Jamie collapsed, clutching his chest.

"Jamie!" Marci screamed. She ran over and fell on her

knees beside him. "Jamie, Jamie," Marci cried.

Stunned, Campbell looked up at Marci but couldn't speak. Pain and confusion was written all over his face.

A calm, but threatening voice emanated from behind Marci. "Alright, Detective, don't move a muscle or you'll be as dead as your partner. I'm not sayin' it again, don't move."

Marci heard him coming closer and closer.

"Okay," the voice commanded, "get up slowly and turn around where I can see you."

She stood, turned around, and stared into the face of the Jerome Barton. He hadn't shaved for days; his clothes were torn and dirty. He locked his eyes on Marci and held her stare. It was if he was looking right through her.

A sinister smile broke across his face. "Now, who's holding the cards, Detective?"

"You killed my partner, you son of a bitch! Why! Why did you have to kill all these innocent people?"

"Because I could," Barton responded, "and besides that, I didn't want no witnesses hangin' around."

"What about me, I'm a witness," Marci said.

Barton gazed up and down Marci's body one inch at a time and said with a wide grin, "Why do you think I stayed in the area all this time. You're all I thought about for the last few weeks. Ever since I first saw you at the Silver Spur with your family, I wanted you. I saw you when you gave your daughter that horse, too, and that night at the rodeo. You looked especially good that night."

"I saw you, too," Marci said. "I followed you up the hill behind the arena and into town, but I lost you."

"I should have let you catch me that night and we could have had some fun together," Barton said.

Marci looked at her partner lying in the leaves and then said, "Jerome Barton, you are under arrest for murder. You have the right to remain silent. Anything you say can and will be used against you in a court of law. You have a right to an attorney…"

Barton laughed. "Are you kiddin' me? Are you readin' me my damn rights?"

"I sure the hell am," Marci said. "Now, do you want to come peaceably or not?"

"I don't believe this. Who's got the damn gun here, detective?"

"I do," Jamie Campbell said. Propped up on one elbow, he had his Glock pointed directly at Barton's chest. "You even flinch and I'll blow a hole in your chest big enough to drive a truck through."

The killer had been so focused on Marci he had forgotten about Jamie Campbell. Marci watched as Barton's finger tightened on the trigger of Bud Beckett's old .45.

Barton challenged, "You're not goin' to shoot me. You know I'll pull the trigger on this bitch detective before I hit the ground."

"Oh, no you won't," Jamie challenged. Barton swung his gun toward the prostrate detective lying on the ground, but before he could pull the trigger, Marci drew her Glock 40 and shot him in the chest, blowing his body back into a cedar tree where it slowly slid to the ground. The lingering smell of cordite hung in the air as a small tendril of smoke curled from the barrel of her gun. Jamie Campbell then closed his eyes and fell back onto the ground.

Marci quickly ran to Barton, kicked the gun farther away from his outstretched hand, and then knelt down to check for a pulse.

Jerome Barton was dead and she turned her attention to her partner.

CHAPTER 107

MARCI CRADLED Jamie into her arms. She could feel his breath against her skin. Marci radioed their position and asked for the coroner's wagon and an ambulance. She prayed that Campbell would be okay.

A few minutes passed and she felt Jamie stir in her arms. "You can stop crying now, it's over," Jamie said as he looked up at her.

Marci peered down into the glazed eyes of her partner. "Help's on the way, you'll be okay. Just hang in there, Jamie."

He looked up at her again and said with a slight grin, "You got one helluva short memory, Detective. Don't you remember telling all of us to wear our vests until this bastard was caught?"

"You mean you're not hurt?" she wailed.

"Hell, it'll take more than a shot in the vest to get this detective."

The always strong, hard-charging Marci McLeod then

broke into sobs as she held him in her arms. Now it was time for Jamie Campbell to console his partner.

After a few minutes, she dried her eyes with the sleeve of her coat. "Can you get up?" she asked and released him from her embrace.

"I think so," he said, "but I like you holding me better."

"Asshole," Marci said with a grin. She then got up from the ground and placed one arm under Campbell and helped him to his feet.

"Wow, don't ever let me do anything like that again partner. It hurts like a son of a bitch," Jamie said holding on to her for support.

After they were both standing, Marci said, "I've got to sit down, Jamie. I have given my all to this case. I'm all used up." She found a tree stump where she could sit while waiting for help to arrive.

Charlie Nichols, the sheriff himself, came in with the first group. He saw his lead detective sitting on a stump alongside Jamie Campbell. "Helluva job here. I knew you two would get that bastard. Good work. I'm proud of ya both," he said so everyone could hear.

The coroner's wagon and ambulance pulled close to the edge of the woods. As the EMTs approached Marci, who was still sitting on the stump talking with the sheriff, she suddenly keeled over and collapsed in a heap onto the ground.

"Marci," Jamie yelled and limped to her side.

"She has a strong pulse sir," the EMT said to the sheriff. "But let's get her to the hospital and have her checked out."

"Don't waste any time," Nichols said, "and take Campbell with you and have him checked out. I'll finish up here with the crime scene boys."

With lights blazing, the ambulance raced down Highway 115 toward Statesville with the two Iredell County Detectives.

Marci regained consciousness on the way to the hospital and looked over at Jamie lying on the other gurney. "What happened?"

"You passed out. You're outta gas, Marci. You've been running on empty for weeks. But, we got our man." With that, Jamie reached over and grabbed her hand and gave it a squeeze. "Now go back to sleep."

"What about Jake, has anybody called him?"

"Why don't you wait and call him from the hospital?"

"Hospital?"

"Yes, they're taking us both there for observation."

Marci lay back on the gurney. "You know, I think that's a good idea." She closed her eyes and slept all the way to Iredell Memorial Hospital.

CHAPTER 108

MARCI AND JAMIE were wheeled into the emergency room where they were examined and then admitted for overnight observation.

After Marci was settled in her room, a nurse entered to take her vital signs again. Marci desperately wanted to call Jake, but she could not hold her eyes open. She asked the nurse to dial her home number and then hand her the phone. After four rings, Marci heard his familiar voice on the other end of the line. "Jake," she said weakly.

"Are you okay, Marci? You sound drunk."

"I'm not drunk, just a little sleepy that's all."

"Sleepy, what're you talking about? Where are you?"

"I'm all safe and sound now," she said."

"Marci, make sense. Where are you?" Jake pleaded.

The nurse, overhearing Marci's side of the conversation; took the phone and explained that the exhausted detective had been given a sedative and would be resting comfortably for the remainder of the day and most of the night.

"What!" Jake said loudly to the nurse. "Somebody better tell me where my wife is."

"She's in room 414 at Iredell Memorial Hospital, sir. She's fine. She just needs rest."

"Room 414." Jake repeated as he slammed the phone down, but then picked it back up and called the reliable Joanie Mitchell.

"Joanie, can you come and stay with Meredith? Marci's in the hospital!"

"Hospital?" Joanie asked. "Is she alright?"

"The nurse assured me she would be fine, but I've got to see for myself."

"I'll be right over," Joanie said. "You just don't worry about a thing."

Five minutes later, Joanie was coloring with Meredith in her favorite coloring book and Jake was on his way to Statesville.

Jake ran from the hospital parking lot all the way to the information desk before stopping to catch his breath. "How do I get to room 414?" he asked impatiently.

The kind woman behind the desk pointed him in the right direction. His heart was beating wildly when he exited the elevator on the fourth floor. Checking the numbers as he raced down the hall, he finally found 414 and barged in without knocking.

Marci lay in the bed with her red hair fanned out over the pillow. She was sleeping soundly and, to Jake, looked just like an angel. He slid a chair over to the bed and gently took her hand in his and prayed.

"Marci," Jake said in a barely audible voice, "can you hear me?" She lay as still as a statue and Jake leaned over and kissed her gently on the forehead. "I love you," he said, "more than anything else in the world."

After seeing Jake barge into Marci's room, the nurse opened the door and motioned for Jake to step outside. "She's just totally exhausted, sir. That's all. She'll be fine," the nurse assured him.

"How'd she get here?" Jake asked. "She was working a murder case in North Iredell."

"You'll have to ask somebody else about that, sir," the nurse said.

"Thank you, nurse," Jake said and silently crept back into Marci's room. He sat beside her bed, holding her hand until he, too, dozed off.

A light peck on the door roused Jake from his sleep. He stood and said softly, "Come in."

Sheriff Nichols strode into the room and looked down at Marci sleeping. "She doin' okay?"

"All I know is what they tell me," Jake said. "The shift nurse said she was just exhausted."

Nichols grabbed Jake's hand and began pumping it. "You got a brave woman there, Jake."

Taken aback, he asked the sheriff, "Brave? What'd she do?"

"You mean you don't know yet?"

"I don't know a damn thing, Sheriff," Jake said.

"Aw hell, Jake, I'm sorry. Jamie said that Marci wanted to call and give you the news herself, so I just figured you knew by now."

"Sheriff, will you please tell me what happened to my wife?"

"Let's step outside," the sheriff said. Nichols told Jake how Marci had called the murderer on the stolen cell phone, tracked him down, and subsequently killed him. "She never gave up, Jake. As exhausted as she was, she never gave up. And the best part is how her hunches paid off. We ain't got anybody else in the department who has the instincts she has."

Jake just stood there dumbfounded.

"You ain't gonna believe this, Jake," the sheriff continued. "That woman of yours stood there while Barton had his gun aimed right at her and she had the balls to read the damn man his rights." Nichols laughed so hard he almost choked. "She was going to arrest the son of a bitch and he was holding the gun on her."

Jake felt weak hearing all this. "Then what happened, Sheriff?"

"Well, even though Campbell had been shot himself," Nichols continued, "he leaned up on one elbow and caught Barton off guard."

"Yeah, and then what happened?"

"I'll tell you what happened. When Barton turned to shoot Campbell, that beautiful wife of yours drew her gun and shot the bastard before he could blink an eye. Ain't that the damndest thing you ever heard? If she was a man, she'd have balls hanging down to here," Nichols said laughing and gesturing about a foot below his crotch.

Jake laughed with the sheriff, but inwardly he ached. Once again his wife had come very close to being killed in the line of duty. "I gotta sit down," Jake said on the verge of collapsing.

"It kinda gets to you, don't it?" Nichols said. "That's one brave woman in there and the Iredell County Sheriff's Department is sure damn proud of 'er."

"I just don't know what to think about that woman," Jake said. "She makes me laugh. She makes me happy. She's a wonderful wife and a fantastic mother and at the same time, she worries the living hell outta me."

The sheriff laughed. "Welcome to being married to a law enforcement officer, my boy," and laughed again. "Jake, you're a lucky man. Marci McLeod is one helluva woman and a damn great detective."

"Yeah, I hear you, Sheriff. I'm tickled to death she got her man, but I'm afraid one day that the thrill of victory is gonna get her killed."

"Don't even talk like that, Jake," Nichols said turning more serious.

"I can't help it, Sheriff. You don't have to live with her and see the way this case has worn her out. She drags home late at night and falls into bed, totally exhausted, but then she doesn't sleep. This case has wrung her out, Charlie. She doesn't have anything left."

"She deserves some time off, that's for damn sure," Nichols said. "Ain't y'all into horses now?"

"Yeah, I guess so. What's that got to do with anything?"

"Well, sometimes just being around horses is good for the soul. Just ridin' through the countryside can be therapeutic. Even smelling hay and horseshit helps get your mind off stuff. Don't sell it short, Jake," the sheriff said.

"I won't," Jake said. "We bought Meredith a small horse that we keep at Love Valley and we all enjoy riding together."

"Why there you go," Nichols said. "That's just what the doctor ordered. Y'all get up there and do some serious ridin'."

"I hope Marci will still want to go back there after all that's happened," Jake said.

"I see what you mean," Nichols said. "You'll work it out, I'm sure. Tell Marci she done good and I'll see her when she gets back to do all that paperwork," the sheriff said as he turned to leave. Nichols stopped, turned back around, looked Jake in the eye and added, "That is one of the finest detectives we've ever had lying in there in that bed. You do what you need to do, Jake, but by God you make sure that woman of yours is happy." With that, Charlie Nichols turned and strode down the hall.

After he left, Jake thought to himself. *What will I say to Marci when she wakes up? How can I tell her how concerned I am for her? She loves her job. It's what she does and she's good at it. Is it fair for me to ask her to quit something she loves?*

The sun had set and the lights from the traffic on Interstate 40 could be seen from the window of room 414. Marci had slept all afternoon and Jake stood at the window staring at his reflection. He called Joanie and told her how Marci and Jamie had finally taken care of the Love Valley murderer. He was confident that the news was now all over Mooresville and most of Iredell County.

"You don't worry about Meredith at all. I'll spend the night at your house with her," Joanie said. "We'll have a ball. Hell, we'll make some cookies. You just stay with Marci and take care of her. She must be plumb tuckered out."

"Yes, she is," Jake said, "and thank you so much, Joanie. I don't know what in the world we'd do without our friends. You all are so good to us."

"That's what friends are for," Joanie said, "now you get you some sleep, too. Everything will look better in the morning."

CHAPTER 109

JAKE STOOD at the window watching semis racing up and down I-40. The sun was shining brightly and he could see a red-tailed hawk soaring over the highway.

"Jake," Marci said barely above a whisper. "What are you doing just standing there staring out at nothing?"

"Marci," Jake said, "you're finally awake."

"Where am I?" she asked.

"You're in Iredell Memorial Hospital," Jake said.

"What am I doing here?"

"I think the best answer I could find from anybody is that you were totally exhausted, both mentally and physically."

"I'll have to admit, I was pretty tired," Marci said.

"Pretty tired!" Jake said incredulously. "You slept all yesterday afternoon, all night last night, and half the morning today. I'd say that it's more than pretty tired."

"Are you mad at me, Jake?"

"Oh, Marci, how could I be mad at you? You just scare the living hell out of me on a regular basis, that's all."

"I'm sorry, Jake. Really I am. I was calling you to explain everything when it hit me like a ton of bricks. I guess everything just finally caught up with me."

"I know," Jake said. "But I was scared to death after the nurse came on the line. I didn't even know you were in the hospital and hearing you talk like that...well, I just lost it."

"I'm sorry," she said. "Come over here and let's make up."

Jake went over to her bedside, leaned down, and kissed her on the lips.

"Now, that's better, isn't it?"

"Yes, dammit," Jake said. "But you don't understand what I went through, either. I came up here to find out from the sheriff that you were reading a killer his Miranda Rights while he had his gun pointing at your gut. Were you crazy?"

"No, it just seemed like a good idea at the time. I thought the son of a bitch had already killed Jamie and I figured I was next in line."

Jake sat down on the edge of her bed and laid his head on her breast. "Oh, Marci," was all he could say.

While gently running her fingers through his hair, she said in a whisper, "Jamie saved my life, Jake. When Barton turned his gun on him, that gave me a chance to shoot the bastard."

Marci and Jake embraced each other, then both broke down and cried.

CHAPTER 110

JAMES AND GAIL Caldwell sat at the kitchen table with Joanie and Ed while Meredith was engrossed in her coloring book on the den floor. "I'm sure glad y'all came over," Joanie said. "They oughta be here any minute."

"How is Marci, have you heard any more?" Gail asked.

"Just that she had passed out and was in the hospital. Probably from exhaustion, that girl has hardly stopped in weeks. Jake said they wanted to keep her overnight."

Gail turned her head at the sound of a car door being shut. "I'll bet that's them now," she said.

"Mommy!" Meredith ran to her mother. "Joanie spent the night! We colored and read books and stayed up real late."

"You did?" Marci said as she swept Meredith up into her arms.

"Uh huh, and we made cookies, too, you want one?"

"Do I not get a hug, too?" Jake whined.

"Sure you do," Meredith said. "Put me down, Mommy, so I can hug Daddy, too."

Jake gave little Meredith a big hug and set her down so she could go back to her coloring.

"What's going on?" Marci asked.

"Ed brought Meredith and me a biscuit from Hardee's and we were having a cup of coffee when Gail and James stopped in to check on you," Joanie said.

Gail and James rose and gave Marci a warm hug. "We just stopped by to drop off a chicken pot pie for your lunch. Joanie said you were on your way home, so we decided to wait and see you."

"Thanks," Marci said to Gail. "You girls are the greatest."

"I've got some coffee made," Joanie said to Marci. "Let's sit at the table and you can tell us all about what happened up there in the woods."

Marci looked to Jake for guidance. She knew she needed the rest, but how could she tell them that another time would be better. Marci shared almost everything that led up to the time of the subsequent death of the killer.

When she got to the part about calling Barton on the cell phone, Joanie said, "You go, girl!"

Then Marci grew quiet and hesitated when she got to the part about shooting Barton.

Jake broke in, "Tell them everything, Marci."

"I thought I did."

"You left out the part about reading Barton his rights while he had his damn pistol trained on your chest."

A small voice was heard in the other room. "We don't say damn no more, Daddy."

"She had to remind me a couple of times about my language last night, too," Joanie confessed. "Now tell me about reading that guy his rights."

There was a knock on the kitchen door and before Jake could answer it, in walked Carson and Debbie Wells. Joanie said. "Grab a chair and a cup of coffee and join us. Marci was tellin' us about how they caught the killer and was just gettin' to the part about readin' the guy his rights."

Fresh coffee was poured and everyone found a seat. Conversation resumed and Marci was about to begin again when Joanie interrupted, "You might as well start over, Marci."

Marci repeated what she had already told for the benefit of the latecomers and then got to the part where Jamie was pointing his gun at Barton and paused.

"What the hell happened?" Joanie asked.

"Marci shot the man. She killed him," Jake said.

Silence…No one knew what to say. Gail rose from her chair and placed her arm around Marci.

Tears fell from Marci's eyes as she thought about her partner being shot and the moment she thought would be her last.

"Are you okay?" Gail asked.

"Yeah, I guess I'm alright."

Debbie said, "I'm sorry. We didn't know."

"Hellfire, I didn't know either 'til right then," Joanie exclaimed.

Jake took over the telling of the story to make it easier on Marci. When he'd finished, Ed Mitchell wiped his eyes with his handkerchief then handed it to Joanie.

"You didn't have a choice, Marci," Carson Wells said. "He would have killed you both."

"I know," Marci said, "but it's still tough. The entire case has taken its toll on me mentally and physically. I don't have any energy. I'm just drained."

Debbie said with some emotion, "Do you think it would help if you saw your regular doctor?"

Gail agreed, "Debbie's right, Marci, it couldn't hurt."

"I might do that," Marci said to pacify the group. She sat quietly for a moment and then added, "I don't want to hurt anybody's feelings, but I think I'll go lie down for a while."

After Marci excused herself and went to the bedroom, Jake said to his guests, "I'm going to make her an appointment with the doctor. She hasn't been herself for several weeks now. I know Marci's been through an awful lot and is totally exhausted, but I want to be sure that's all it is."

"I'll say she's been through a lot," Joanie agreed and then added, "why don't you do it now before you forget? I know how you men are."

Everyone smiled at Joanie. If she thought it, she said it. She rose from the table and began carrying coffee cups to the sink while Jake obediently went to make the call to Marci's doctor. Gail joined Joanie at the sink and asked her in a low voice, "Do you think Marci is okay?"

"She's not the same ol' girl she was before all this happened in Love Valley, that's for sure," Joanie said.

Jake returned to the kitchen and announced "I've made Marci an appointment with her doctor for Friday of next week. Before you say anything; that was the earliest one I could get."

"Well, it is what it is," Joanie said. "At least you got one, Jake, I'm damn proud of ya."

"We don't say damn no more," was heard again coming from the den.

"That child is gonna have me cussin' if she don't quit correctin' me."

Gail joined in, "You can't change, Joanie, admit it. That would be like a leopard changing his spots."

"Why I can sure as hell try, can't I?"

The same small voice was heard from the den, "We don't say hell no more, Joanie."

Everybody laughed and Gail said, "Let's let Jake get some

rest, too."

Jake thanked them for their support and suggested they all go to Love Valley the first Saturday that Marci was up to it. "Meredith has been begging to ride Freckles and we can all spend a relaxing time together."

They all agreed that it was a great idea and hoped it would not be long until Marci was her old self again.

After they left, Jake joined Meredith on the den floor with her coloring books and crayons. "Is Mommy alright, Daddy? She went to bed and the sun is shinin' outside."

"Yes, darling," Jake said gathering her in his arms, "Mommy's fine. She's just tired, that's all."

CHAPTER III

THE FOLLOWING Friday morning found Marci sitting in the waiting room at Dr. Melanie McCaskill's office reading the latest edition of *Our State* magazine. Dr. McCaskill was relatively new in Mooresville; Marci had been seeing her two years and liked the young doctor very much. They had become friends and Dr. McCaskill was someone that Marci could talk with on just about any subject.

Marci's name was called just as she had gotten absorbed in an article about the Outer Banks. She was led into an examination room where she had to wait again. It was a good thing that she had the foresight to take the magazine with her from the waiting room.

"Well, how're you doing, Marci?" Dr. McCaskill asked as she breezed into the room. "I see where you took care of the situation in Love Valley. Congratulations!"

"I think I am feeling better, but Jake insisted that I come to see you anyway."

"Jake's a smart man. You did very well in the husband department, if you don't mind me saying."

"Oh, I don't mind at all. He's a wonderful man."

The doctor examined Marci very carefully, checking all her vital signs, and pushing and probing. After taking her stethoscope from her ears and looping it around her neck, she asked, "Have you been feeling a little weak, lately?"

"Why yes, I have. Why do you ask that?"

"Have you missed a period, Marci?"

"Why yes. Yes I have. I thought maybe it was from all the stress."

"Well, I think it's a little more than stress," Dr. McCaskill said with a grin.

"What is it then?" Marci said getting more anxious.

"You're pregnant."

The usually fearless Marci McLeod fell back on the examination table in a dead-faint.

"Marci, you're gonna be alright," she heard as she opened her eyes and saw Dr. McCaskill holding her hand.

"What happened?" Marci said looking bewildered.

"You fainted," the doctor said smiling.

"I've never fainted in my life," Marci said with defiance as she sat up. She hesitated and then added, "Unless you count the two times I collapsed while working that murder case."

"Well, you just fainted right here on the examination table, Marci, and it's nothing to be ashamed of. You've just had quite a shock."

"Did you just say that I'm pregnant?"

"I did!"

Marci lay back on the table again and took a deep breath. "Is that why I have been feeling so out-of-sorts?"

"More than likely."

"Well, what in the world am I going to tell Jake?"

"Tell him, 'Congratulations, you're going to be a father again.'"

Marci laughed. "I'm not too old to have this baby, am I?"

The doctor laughed, "No, Marci, you're not too old. You'll be fine. Jake's the one I'm worried about. He might have a heart attack when he gets the news."

"I think I will wait until the time is right to break the news to him. He's had a lot to deal with lately."

"You're not that far along yet, tell him when you feel the time is right." The doctor squeezed her hand as happy tears coursed down Detective Marci McLeod's cheeks.

CHAPTER 112

THE STATESVILLE RECORD and Landmark ran a feature story on the manhunt. Pictures of Marci McLeod, Jamie Campbell, and Sheriff Charlie Nichols covered the front page. The "regulars" who gathered around the stove at Andy's Hardware talked of little else.

The tragedy that had shaken the small community to its core had also drawn it closer together. Their lives would never be the same, but thanks to the bravery of two Iredell County detectives, the fear that had once overshadowed their lives was now gone. An audible sigh of relief could almost be heard throughout the tiny town of Love Valley.

The main street was once again crowded with visitors. People dressed in their best western clothes sat on benches in front of the General Store laughing and talking. The clip-clopping of horses' hooves resounded up and down the dusty street. This was the Love Valley that drew people from all over the surrounding counties on weekends—a peaceful place made especially for people who love horses and the atmosphere of the old West.

Tori Callanan and Beth Nance had decided a celebration was in order. Of course it didn't take much for the folks of Love Valley to throw a party anyway. So on the Saturday after Easter, red, white, and blue bunting was brought out of storage and hung from store balconies along the main street. American flags hung on practically every post in town. Excitement filled the air in downtown Love Valley.

Marci was feeling much better and the Mooresville Bunch arrived early that morning and parked their cars beside Tori Pass. Jake had called ahead and told Wish when they were coming. Meredith bounded from the car and headed straight for Wish, who was standing alongside Freckles, grinning broadly.

"Hey there, little girl," Wish said as he hefted her into his arms. "Have you missed me?"

"Oh, yes, I've missed you and Freckles, too."

"Freckles has missed you, too," Wish said, "you wanna hop on her right now?"

"I sure do," Meredith said with glee. She let Wish place her onto the saddle and she grabbed the reins with both hands. "I'm ready," she added giggling.

"Let Wish hold the reins and ride you around until we get our horses," Marci said.

"Okay, Mommy," Meredith agreed and off they went up the main street with her waving at anyone who would wave back and some who wouldn't.

"That's one happy little girl," Joanie said.

"She surely is," Marci said, "I wish we could stay like this forever."

Marci's musings were interrupted when she heard someone shouting her name. "Hey, Detective McLeod!" She looked behind her to see Dewayne Allison and Shorty Parsons walking toward them at a fast clip. Allison was grinning from ear to ear. "Boy am I glad to see you," he said reaching for her with outstretched arms.

Marci smiled at Dewayne and welcomed his embrace. "It's good to see you, too, Dewayne," she said. "How have you been?"

"Oh, I've been fine. Me and Shorty have a pretty good business goin'. We're the ones that people call when they need somethin' fixed up or some small building projects done. I want you to know that neither me or Shorty have had another drop to drink."

"That's wonderful, Dewayne. I'm really proud of you," Marci said.

"Well, I'll see ya. I just wanted say howdy and tell you how much I appreciate all you've done for me. You take care of that little girl now, y' hear."

"I will, Dewayne, and congratulations. I'm sure we'll see you more often now that Meredith has a horse here. We will more than likely buy one for ourselves too; so you'll probably be seeing a lot of us."

Jake overheard what she had said, but bit his lip and just smiled.

"That's great," Dewayne said. "See ya later." Dewayne and Shorty strolled up the street toward the General Store and left the Mooresville Bunch staring at each other in disbelief.

"Is that the same Dewayne Allison we met a couple of months ago?" Joanie asked.

"One and the same," Marci said smiling. "You know, it's funny how things work out. I used to despise the man, but now I admire him. He's turned his life around and is making something of himself."

Gail added, "It's just another example of what God can do if people will just let him help them."

"Hey, McLeod, wait up!"

Marci turned to see Chief Sam Kinkaid coming her way. She stared in disbelief as he strode purposely toward them. "Why, Sam, what in the world are you doing down here in Love Valley?"

"I came to see you, what else?"

"To see me? What on earth for?"

"You mean you don't know?"

Perplexed, Marci furrowed her brow and asked, "Know what, Chief?"

"Hells bells, woman. They've declared this Marci McLeod Day in Love Valley!"

"What?"

"Yeah, Sheriff Nichols kept me updated about the case. Hell, we're all so proud of you!"

Marci was speechless. "You are kidding, right?"

"No, ma'am. I'm on the level," Kinkaid said. "Have you decided what you're going to do now? I was surprised to hear you had resigned from the department."

"It was just time," Marci said smiling at Jake.

Jamie Campbell and Sheriff Nichols came striding up the hill on Tori Pass and waved at the crowd that had gathered. "Well, Marci," the sheriff said grinning, "welcome to Marci McLeod Day."

"But wait, I didn't do anything without Jamie by my side. This should be for him, too!"

"Jamie got a promotion and you're out of a job, so hush up!"

Jamie just laughed at Marci's discomfort and then hugged her fiercely.

Andy and Ellenora Barker joined them on the dusty street. Andy, as usual, opened his arms wide, ready for a hug. "Come here, darlin' and give me some luvin'," he said and wrapped his long arms around Marci in a warm bear hug.

"That man'll never change," Ellenora said laughing.

The mayor took Marci's hand and led her and her friends up the main street lined with well-wishers and stopped in front of Tori's gift shop. Marci felt weak and wanted desperately to sit down on the bench in the shade.

All her Love Valley friends were there: Beth Nance, Bob and Judy Adams, Dewayne Allison, Shorty Parsons, Angela Chapman, Sue Ladislaw, and Jack and Linda Jolly. Wish and Meredith came down the street and joined them. Meredith was just pleased to be sitting astride Freckles and had no idea what all the excitement was about.

The mayor's granddaughter, Tori Callanan, pushed Bryan Sherrill out of her shop in his wheelchair onto the sidewalk so he could join the rest of those who had gathered to honor Marci. Thankfully, Sherrill was much better, but needed the wheelchair occasionally. They all waited in anticipation for Mayor Barker to begin.

"Could I get you folks' attention?" Mayor Barker said in a loud voice. "Can we all get quiet for a few minutes?" The assembled crowd gradually grew silent.

"The people of Love Valley lost some good decent folks by the hand of one malicious individual. Chief Sam Kinkaid, Police Chief of Galax, has joined us today as we pay our respects to these victims: Bud Beckett, Hazel Colebrook, and Walter and Maudie Cameron. And let us not forget that Chip and Tiffany Davenport and Beatrice Barton who also lost their lives. Please join us now in silent prayer for each one of these innocent victims." Throughout the crowd, cowboy hats were removed and everyone bowed their heads in reverent silence as the mayor requested.

After a brief period of silence, Sam Kinkaid stepped up. "Thank you, citizens of Love Valley, for allowing me to not only share with you in this time of grief, but for giving me the opportunity to help honor a couple of your local heroes. Mayor Barker, it is now time for you to do the honors."

The crowd applauded Chief Kinkaid for his words as he stepped aside for the mayor.

Andy Barker raised his hands again to quiet the crowd. "The people of Love Valley wanted to show our appreciation to some special people who have brought us through a fearful time in the life of our community. First let me call up Jamie Campbell, the new Chief of Detectives."

Jamie, embarrassed, walked up and shook the mayor's hand. Barker began, "Detective Campbell fought along side Detective McLeod all the way and was instrumental in the apprehension of the murderer. Since he is still an employee of the county, I don't suppose we can heap any fine gifts on him, but we can give him a plaque commemorating the bravery he exhibited while carrying out his duties."

Jamie looked as if he wanted to crawl into a hole and hide. The mayor grabbed Campbell and gave him a big bear hug and then raised the detective's hand high in the air. There were cheers and applause from the crowd as Detective Jamie Campbell accepted his award. After the crowd grew quiet, Sheriff Nichols stepped up and congratulated his new chief Detective.

As the sheriff and Jamie Campbell melted back into the crowd, Mayor Barker motioned for Marci to join him. He wrapped one arm around her as he began speaking to the hushed crowd. "The people of Love Valley have spoken and have declared this to be Marci McLeod Day," the mayor said. The crowd applauded with enthusiasm and Marci looked uncomfortable with all the attention. The mayor waited for the applause to die down and then resumed his speech. "The children ofo Walter and Maudie Cameron and some of us got together and we have a little something for you," he said grinning and looking at a confused Marci McLeod.

All eyes turned to see Charlie Nance and Mutt Burgess leading a beautiful buckskin horse through the crowd. Mutt was carrying a white Resistol hat in one hand and a new pair of women's western boots in the other.

Charlie greeted Marci who was barely standing now, "How you doin', darlin'?"

"I'm in shock right now, Charlie," she managed to say. He handed the reins to Marci and gave her a big hug. With tears in his eyes, he said, "Here's just a little something to show you how much we love you. Her name's Lady."

For a moment, Marci just stood there, holding the reins, looking at Charlie, then Andy, and then Jake for help. She was at a complete loss for words. Jake walked over to her with tears freely flowing and wrapped his arms around her. He looked into those big liquid eyes of hers and said, "Marci McLeod, you're something else did you know that?"

Marci choked back the tears as she attempted to speak. She managed to say: "Thank you wonderful people of Love Valley for all you have done for me and my family. I will cherish Lady forever, ride her frequently, and think of your generosity every time I look at this beautiful animal. God bless you all and thank you again."

CHAPTER 113

THE DAY WENT by in a blur for Marci. The mayor explained that the Camerons' children were selling their parents' home in Love Valley and had little interest in horses. So when the good mayor suggested to them that their prized buckskin could be donated to a worthy cause—the worthy cause being, Marci McLeod—they heartily agreed.

Throngs of people stood in line to give Marci a hug and to wish her well. Everyone felt safe and secure again and was grateful to Marci and Jamie for making that happen.

Finally the Mooresville Bunch was able to speak to Marci.

"Hellfire! Woman, you could run for governor right now and win," Joanie said.

Of course, everyone laughed, but it was obvious that everyone did seem to love Marci McLeod.

A small lady with white hair who appeared to be in her eighties came up to Marci, threw her arms around her and cried,

"Thank you so much for letting me get a good night's sleep again. I'm glad you stopped that son of a bitch, excuse my French, and I'm glad you blew him away. I would have shot the bastard myself if he had come into my house. I keep a .45 right beside me all night." The woman winked at Jake and said to Marci, "If you get tired of your man there, send him over to my house," and walked away laughing.

"Who was that?" Marci said laughing in spite of herself.

"I have no idea," Jake said.

"I better keep a tight rein on you, Buster. It looks like I have some competition," Marci said and grabbed Jake's hand.

"Not to worry, my dear," he said, "you're more than I can handle."

"And don't you forget it," Marci said and laughed.

Most of the afternoon was spent riding along the trails that wound through the woods around Love Valley. Marci felt alive again. She breathed in the Brushy Mountain air with relish and rode alongside Meredith who was having the time of her life. Jake rode a rented sorrel and the rest of the Mooresville Bunch followed along on their mounts. As they headed up Mitchell Trail, a sad-looking hound dog was standing in the middle of the bridle path.

"Look, Mama!" shouted Meredith. "Look at that poor dog. He's lost."

Marci exclaimed, "Why that's ol' Rounder."

"How'd you know that dog's name?" Meredith asked.

"I'm a detective, honey. I know everything," she teased.

"Oh, Mama," Meredith said. "Do you know whose dog it is, Mama?"

"I don't think Rounder has a home now," Marci explained to Meredith.

They reined in their horses and Marci dismounted, stretched out her hand, and called the dog's name. The old hound slowly ambled over to her and plopped down on the dirt. "You poor thing," Marci said as she rubbed him between the ears. "You're all alone now and have no one to scratch behind your ears?"

"Help me down, Mama," Meredith said. "I wanna rub him, too."

Eventually the rest of the party gathered around to witness Marci and Meredith seated on the ground with a melancholy hound dog sprawled between them.

"Well, what do we have here?" Joanie asked.

"This was Bud Beckett's dog," Marci said. "He's homeless now."

"Why the poor thing," Joanie said, "it looks like he's starved half to death."

Before Jake could protest, Marci declared, "Well, Meredith, it looks like we now have a dog in the family, too."

"Really, Mama?"

"I guess so," Marci said as she glanced at Jake for an approving nod.

"Now, I got a dog and a horse," Meredith said. "I'm rich!"

When they returned downtown, a huge feast had been set out in the vacant lot between Mutt's Tack Shop and Tori's Moonshine Gifts.

They tied their horses to the hitching posts and strolled over to the crowd that had gathered. There were plenty of grilled hamburgers and hot dogs for everyone.

"Oh boy, hot dogs," Meredith said and she ran over to Tori and gave her a big hug and asked for a hot dog without a bun.

"Don't you want a bun for your hot dog?" Tori asked.

"It's not for me," Meredith answered, "it's for Rounder, my

dog." She grabbed the meat in her little hand and said, "Thank you, Tori," and then raced to the forlorn hound with the sad eyes.

Meredith knelt beside the dog and presented her offering which was wolfed down with great appreciation. She stayed beside her new friend and rubbed him gently behind his ears. Rounder edged closer to Meredith and eventually laid his head on her lap and closed his tired eyes.

The ordeal was over for Rounder, too. His master's killer had been brought to justice and finally he could get back to just being a lazy hound. His new job from now on was just to be a little girl's best friend.

Dewayne Allison walked over to Meredith and Rounder and began rubbing the dog between his ears. "That sure is a nice dog. If you like, Meredith, he can stay here with me so he won't be lonely no more. He can still be your dog, though."

Meredith reached up and gave Dewayne a big hug. "That's a good idea! We live in town and I don't think he would be as happy there. Thank you. I'll ask Mama, but I'm sure it will be okay."

Dewayne stood with tears in his eyes and patted Meredith on top of the head and gave Rounder one last scratch for good measure and then ambled off.

The newly retired detective overheard Joanie ask Ed, "Will you rub my butt tonight, honey. I'm gettin' saddle sores."

It looked as if everything was getting back to normal.

CHAPTER 114

MONDAY MORNING Marci sat at the kitchen table drinking coffee, enjoying the quiet time while Jake and Meredith were still in their beds.

Marci's spirits had lifted dramatically after the outpouring of love shown by her friends and the citizens of Love Valley. She felt truly blessed. It was a relief that she had finally made the decision to resign from the sheriff's department. Resigning had been a difficult thing for her to do, because she liked her job…she was good at it…and she wasn't a quitter.

I'll miss the detective work. My job was always so interesting. I'll really miss my friends at the department, too. Maybe the sheriff will let me drop by once in a while.

A knock at the kitchen door brought Marci to back reality. Before she could respond, Joanie burst in. "How's it goin', girl?"

"Hey, Joanie, you scared me. I'm not used to having visitors this early in the morning."

"Hells bells," Joanie said, "it's past seven o'clock. A whole

n ⸻ ⸻ ⸺ longer? I'm not even dressed

⸻ Joanie continued,

⸻ na ask me if I want

⸻ ci said smiling.

⸻ said. "Thank you, I'd

⸻ ieved a ceramic mug,

⸻ own at the table across

⸻ coffee cup and then put

⸻ hat's still hot," she swore

⸻ and said, "Y'all make the

⸻ the time."

⸻ ng.

⸻ her custom. "What're you
gonna now that yo⸺ ⸺ ⸺⸺ ⸻?"

Marci shrugged, "I have a ⸺ ple of ideas I've been thinking about, why?"

"Well, I've got a humdinger of an idea for you."

"I can imagine," Marci responded. "What kind of idea?"

"You and me can open up a detective agency. Can't you just
see it now? 'The Mitchell and McLeod Agency,' written in big letters."

Marci was taking a drink of her coffee and almost choked
when Joanie made her proposal.

"What? You can't be serious?"

"And why in the hell not?" Joanie exclaimed. "With your
experience and my bullshit, and not to mention your newfound
reputation, we'd be a cinch."

Marci stumbled for words and then laughed. "Joanie

Mitchell, you're something else, did you know that?"

"That's what your old man always says about you. I'm serious, Marci. Just think about it, okay?"

"If you're serious, Joanie, how about McLeod and Mitchell Detective Agency, doesn't that sound better?"

"Damn, Marci McLeod. Jake's right, you are something else!"

They both laughed until tears rolled down their cheeks. And then a small voice was heard from the hallway, "We don't say damn no more, Joanie."

"Well, look who's up. Come here sweet pea and give me a hug," Joanie said embarrassed by her faux pas.

Meredith wiped the sleep from her eyes and walked over to Joanie. "Hey, Joanie," she said with a big grin and crawled onto her lap. "What are y'all laughin' about?"

"Oh, nothing, sweetheart, we were just wishin'."

"I wished for a horse and now I have Freckles," Meredith declared. "I hope you get what you wish for, too."

They were all still laughing when Jake stumbled through the door from the hall, "You guys got a cup for me?"

"Sure we do," Joanie said, "let me get you one."

"Just sit still," Jake said. "I can get my own coffee, I'm not helpless yet!" He filled himself a cup and joined them at the table.

"What are you two ladies up to? It sounded like a bunch of laughing hyenas in here."

"Oh, Jake," Marci said, "Joanie and I were talking about opening up the McLeod and Mitchell Detective Agency."

Jake choked on his coffee. "You can't be serious?"

"Well, it just came up in conversation and we started thinking about it, that's all," Marci explained.

"I think it is a great idea," Joanie said. "Can't you just see us now…the female caped crusaders."

"How about the Silly Snoops," Jake said.

"That's not funny," Marci retorted.

"I was just kidding. You weren't serious anyway, were you?"

"Well, we might be," Marci said.

CHAPTER 115

THE SUN SHONE brightly through their bedroom window when Marci rolled over in their king sized bed and hugged Jake and kissed him awake. She ran her right hand up under his t-shirt and massaged his chest then slowly inched it down his belly.

"What's going on here?" Jake asked.

"Well, this is as good a time as any to tell you, darling."

He propped up on one elbow. "Tell me what?" he asked, his eyes getting wider. "Let me guess. You two super sleuths have started your business and have your first client?"

"No, not that," she said. "Come closer and I'll tell you."

Jake leaned over and kissed her on the mouth, "Okay, what is it?"

Marci put her lips close to his ear and whispered.

"You're what?"

"I'm pregnant. We're going to have a baby!"

Jake McLeod opened his eyes even wider in disbelief. Marci

took his hand in hers and placed them over her slightly swollen tummy. Tears had formed in his eyes and had begun to course down his cheeks. "What can I say, Marci?"

"Just tell me you're happy."

"Are you kidding?" Jake said. "Marci, I love you and Meredith more than anything in the world and I couldn't be happier. We've wanted another baby for quite a while and now our family will be complete." A big smile played across his face and he flopped over onto this back and added, "And I guess we'll have to get another horse."

Marci laughed and kissed his tears. "Another horse? She took his face in her hands. "Nothing could be farther from my mind right now," she said teasingly. "Since Meredith is still asleep and just in case the doctor is wrong about me being pregnant," she continued, "don't you think we should make sure?"

With a wide grin Jake said, taking her hand, "You're something else; did you know that?"

ACKNOWLEDGEMENTS

There are so many good friends to thank I hardly know where to begin. I owe a special thanks to the gracious and wonderful people of Love Valley, North Carolina. Mayor Andy Barker and his wife, Ellenora always were there for me to answer any questions about their town.

This book could not have been written without the help and patience of Beth and Charlie Nance who answered so many questions about rodeos and horses and anything and everything about Love Valley.

Thanks go to many people of the town who offered their names for this book: Andy and Ellenora Barker, Tori Barker Callanan, Charlie and Beth Nance, Bob and Judy Adams, Angela Chapman, Sue Ladistow, Mutt Burgess, Danielle Cadigan, and Jack and Linda Jolly.

I wish to thank Captain Darren Campbell of the Iredell County Sheriff's Department for his help and willingness to answer any and all questions about procedure, protocol, crime scenes, and anything that came up about law enforcement.

Thanks also to Amy and Kelly Williams, Beth and Charlie Nance, Laurie Lund, John Vest, Teena Griffin, and Nancy Wakeley for reading my manuscript and offering suggestions.

I want to thank Leslie Rindoks of Lorimer Press for her guidance and expertise through the publishing process of my second novel.

I could never thank my wife Vickie enough for the countless hours she spent reading and re-reading the manuscript and straightening me out on overlooked facts, story line, and inconsistencies. I shudder to think what the final book would have been like without her guidance and input. Her tireless effort in making this a better book is, and shall be forever, greatly appreciated. A simple thank you will never be enough to show my appreciation.

About the Author

"Cotton" Ketchie published his first book, *Memories of a Country Boy*, in 2006. This memoir was soon followed by *A Country Boy's Education* in 2007. Both books provide an amusing glimpse into the life of a country boy growing up in North Carolina in the 1950s. His first novel, *Little Did They Know*, was published in 2009.

Ketchie is also a nationally known watercolorist and was selected as the featured artist for the 2004 North Carolina Governor's Conference on Tourism. His works, which celebrate the beauty of the country, can be found in collections throughout Europe, Asia, the United States, and Canada. In 2001, he received the coveted Order of the Long Leaf Pine for working to preserve the legacy of his state and his community.

"Cotton" and his wife Vickie invite you to visit Landmark Galleries in downtown Mooresville, NC, where his original watercolors, limited edition prints, and photography are on display.